W~~elcome to the darker side of ro~~

12 SHADES OF
SURRENDER

Two volumes of intense, unforgettable
short stories from top erotic authors, including
Megan Hart, Tiffany Reisz, Saskia Walker
and Portia da Costa

12 SHADES OF
SURRENDER

BOUND

TIFFANY REISZ
LISA RENEE JONES
ALEGRA VERDE
ADELAIDE COLE
ELISA ADAMS
PORTIA DA COSTA

Mills & Boon, an imprint of Harlequin (UK) Limited,
Eton House, 18-24 Paradise Road, Richmond, Surrey TW9 1SR

12 SHADES OF SURRENDER: BOUND
© Harlequin Enterprises II B.V./S.à.r.l. 2012

Seven Day Loan © Tiffany Reisz 2010
Taste of Pleasure © Lisa Renee Jones 2011
Taking Her Boss © Esperanza Cintrón 2011
A Paris Affair © Adelaide Cole 2011
For Your Pleasure © Elisa Adams 2010
Chance of a Lifetime © Portia da Costa 2008

ISBN: 978 0 263 90461 1

084-0812

Printed and bound by
CPI Group (UK) Ltd, Croydon, CR0 4YY

CONTENTS

Seven-Day Loan

By Tiffany Reisz

Tiffany Reisz lives in Lexington, Kentucky. She graduated with a B.A. in English from Centre College and is making her parents and her professors proud by writing erotica under her real name. She has five piercings, one tattoo, and has been arrested twice. When not under arrest, Tiffany enjoys Latin Dance, Latin Men, and Latin Verbs. She dropped out of a conservative seminary in order to pursue her dream of becoming a smut peddler. If she couldn't write, she would die.

"At twenty-three years of age, I would have hoped pouting would be far behind you, Eleanor."

Eleanor turned her face to the car window and rolled her eyes. She didn't pay any attention to the soft winter woods gliding past her; she simply didn't want him to see her childish response to his rebuke. She was in enough trouble with him already. Him—she wouldn't even think or speak his name.

"I'm not pouting...sir." She delayed adding the term of respect for as long as safely possible. "Pouting is what I do when you send me to bed without supper. You're leaving me for a week and just pawning me off on some stranger. Pouting is not what this is."

She heard him sigh and felt a tug of sympathy that she quickly forced aside. She knew she was being difficult, but he was being impossible.

"Then what is it?" he asked.

Eleanor kept her jaw tight. "Righteous indignation."

"Righteous indeed," he said. "You realize that Daniel is only a stranger to you," he reminded her, but Eleanor only stared out the window again. Daniel…something. She didn't even know his last name or anything about him. He was rich apparently. He'd sent a limo to bring her to him. She'd thought the limo was a little ridiculous, but at least it gave her the privacy to vent her frustration at him during the whole drive. "He is an old and dear friend," he continued. "One of the best men I have ever known. As I've told you before, his wife died nearly three years ago. He's been something of a recluse ever since."

"So giving me to him to fuck for a week is supposed to mend his poor broken heart?" she challenged. "You must think I'm pretty damn good in bed."

"Although considerable, it's hardly your prowess in the bedroom that I imagine will help Daniel return to the outside world again. I merely wish you to keep him company while I'm away. Whether or not he chooses to sample your talents is his decision."

"So I don't get a say?"

Eleanor started at the sound of the tinted window separating them from the driver being raised. But she wasn't surprised when he grabbed her by the knees and wrenched her toward him. She ended up on her back stretched across the dark leather of the seat, his hands lifting her skirt and prying her thighs apart. With two fingers he penetrated her quick and hard.

"Who do you belong to?" he demanded, his voice quietly threatening.

She forced herself to breathe, forced herself to meet his eyes—eyes gray and ominous as a rising storm.

"You, sir," she answered through teeth gritting against the sudden violation.

"And this," he said, spreading his fingers open inside her. She felt herself growing wet at his touch and had to curse her betraying body for being so endlessly responsive to him. "Who does this belong to?"

"You, sir."

"Mine to keep?"

"Yes, sir."

"Mine to give away?"

She swallowed before answering. "Yes, sir."

"And mine to come claim again?"

Tears tried to form in her eyes but she forced them down. She nodded and whispered, "Yes, sir."

Slowly he pulled his fingers out of her. She sat up and straightened her skirt while he wiped her wetness off his hand with a black handkerchief.

"Now," he said without bothering to look at her, "you've had your say."

Eleanor said nothing else as the limo pulled into the long, winding driveway of a snow-covered colonial manor. At least he's got a nice house, Eleanor told herself. She'd almost expected it to look like a prison. But still, a pretty home was cold comfort for spending a week alone with a man she'd never met.

The limo stopped at the front door and a man, presumably Daniel, came out to greet them. She stood to the side shivering as she let the old friends exchange greetings and handshakes. Out of the corner of her eyes she studied Daniel. She guessed he was thirty-six or thirty-seven; he certainly looked no older. And, she grudgingly conceded, he was very handsome. Far from the thin pale hermit she'd imagined, he was well-muscled with a face as chiseled as an old Hollywood movie idol. His blond hair made him seem slightly less threatening but when he turned his attention to her, she stiffened in fear. His eyes were neither cold nor cruel, but flush with sorrow. The sadness rendered him immediately human to her and that was the last thing she wanted or needed. To get through this week, she needed to keep her guard up. She'd let him have her body if he demanded it of her. She'd give him nothing else.

"So this is Eleanor," Daniel said as he offered her his hand. She shook it briskly and quickly before dropping it and pulling her arms tight in around her.

"My Eleanor, yes," he said with a smile of affection and pride. His obvious love for her didn't stop her from still thinking of him as just *him*. Faced with the reality of the week ahead, she was more furious at him than ever.

"It's very nice to meet you," Daniel said. "It'll be nice to have a houseguest again. I've been a bit of a Miss Havisham lately."

Eleanor bit her lip not wanting to laugh at his astute,

if ridiculous, literary reference. She hadn't expected him to be a Dickens fan.

"I'll be sure not to eat the wedding cake," Eleanor said before she could stop herself. She was naturally chatty and even a bad mood couldn't quite keep her from bantering.

"Ah, she reads," Daniel said. "Good. I'm trying to reorganize my library this week. An extra pair of hands will be a great help."

"Eleanor loves books," he said. "She even works in a bookstore so at the very least you'll have a perfectly alphabetized collection."

"Oh, it's already alphabetized," Daniel said as he ushered them inside the house. "I'm just not sure which alphabet. Certainly not the English one."

Eleanor glanced around Daniel's home as they made their way to what she guessed was the drawing room. The house seemed vast but warm and would have been cozy but for its enigmatic master. In the presence of such pain, Eleanor doubted she could ever feel at home.

Daniel gestured toward a chair and he sat down. One glance from him brought her to her knees at his feet. In private she always sat at his feet. That she was to take the standard submissive posture in front of Daniel meant only one thing—Daniel was one of them. Or had been, at least, before his wife died.

"Could I offer either of you a drink?" Daniel asked, taking a seat on the sofa across from them.

"No, thank you." Eleanor let him speak for her. "I really must be going. My flight leaves in three hours."

"Back to Rome again?" Daniel asked.

"Again," he said, sounding tired of it all.

"I'll walk you out."

Usually he would never leave her without a long and intimate goodbye. But this time he merely stood, brushed a finger gently across her cheek and chin, and left her alone in the room. She waited on the floor although she desperately wanted to run after him and beg him to take her with him. But she was far too well-trained to break a submissive posture for the sole purpose of engaging in what she knew would be a futile emotional outburst.

After a few moments, Daniel returned to the drawing room. He said nothing at first and Eleanor could only keep her silence and her eyes lowered.

"Please, sit," he said, his voice kind and quietly amused. "In a chair."

"Oh, a chair. How extraordinarily generous," she said, unable to maintain her submissive comportment now that she was truly alone with Daniel.

"I understand that you're upset with this arrangement."

Eleanor smirked. Upset?

"I get it," she said as she sat in the armchair behind her. "This is good cop, bad cop, right? Bad cop works me over and leaves and then good cop comes in and offers me the milk and the cookies and the nice comfy chair. How cute."

"He warned me you were smart. He neglected to mention you were a smart-ass as well."

She had to give Daniel some credit. He was impressively unimpressed by her sarcasm. Tougher even than he looked.

"He may live to be a hundred and the word 'smart-ass' will never pass those perfect lips of his and you know it," she said.

Daniel half laughed. "He is a bit too proper for that, isn't he? I suppose he would say you were—"

"Impudent," she suggested.

"A fair assessment, I think. He could have warned me you were impudent."

"I guess he thinks it goes without saying. Since you're playing good cop, should I expect a big dinner now? A massage maybe? Or how about the sob story about your poor dead wife and how you're so sad I should blow you nine ways to Sunday?" she asked, deliberately trying to get a rise out of him. But he still seemed unmoved. That scared her even more than an emotional reaction would have. His pain was too deep to be touched. It made him seem far beyond her.

"I think we've left the kingdom of impudent and entered the realm of bitchiness."

She almost laughed. Bitchiness—another word she would never hear him say.

"A fair assessment," she said, repeating Daniel's words.

Daniel inhaled and exhaled heavily. She could tell he was considering his next words.

"I won't burden you with a sob story," he said. "But you deserve some explanation for your presence here. I was married, blissfully, for seven years. My wife and I were as you and—"

"If you want to get on my good side, please don't say his name. I'll make it through this week a hell of a lot easier if I don't have to hear about him or talk about him."

Daniel nodded. "As you and he are," he continued. "She was more than my wife. She was my property, my possession…and my best friend. She died three years ago. I have been with no one since. When I confessed this to S—to him, he insisted that some time with you would be therapeutic. As you belong to him, there is no threat of romantic entanglement. And as you are already familiar with the specific requirement of the lifestyle—"

"I'm kinky. You don't have to resort to euphemisms."

"Then the transition from celibacy back to sexuality would be far smoother."

"So you do plan to fuck me then?" she asked although she knew the answer already.

"When you're ready and if you have no objection."

"I'm here, aren't I? Nobody's got a gun to my head."

"Force is for amateurs. I will sleep alone for eternity before I would ever take an unwilling partner to bed. He has shared you with others before, hasn't he?"

"Yeah, of course. But—" she said and took a breath "—he was always there."

"I understand. As I said, when you're ready. And not until then."

"So what now?" she asked after a moment's pause. Daniel stood up and went to the door. She quickly joined him.

"I'm sure you need to unpack and rest. So I suppose for the night I'll simply send you to your room."

"Send me to my room? After what a bitch I've been?" Eleanor scoffed. "From good cop to cop-out. Fine, I'll go to my room." She moved to take a step but Daniel caught her by the chin. She gasped at the sudden unexpected movement, shocked by the sudden change in his demeanor.

He forced her to meet his eyes.

"I haven't played this game in years," he said, his voice low and forbidding. "That does not mean I've forgotten how."

Eleanor didn't dare to blink or breathe. Daniel loosened his grip on her chin but did not let her go.

"I may not touch you again for the rest of this week," he said. "Or I may fuck you blind, deaf and dumb. But you will be respectful of me while you are here no matter what the sleeping arrangements prove to be. Understood?"

Eleanor blinked and nodded. "Yes, sir," she said through trembling lips.

"Good. Your room adjoins mine. It is at the top of the stairs, the second to the last room on the right. Your bags are already there."

"Thank you," she said, her voice little more than a squeak.

Daniel smiled but it was not a kind smile. It sent a chill into her stomach even as his fingers against her skin made her uncomfortably warm. "You flinched," he said. "This must not be how he usually gets your attention."

"It isn't. He grabs my neck. Or my wrist."

"Which do you prefer?"

She shrugged. "I hate them all the same."

Daniel's eyes momentarily brightened with suppressed laughter and Eleanor was struck again by how handsome he was. This was going to be a long week.

"Go," he said. "I'll see you tomorrow."

Relieved to be dismissed from his unnerving presence, Eleanor practically bolted toward the staircase. Taking two steps at a time she made it to the top and down the hall to her room in no time. She threw open the door and slammed it behind her, grateful to be safe and alone for once that day. Well, perhaps not safe, she told herself. But at least alone.

He had told her why she was here, what would be expected of her. But only now did the realization that she would be Daniel's sexual possession this week truly register. She went to the window and peered out, trying to see where Daniel's property ended and the outside world began. But a new snow had begun to fall and Eleanor had lived in New England all her life. She knew those heavy dense flakes dropping from a deep gray sky meant a snowstorm. She was trapped here, trapped with him. She was here and for now she was his.

Unpacking had only taken a few minutes and although her bedroom was elegant and spacious with an equally elegant bathroom attached, there was little to be explored. Eleanor tried to read—she'd packed one whole suitcase full of nothing but books—but her mind wandered too much down too many dangerous paths. She was consumed by thoughts of Daniel. Lying on her bed she stared at the ceiling, recalling the rough grip of Daniel's hand on her face. She'd felt the force in him, felt he was a man to be reckoned with. She lay there until she fell asleep and dreamed she was drowning in a sea of black snow.

An hour or a day later, she awoke shivering in the dark. She glanced around trying to get her bearings.

She reached for the bedside lamp and tried to switch it on. Nothing happened. She stumbled to the wall and flipped that switch, but again the darkness remained untouched. Wearing only a white cotton nightgown, she dove under her bedclothes, desperate for what warmth they could offer her. In bed she noticed a light streaming from underneath the door that separated her room from Daniel's. How did he still have electricity when she didn't? Curiosity overcame fear and she eased out from underneath the covers and trod quietly across the floor. She considered knocking but the silence in the house seemed too pervasive to break. With a shaking hand, she turned the door handle and found the door unlocked. She took a deep breath and slipped inside.

"Can't sleep?" Daniel's voice came from a chair in front of an imposing fireplace. The orange and roaring fire was the source of the light she'd seen.

"I'm cold," she said and moved nervously toward the sound of his voice. "What happened to the lights?"

"Just a line down from all the snow." He sounded world-weary, tired. "They'll be back on by morning, I'm sure." Eleanor found him still dressed but with an extra button undone on his dress shirt and a glass of white wine in his hand. "You're welcome to share my fire. I won't even charge you rent."

She gave him a tight smile, knowing exactly what he meant by rent, and sat down on the plush rug in front of the fireplace. She wrapped her arms tight about her and breathed the smoky heat into her lungs.

They sat in silence for what felt like an hour, the only sounds in the room the popping and spitting of the wood being consumed.

"I'm sorry." Eleanor finally broke the silence.

"For what?" Daniel asked, taking a leisurely sip of his wine.

"For what I said about your wife. That was uncalled for."

"Uncalled for? Yes, I suppose it was. Still, this can't be the most comfortable situation for you."

She shrugged. "No one held a gun to my head. I do what he tells me to do, what he wants me to do. Because I love him. That simple."

"Simple…is it? We've never met before today, Eleanor. He expects you, wants you to give yourself up to me. Not very simple from where I sit."

"He's infuriating but I've known him and loved him since I was a kid."

"You're twenty-three, yes? You're still a kid."

"But he's never taken me anywhere I was too young to go. Never asked me to do anything…" Her voice trailed off as she realized the implications of what she was saying. She took a quick breath. "Anything I wasn't ready to do."

Eleanor met Daniel's eyes for the briefest moment and glanced back at the fire.

"Are you ready?" Daniel asked and sat his glass on the table next to his chair.

She counted to ten before answering. She knew the answer at "one" but the little feminine pride she had made her wait nine more seconds.

"Yes."

If Daniel was pleased by her response, his face didn't show it. His expression was inscrutable.

He sat forward in his chair. Eleanor studied him as he moved. It seemed he was looking only at his own right hand. He fanned his fingers out, gazed at his own palm. His hand curled tight into a fist. But it was the sound of his fingers snapping, loud and unexpectedly sharp, that really demanded her attention. He snapped and pointed at the floor. She responded with well-trained obedience, rising off the rug and kneeling again at his feet.

She inhaled as he laid a hand on the side of her face. His thumb caressed her cheek.

"I won't kiss you if that makes you uncomfortable."

"To be honest, I think not kissing would make it worse."

"Honest," he repeated. "Yes, be honest. It's been over three years for me, you realize. I need you to tell me if it's something you don't like."

"What if…" She stopped and took another breath. His hand was on her neck now, his muscular fingers kneading her skin in a way that made her stomach knot up and the flesh between her thighs damp. "What if I do like it?"

Daniel smiled at her question and for the first time she thought she caught a glimpse of the man he must have been before the pain burrowed in and made a home out of his heart.

"Then tell me that too. Understand?"

She smiled back at him. "Yes, sir."

"Sir...I haven't been called that in so long. I've forgotten how much I like it. Stand up, Eleanor," he ordered and she came immediately to her feet. He reached out and untied the ribbon at the neck of her nightgown. The fabric loosened and gave way to his hands. He slid the gown down her shoulders and let it fall to the floor. She wore nothing under her gown so she now stood naked before him, shivering, even, despite the fire.

Daniel placed his hands against her stomach before letting them roam slowly over the contours and curves of her body. The act felt strangely unsexual. She felt as much wonder and curiosity in his touch as she did desire.

He gathered her breasts in his hands, cupping them gently. He brushed his thumbs across her nipples and she flinched with pleasure. He took her by the hips and moved her even closer to him, close enough for him to take a nipple into his mouth. She grasped his shoulders to steady herself as he sucked at her breasts, alternating between his mouth and his fingers as he pinched them and kissed them until her nipples were painfully swollen.

Eleanor took slow breaths as he continued his assault on her senses. He slipped a hand behind her knee and lifted her leg, placing her foot on the chair next to his thigh.

Still holding onto his shoulders for balance, she looked down and watched as Daniel slid a single finger into her. She heard a sigh of pleasure but wasn't sure if it had escaped from his lips or hers.

A second finger joined the first and Eleanor began to pant as Daniel moved them in and out of her until they shone with her wetness against the light of the fireplace.

With his other hand he explored her clitoris, probing gently and slowly until he found her rhythm, the prefect pace and pressure that brought her to the edge of orgasm.

"I can't…" she gasped. "I can't stand."

Daniel immediately took his hands away from her. He gathered her in his arms and carried her to his bed. It was dark away from the fire, and cold. She wriggled under the covers as Daniel lit a smattering of candles.

She saw now that his room was both masculine and elegant; dark wood furniture contrasted with the off-white linens and rugs. But as he stood next to the bed and started to undress, her appreciative eyes fell only on him.

Daniel's naked chest was even more broad and strong than his clothes had hinted at. His stomach was a flat hard plane of muscle. Candlelight flickered over his skin, throwing every line and angle into sharp relief. Eleanor pulled the heavy covers to her chin, suddenly uncertain at the prospect of seeing all of him.

She rolled onto her back and stared into the darkness that hovered at the high ceiling as he discarded the rest of his clothing. She knew from the shifting of the bed that he had joined her. Then it was his face, his naked body that claimed her field of vision. He pulled the covers down her body, revealing every inch of her to his sight again.

"Spread your legs," he ordered and it was, without question, an order. She heard the imperative in his voice, the tenor of command. She obeyed. She was trained to obey, trained to want to obey.

As she spread her legs, Daniel reached for one of the candles that burned on the bedside table. He brought it to him, careful to spill no wax. He settled between her open thighs and looked down at her.

"Use your hands," he said. "Open yourself."

Eleanor reached down and with trembling fingers spread the lips of her vagina as wide as she comfortably could. "Your clit," he said. "Show me." Eleanor blushed in the semi-dark, but embarrassment did not stop her from using her thumb and pulling back the hood of her clitoris. Now nothing of her secret parts remained hidden from his view.

She looked at Daniel as he looked at her. His eyes seemed to devour her. She'd rarely felt so exposed in her life.

"I'd forgotten," he said quietly, "how beautiful this is."

He moved the candle to his left hand and with his right he touched her. One by one he dipped every finger into her—his thumb, his index finger…sliding one in, pulling slowly out, and then pushing in the next as if he had to experience her from every angle. With a single wet fingertip he widened her tight entrance with spiraling circles. She was so wet she could hear herself.

Again he pressed two fingers into her. She arched her hips into his hand. He probed along the front wall of her eager body. She gasped when he suddenly pushed hard into her g-spot, her inner muscles clamping down on him.

She heard his soft laughter and she blushed again, this time at her own blatant need for him.

"Responsive little thing, aren't you?" Daniel teased as he pulled out of her once more and leaned forward to set the candle back on the table. "I wonder how you'll respond to this.…"

Now it was his mouth on her, his tongue inside her. She balked in shock from the sheer ferocity of it. He took her clitoris between his lips and sucked. She dug her hands into the bed, desperate to hold onto something, anything to steady herself as a current of pleasure—so strong it felt as if it would drag her under—washed over her again and again. Daniel brought her once more to the sharp edge of orgasm and stopped. He crawled up her body and pressed his lips, wet with her desire, to her mouth. She tasted herself first, then him. As he kissed her with desperate hungry lips, she felt him reach for her knees. He brought her legs up, positioning them over his shoulders. He leaned in to kiss her again, a move that pushed her knees nearly to her chest.

Now it was Daniel who reached between her legs and spread her wide. She felt the wet tip of his cock against her. She barely had time to brace herself before he thrust into her so hard, so incredibly deep that she nearly cried.

Eleanor tried to breathe as Daniel rode her with long driving thrusts. He was big but she was well-accustomed to a large size. She was shocked instead by his insistence; every thrust going deeper and deeper until it seemed he pounded into the pit of her stomach. It quickly left the realm of sex and devolved into pure fucking. And he fucked her like a starving man ate. Three years of celibacy and sorrow had turned his body into a vessel of pure hunger. He gripped her wrists as he took her, holding her down hard. If she wanted to escape him she couldn't. No part of her wanted to escape. Still some lingering defiant spark in her fought off the climax that was threatening to erupt from within her. He was so suddenly possessive of her and she so aware that no matter how he took her, she was not his, that she refused to give him the satisfaction of giving her satisfaction. But no amount of slow steady breathing could stop her. She came and when she came it felt as if her orgasm was wrenched from her. He took it from her body rather than giving it to her. His pace grew faster, harsher, and she held onto the bars of the headboard as he spent his pleasure in her, filling her stomach with his liquid heat.

Eleanor's heart still raced even as her ragged breathing settled. She looked at Daniel who still lay embedded in her. His eyes were closed and his brow was furrowed in concentration as if he were trying to imprint in his memory this one moment inside her. Eleanor stared at his face. Long blond eyelashes lay on pale cheeks like sunlight on snow, and she felt an unexpected stab of tenderness toward him.

Daniel opened his eyes slowly. Eleanor tried to smile at him but the look he gave her was one of shock. He seemed to be seeing a stranger, and Eleanor realized with a sick churning in her stomach that he was.

"It was her you were fucking, wasn't it?" she asked, her voice soft and without accusation. "Your wife, right? Lucky lady."

Daniel's only answer was to slip out of her. He left the bed and threw on his clothes.

"Keep the bed," he said without looking at her. "Tonight this is the warmest room in the house."

"But where will you—" Eleanor started to ask, but he was already gone.

She groaned in frustration and collapsed back on the bed. She blew out the candles and yanked the covers to her chin. After a few minutes in the dark, she felt the presence of ghosts in the room—the ghost of Daniel's late wife and the more fearsome ghost of the man Daniel had been before her death. Eleanor knew she lay with them in the ghost of their marriage bed. She tossed the covers aside, found her nightgown, and returned to her own bedroom. She crawled back into her freezing bed where at least she knew that the only cold body between the sheets would be her own.

Eleanor awoke the next morning and heard the faint but reassuring hum that indicated the power had been restored to the house. She showered and dressed and scrounged for breakfast in the grand but near-empty kitchen. Still…although the kitchen felt abandoned, something told her she wasn't alone in the house. Last night's snow had been far too thick and heavy for the roads to be safely passable yet. Once her stomach was comfortably full, she began a cursory exploration. Ears attuned to the slightest sound, she paused outside a closed door near the backside of the house and heard the unmistakable sound of books sliding across a shelf.

She let loose a wolf whistle as she entered. The library was far larger inside than the unobtrusive door had presaged and was stocked with row after row, case after case of books. Enough books to start her own bookstore.

"I knew I heard books," she said to no one in particular.

"You hear books?" Daniel's lightly sarcastic voice came from the far left corner of the library. "Interesting. Most people actually have to read them."

"It's a gift," she said, shrugging. "What are you doing?"

Daniel stood behind a desk stacked shoulder high with books.

"I am draining all the alphabet soup out of my library." She raised an eyebrow at him as she walked to the desk. "I thought you were a bibliophile," Daniel taunted in response to her puzzled look.

"I am a bibliophile. A bibliophiend even. But I still have no idea what you are talking about."

"Well, as your book knowledge comes from the retail side of the industry then I'll pardon your ignorance." He winked at her and she fairly flushed as a sensory memory from last night hit her lower stomach with soft but insistent force. And the light, that certain white light created only by the morning sun reflecting off new-fallen snow rendered Daniel's handsome features almost luminous. She almost forgot what they'd been talking about. "Let's see, at your bookstore your books are divided by subject and then alphabetized by author's last name, yes?"

"Right. With a few exceptions."

"Well, libraries aren't allowed any exceptions. The books have to be in perfect order at all times. You can't do that with just sorting by genre and then alphabetizing."

"Yeah, that's what the Dewey Decimal system is for, right?"

"But there isn't just Dewey. There's the Library of Congress classification system. Dewey is a clean, efficient system, ten main classes divided by ten and so on. The Library of Congress is alpha-numeric and based on 26 classes, one for each letter of the alphabet. Compared to Dewey it is crude and confusing, and I only had the library that way because of Maggie. It's what she was used to."

"Alpha-numeric—so that's your alphabet soup."

"Yes, and this library has been disorganized soup for far too long." Daniel shook his head as he wrote out a series of numbers on an index card and slipped it inside the front cover of a book.

"Oh my God," Eleanor said, sounding utterly shocked.

"What?"

"You're a nerd."

Daniel only looked at her a moment before laughing.

"I am not a nerd. I'm a librarian."

"No way," she said, recalling again the ferocious passion and the skill he'd demonstrated last night. "Guess they were right."

"Who?"

"You know, whoever said 'it's always the quiet ones.'"

Daniel's mouth twitched to a wicked half grin. "I'm the quiet ones," he said, flashing a look at Eleanor that nearly dropped her to her knees.

She coughed and shook herself out of the erotic reverie she'd fallen into.

"Okay," she said, walking toward him with more gusto than guts. "I can accept that you're a librarian and a sex god—"

"Well, considering your lover is a pr—"

"Nope. Nyet. Halt. I told you last night—"

"Oh, yes. I had forgotten. Our mutual acquaintance is off-limits to discussion."

"If you want me to survive this week with what passes for my mental health intact, then yes."

"Which I do. So I apologize. But as we barely know each other, finding a topic of conversation apart from our mutual friend might be difficult."

"Oh, I doubt that," she said, sitting on the table next

to a stack of books. "We've got books in common, sex…" She ticked them off on her fingers.

"All of two," Daniel said skeptically.

"Well…" She stuck out her foot and tapped his leg lightly. "We've got you."

"Me?"

"Yeah. I'm curious. You're a curiosity. As long as you don't mind answering personal questions—"

"How personal?" Daniel interrupted.

"Unapologetically intrusive, knowing me. Unconscionably so."

"You have a large vocabulary, Eleanor."

"And you have a large…" She paused as he gave her a warning look. "House."

"I do."

"How does a librarian afford a house like this? That was the first unapologetically personal question, for those of you keeping count."

Daniel smiled but Eleanor saw the pale ghost of pain pass across his eyes.

"Librarians can't afford houses like this. But a partner in a Manhattan law firm can."

"Your wife? She was a lawyer?"

"She was. A very powerful attorney."

"You married a shark?" Eleanor asked, laughing.

"A corporate shark, in fact."

"Wow," Eleanor said, duly impressed. "How did you meet her?"

"At the library, of course."

"She read?"

"She gave," Daniel said with great emphasis on the last word. "She gave balls, galas, parties, charity events, fund-raisers of every stripe. She actually had a heart and a conscience. She was the human face of an otherwise very imposing old firm. She held a gala one year to raise money for a literary charity at the NYPL—"

"Holy shit, you worked at the NYPL?"

"Fifth Avenue, Main Branch," he said with barely concealed pride.

"With Lenox and Astor?" she asked, naming the two famous lions that guarded the legendary library.

"On warm days I ate my lunch outside with Astor."

"Why not Lenox?"

"He asked too many personal questions."

"I like him already. So you were both guests at the party?"

"Oh no. She was the hostess. I happened to be working late that night in the Map Room. Lowly archivist. Not important enough for an invitation."

"So you were tucked away in a dusty corner alphabetizing 18th century maps of Tierra del Fuego…"

"Something to that effect—"

"And she slips away from the suffocating crowd of the geriatrically wealthy—"

"Has anyone ever told you that you should be a writer?"

"No one who's ever tried it themselves. But back to you and her. So you're up to your elbows in Fuego and she rushes in all disheveled elegance, out of breath, desperate for just one moment of solitude…"

"Actually I was examining a map of Eurasia for signs of wear; she strolled in quite calmly, apologized very politely when she saw me and said she simply wanted to see the library by night."

"I like my version better. But still that is romantic. You gave her a tour? It was love at first sight?"

"Intrigue at first sight. I assumed she was just a guest at the gala. She was lovely, intelligent, a very young-looking thirty-nine."

"Ohh…an older woman. I love it."

"Her age or mine was never a factor. Or perhaps it was. She was older than me, powerful, wealthy…but at night when we were alone…"

"She was your slave," Eleanor said, finishing his sentence.

"My slave. My property. My possession."

"Your possession…I know how she must have felt. Pressure to be in charge of the world. So much responsibility. The whole world on her…to let go and just give herself to you, to give up to you…"

"I'm glad you understand," Daniel said as he started sifting through another stack of books. "Few women do."

"Oh, they do. They're just afraid to admit it. Yeah,

equal pay for equal work and our bodies our selves and Gloria Steinem and all that jazz…but in that dusty dark little corner of every woman's heart where we keep our maps of Tierra del Fuego lives the hunger to fetch a powerful man his slippers on her hands and knees."

Eleanor was pleased to see her words had a similar effect on Daniel as his did on her. His breath quickened just slightly as his hands deliberately stroked the leather binding of the book in his hand.

"So you," she said, meeting his eyes, "are a librarian. What does that make me then? A seven-day loan?"

Daniel laughed as he set his book aside. He moved toward her and lightly gripped her knees.

"Seven-day loan…I'm not sure I like the thought of giving you back." He slid his hands up her thighs and took her by the hips.

"But what about the overdue fines?" she asked, playfully flashing her eyes at him.

"I think I can afford them," he said. Eleanor tried to voice another protest but his mouth was already on hers.

He kissed her with an urgency she hadn't felt last night. Last night he'd discovered, taken for his own. This morning she felt the need to have her. It wasn't about her body as a stand-in for his wife. Eleanor had made him laugh, given him a break, if only momentary, from three years of pain. This time he wasn't conquering. This time he was just grateful.

Daniel pulled her from her seat on the desk. She

wondered if he would take her on the floor or take her back to his bedroom. Instead he turned her so she stood with her back to his chest. He laid one slow, possessive kiss along the length of her neck before pushing her forward onto the desk.

Eleanor forced a deep calming breath as Daniel stripped her naked from the waist down. She braced for his entrance, expecting it to be as sudden and fierce as last night's. But he waited, running his hands over her thighs, across her lower back, slipping a hand between her legs to caress her outer lips until she was so eager for him she stood on her tiptoes in readiness. When he finally penetrated her it was slow and methodical. He gripped the back of her neck as he began thrusting. He didn't go as deep today as last night either but moved in spirals in and out of her, reaching every corner inside her.

She moaned quietly, her hot breath steaming a patch of the cool mahogany of the desk under her cheek.

"You like it from behind," he said. It wasn't a question.

"God, yes," she confessed without shame.

"There's more than one way to enter from behind."

"If you think that's a threat, then you don't know me very well," she said, smug even while squirming underneath him.

"I don't," he admitted, slightly breathless, but still in control. "But that will change."

As if to prove his point, he pushed down and deep into her, eliciting both a muscle spasm and a sharp gasp.

She closed her eyes. He increased his pace. When she came she came as quietly as she could but still loud enough for Daniel to hear and laugh just before he let himself come with three final thrusts and a muffled grunt at the back of his throat.

Eleanor's breathing slowly settled. She blinked and raised her head. All she saw were thousands of books stacked and shelved and neatly scattered. Daniel was still inside her.

"God I love a man who reads," she breathed and laid her head on the desk, spent.

The sex out of their system—for the moment, at least—Eleanor and Daniel made diligent progress on his library. Daniel sorted, reclassified while Eleanor dusted the bookcases in question and reshelved the newly Deweyed books in proper order.

Sometimes they talked as they worked: Eleanor learned about Daniel's childhood in Canada, the source of his imperviousness to New England winters, and Eleanor confessed her frustration with her lack of ambition. She wanted, in theory, to do more than work in a bookstore but was so happy, most of the time, with him that she couldn't bring herself to make any sort of profound change.

"Contentment can be the enemy," Daniel agreed and

he sounded like he knew what he was talking about. "But don't worry. Life, death, or an act of God will eventually intervene. Enjoy the contentment while it lasts. It won't last forever."

Eleanor shivered at the bitter truth of his words.

"You've been content to be alone for three years. So am I the life, death, or act of God sent to shake things up?"

"You," he said, "are a force of nature." He slapped her bottom and ordered her back to work.

They worked mostly in silence, companionable silence after that, speaking only about the books and how they should best be arranged. During a back-stretching break, Eleanor wandered into the corner of a windowless alcove. Two dozen or more cardboard boxes were neatly stacked.

"What are these?" she called out to Daniel.

"Discards," he said, coming to her corner. "Maggie's old law books. There's a business college with a paralegal program in town. I was going to donate the books to their little law library."

"Going to?"

"Well, I still am. I just haven't quite…"

Eleanor gave him a flat, steady stare.

"How long have these been sitting here in those boxes?"

"A year, I suppose."

Eleanor continued to gaze blankly at him.

"You do recall I am the dominant in this particular relationship, yes?"

Eleanor wasn't intimidated. "Then act like it."

"I will." At that, Daniel scooped her up and threw her over his shoulder, carrying her squirming self back to the case they'd been working on. "Back. To. Work," he ordered as he put her down, gently but firmly, on her feet.

"Yes, sir." She turned and climbed nimbly up the library ladder.

"Eleanor," Daniel said, after a few minutes of actual work had passed.

"Yes, sir?"

"I'll call the college tomorrow."

Eleanor smiled a smile only the shelves could see.

"Yes, sir."

Eleanor groaned in unconcealed ecstasy.

"My god…this is so good…."

"I know," Daniel replied, taking another bite for good measure. "I have a neighbor, an older lady on the property adjacent mine. She made this."

Eleanor licked her fork and dove into the lasagna yet again. "God bless her. Did you go get this while I was in the shower?"

Daniel's eyes flashed at her innocent question. After an entire day of dusty library work, Eleanor had spent a solid hour showering and changing into her nightclothes, and when she emerged Daniel had dinner waiting for them.

"No." His voice was even. Whatever she'd seen had come and gone. "Her husband brought it by. He does some of my property maintenance. And he brought more firewood." He took another log and threw it on the warm orange fire. The wood crackled and sizzled; Eleanor breathed in the raw smoke with pleasure. She was silent for a long moment. When she was sure Daniel was watching her she said, "I was thinking."

"Always a dangerous pursuit."

"Tell me about it."

"What were you thinking about?" Daniel asked, a wary note in his voice.

"Why am I here? Really? I mean, you seem okay. Sad still. Very sad. But hardly a desperate case. What am I doing here?"

"You don't know?"

"No. I mean he," she still wouldn't say the name of her love who'd abandoned her here, even if she was enjoying herself far more than she wanted to admit. "He said I'd be good company for you, that I'd help you get back out into the world. But like I said, you don't seem like you need that much help."

"Back out into the world? Quite a way with words that one has. Only he could tell the absolute truth and still keep everything a secret."

"So what's the truth? And what's the secret?"

"Back out in the world…" Daniel said again. "It's a cliché. Somebody gets divorced or dumped, widowed. And after awhile it's time to get back out there. Date again, make new friends, find someone new. It's figurative, not literal. But me…"

She knew the secret before he could tell her.

"Daniel? How long has it been since you left the house?"

"Oh, I leave the house all the time. But I have eight acres and—"

"When?"

"My wife died three years, five months, and eleven days ago. So it's been…"

"Three years, five months and eleven—"

"Nine days. I made it to the funeral. I was on the human equivalent of a horse tranquilizer but I made it."

Eleanor shook her head. "I'm so sorry. I didn't know. But how? Over three years?"

"Maggie left me a wealthy man. Money, good neighbors, and the internet is all you really need. They've been my wardens, my guards on the tower. A pleasant prison," he said, glancing around at the exquisitely furnished living room they lounged in. "No bars necessary. I suppose our mutual friend was hoping a week with you would give me a taste of what I was missing."

Eleanor snorted in derision. "He's not that altruistic.

Not when it comes to me. He thinks you'll fuck me until you fall for me. Hook, line and sinker and then when I go, you'll follow."

"I've grieved in this jailhouse every day for three years and he thinks I'll be in love with you in a week?"

Eleanor shrugged and looked away from his face and into the fire. She started when she felt Daniel's fingers slide under her hair and touch the nape of her neck.

"I don't know," Daniel said. "Maybe he's right."

He bent in and kissed the sensitive spot below her ear, misdirecting her attention as he took her plate of lasagna from her and set it aside.

"But I wasn't done," she pouted, no longer hungry for anything but him.

"Yes, you were."

"Yes, sir."

"Lay down on your back."

"Very yes, sir."

Daniel smiled down at her once she'd positioned herself on the plush rug by the fireplace.

"You could at least pretend to be intimidated."

"No offense but I've had scarier gym teachers than you. And remember who I belong to," she said, not really wanting to remember at just that moment. "He makes you look like a floppy-eared fluffy baby bunny."

"Ouch. Not even an adult rabbit but a baby bunny."

"Yup." She reached up and grazed his cheek. He really was unnecessarily handsome.

"That bad, is he?"

Eleanor shook her head. "That good."

Daniel laughed. "I keep forgetting who I'm dealing with. The Queen of Kink."

"I'm a trained submissive. More like King's Consort. I'm not worthy to hold actual rank," she said with a wink.

"Well, I'm honored to consort with you."

Eleanor gave him her best wicked grin. "Then consort with me already."

Daniel grinned back. "Yes, ma'am." He looked her up and down and something changed in his eyes like he suddenly had a very good idea.

"Where are you going?" Eleanor asked when Daniel stood and moved to leave.

"To get supplies. Stay."

Eleanor stayed flat on her back in front of the fireplace. She closed her eyes and wondered what sordid things Daniel did to his wife on this rug. She opened her eyes and saw Daniel standing over her. He sat a tube of lubricant and a towel on the floor by her hip. Deliberately he began to roll up the right sleeve of his shirt.

Eleanor didn't have to wonder anymore.

"You've got to be kidding," she said, her heart racing.

"Does it look like I'm kidding?" Daniel dropped to his knees. He eased her pajama pants down her legs and tossed them aside. With a flourish he unfurled the towel and slid it under her hips.

"Surely he's done this to you before," Daniel said.

"He has…on special occasions."

Daniel pried her knees apart. "Consider this a special occasion. Now are you intimidated?"

Eleanor took a deep breath. "Yeah. Happy?"

"Very."

She took another breath and stared blankly at the ceiling. She flinched at Daniel's first touch. "Sorry. That stuff is cold."

"I know. But it's necessary. Just relax."

"The guy always says relax. Would you be relaxed if someone were about to stick their whole hand in you?"

"I can't say I would be relaxed, but I'm quite certain I wouldn't be argumentative."

"Point taken."

Daniel stopped touching her. "Close your eyes," he ordered softly. "Just breathe in and out. Tell me if anything hurts."

She nodded but didn't answer. She began to breathe slowly—in…then out, in…then out. She could do this, had done this. If she was being honest she'd even admit that she loved this.

Daniel's fingers returned to her. He pressed her outer lips apart with his left hand while he pushed two fingers from his right hand deep inside her. Eleanor kept breathing. She'd learned the secret. She knew she couldn't allow herself to become too aroused. The vaginal muscles tightened when aroused. She had to stay calm, empty herself, let him completely in, push nothing but fear out. The perfect passive act for a true submissive.

Inside her Daniel made slow spirals with his hand… spiraling outward pressing against her inner walls, opening her until three then four fingers were inside her.

"Are you okay?" Daniel asked, gentle concern in his voice.

"Very okay."

"Are you ready?" She didn't have to ask him ready for what….

"Yes."

If the four fingers filled her, it was nothing compared to the sensation of his whole hand, his whole fist inside her. Her calm broke for a moment and she gasped at how he now filled her. She spread her thighs wider, pressed hard into his hand. She felt her own fluid cool and slick on her thighs.

Daniel barely moved. He didn't need to. Eleanor writhed around his hand, her body torn between the twin needs to push him out or pull him in deeper and deeper.

She leaned up and gripped her own knees. For the first time she looked down and saw Daniel's wrist deep inside her. She collapsed on her back, lifted her hips and orgasmed so fiercely even Daniel gasped.

As she panted, he pulled gingerly out of her. He used the corner of the towel underneath her to dry his hand. He rolled her onto her stomach, Eleanor limp as a rag doll. She felt the cold liquid on her again, this time inside her ass. Then it was Daniel inside her thrusting hungrily. She was too tired to enjoy it. She merely waited patiently underneath him as he used her for his own pleasure and spent himself inside her once and then again when once proved inadequate to sate his appetite for her.

Finally they lay naked, near each other, sore and tired and smiling.

"I was thinking," Eleanor said turning to drape herself over Daniel's chest.

"Always a dangerous pursuit…what were you thinking?"

"Your wife. I know she died of cancer but still—"

"Still what?"

"I kind of envy her."

Eleanor spent the next three days in a haze of sex and books and happiness. There was no room of the house they did not christen; there was nothing they were afraid or unwilling to do to each other. The fog grew so thick that Eleanor had to keep reminding herself what day it was and how long she'd been there.

Arrived on Saturday, today was Wednesday, leave on Friday…leave on Friday.

Wednesday night Daniel came for her and brought her back to his bedroom. He stripped her naked and left her standing by the bedpost. She relaxed and breathed knowing exactly what was coming.

"Tell me your safe word, Eleanor," Daniel commanded as he yanked her arms behind her back, bent her over the bed, and put bondage cuffs on each wrist.

"Doesn't matter," she said. "Do your worst. You won't hear it."

"Arrogant, aren't we?"

"Not arrogant at all," she countered. "Just very well-trained, sir."

He pulled her up to her feet and chained her arms high over her head to the bedpost. The first blows of the flogger landed on her back softly. Daniel was well-trained too. A long hard beating was always prefaced by a gentle one to desensitize the skin. Breathing in and out slowly, she let the pain wash over her as she'd been trained to do. The pressure intensified, the pain grew. Daniel paused only long enough to penetrate her from behind with short hard thrusts. He came on her thighs, pulled roughly out of her, picked up the flogger, and beat her again.

An hour later he finally released her and let her fall to the floor. He was everywhere with vicious hands and probing fingers. He bit at her neck and breasts and thrust until she nearly cried from the mix of pleasure and pain. She felt Daniel coming more and more back to life every time he took her. Pushing her onto her stomach, he forced himself into her again. Her thighs were wet as his fluid mingled with hers. Her back burned with welts. Underneath him, pinned to the floor, a part of her wanted to stay there forever.

An hour...three hours later...she lost track of time. She forgot her name, forgot where she was...and most dangerously forgot momentarily who she belonged to. Bucking her hips hard into Daniel's, Eleanor came so hard he gasped from the intensity of the muscle contractions that gripped him like a hand. When Daniel came, it was with a force that tore into her stomach and sent her calling out his name. For a long time after they lay tangled together, Daniel still inside her.

She lay in his arms and tried not to say what she knew needed said.

"I leave Friday morning." It wasn't a reminder or a taunt. She just had to say it to remember it was true.

"Friday," Daniel said, leaning over her to blow out the two candles that burned on the bedside table. A clear signal that it was time for sleep. "Still time."

Daniel eased into the covers and pulled Eleanor close to him.

"Time for what?" she asked, already half asleep.

"Time to change your mind."

***

Daniel and Eleanor spent the next morning finishing his library. All the books had been recoded and properly shelved. The work progressed quickly as, for once, Eleanor toiled in silence. She couldn't get Daniel's words out of her mind. He wanted her to stay with him...here in his exquisite prison. It was unthinkable. She belonged to someone else, belonged to *him* like her heart belonged to her chest. She would no more leave him than she would amputate her own arm. Unthinkable...and yet, she *was* thinking about it.

"Want to break for lunch?" Daniel asked shortly after one.

Eleanor didn't answer.

"Elle? Eleanor?"

She exhaled slowly. "Seven-day loan, remember?"

"What was that?"

Eleanor turned to face him. "Seven-day loan. That was the deal."

Daniel nodded, but it was clear he wasn't quite nodding in agreement.

"That was the deal. The deal can change."

"No. It can't," Eleanor said, suddenly angry. "It's not a joke. I'm not a library book. I'm not a part of the permanent collection."

Daniel said nothing for a long time. "You could be."

Eleanor just shook her head. "I can't believe this. You're his friend and I'm his everything and you're doing this." She left the library and kept going down the hallway, stopping only to grab her coat. She was out the door and in the snow. She headed down the long winding driveway. Soon she heard footsteps behind her.

"Eleanor, get back in the house."

"You get back in the house. It's your goddamn prison. Not mine." She kept walking. It was cold out but she was too upset to notice or care.

"You're in a jacket and jeans and it's twenty-five degrees out."

"Well, you should have thought of that before you asked me to stay."

"That makes no sense whatsoever." They were nearly to the edge of the long driveway. "I'm not the one running away."

Eleanor turned around and stopped. She was at the end of the drive. Two steps back and she would be off his property and in the road.

"No. You're not running away. You're not running or walking or strolling or going anywhere. You're staying and rotting and hiding. And there's not much you and I haven't done together this week, but I will not do that with you."

Daniel took a step toward her. Just one but she took another step back.

"Eleanor." Daniel's voice was calm, controlled. He sounded like a jockey trying to gentle a spooked horse. "We can talk about this. Nothing has to be decided today. Just come in out of the cold. *I'm* cold, too, and

I'm never cold. I know you have to be freezing. Come inside."

Eleanor only looked at him. Even so angry at him, and cold and scared, she couldn't deny he was breathtakingly handsome. Grief had left its mark on him. His eyes were haunted and his body lean and cold…like granite. She knew about granite, how you could build on it or be broken on it.

Still without a word she took the last steps back off his property.

"If you want me back in the house, come and get me." She wasn't mocking him. All she wanted was to help him.

"Don't do this to me." Daniel looked at her so gently that she was instantly ashamed of herself. But still she didn't budge.

"You're doing this to me," she countered. "I love him with all that I am and you're asking me to let that go, to leave him. I won't do it. I can't do it. I love him as much as you loved her. More maybe because if he died I would live like he would have wanted me to and not like some hermit in a cave."

"Then just say 'no' to me. Let me ask you to stay and just tell me 'no.' No frostbite or theatrics required."

"I can't let you ask me," she said.

Daniel took a half step toward her.

"Why not?"

"Because," she said looking down at the snow that

caked her shoes like white icing. "I'm not sure I'll be able to say 'no.'"

"Why not?" Daniel asked again as he inched another minuscule step forward.

"Who he is and what he is…" she paused and tears flooded her eyes. "Every single second I spend with him I have to steal. I sleep in his bed and know there's no place in the world I'd rather be but it's the last place in the world I should be. I get Saturday nights with him, sometimes a Thursday night if I'm lucky. But never the mornings. What I wouldn't give for a Wednesday or a Sunday morning…"

"You're in love with a priest, Eleanor. What did you expect?"

"Not to be in love with a priest for starters," Eleanor said, half laughing, half crying. "Every morning this week you've made love to me. You're all mornings and afternoons and evenings and I didn't have to steal a single second of it. You just have them all to give. So if you ask me to stay…Please, Daniel, don't ask me to stay."

When Daniel nodded, it was in agreement this time.

"The only thing I'll ask is that you come back inside with me." He was still on his property but when he reached out his hand it crossed over to her side. She took it and hated how good her small cold fingers felt wrapped up in his warm large hand. She hated it but didn't let go until they were back inside.

Daniel let go of her hand but only so he could take

her by the shoulders and pull her to him. He kissed her and undressed her at the same time. She was pinned to the front door before she knew it.

"I'll let you leave," he said into her ear as he lifted her by her thighs and pushed his cock into her. "But I'll make sure you miss me."

He was relentless. Eleanor gripped his shoulders. He was still dressed. Only she was naked and spread out against the unforgiving front door. Only she was taking and taking as he was giving more and more of himself each time he pushed into her: she took his need, his sorrow, his determination to keep her, his anger that he couldn't, his fingers on her clitoris, and finally his cum that poured into her as she shuddered from the orgasm that he'd also given her.

Eleanor wrapped her arms around Daniel's neck as he lowered her feet to the cold floor. She leaned into him and inhaled his scent—warm and clean with the slightest hint of fireplace smoke—and committed it to memory.

"Don't worry," she said, finally letting him go. "I miss you already."

Eleanor and Daniel lay in bed Thursday night, their last night, with their arms and legs wrapped around each other so that it was nearly impossible to tell where one ended and the other began. Tomorrow morning the car would come for Eleanor and take her back to the outside world and to him who she missed with every other breath and cursed with every breath in between.

"What will you do after I'm gone?" Eleanor asked, not knowing how else to keep avoiding the topic.

"What do you think I should do?" Daniel asked as he pulled Eleanor even closer than she already was.

"I don't know. You've got money, no job, and it's fucking freezing outside. Go to Tierra del Fuego or something. I hear it's nice this time of year."

Daniel laughed and the movement of his chest from the laugh against her back nearly sent her reeling again. Could he stop being sexy for one moment? "Tierra del Fuego is nearly the southernmost tip of South America, a stone's throw from Antarctica. It snows there in summer."

"Wow. Anyway, you should be used to all that cold. I bet it's pretty there."

"Yes, I imagine it is. The natives burned fires constantly to ward off the cold—hence the name Land of Fire."

"How do you know all this stuff?"

"Librarian, remember?"

"I keep forgetting." She reached between his legs and stroked him. "I'm really going to have to renew my library card when I get back."

"You should," Daniel said pressing her onto her back and sliding into her. "Watch out for those overdue fines."

Eleanor laughed softly as she wrapped a leg over Daniel's back to coax him in even further. "Oh, I think I can afford them."

Morning came too early for both of them. Eleanor awoke with her stomach pressed to the mattress and Daniel inside her, gently thrusting. He was too desperate for her to even wait for her to wake up on her own. They made love in silence, mute from the pain of having to part too soon.

Daniel pulled out of her at last with a reluctance they both felt. He ran a hot bath for her and with soap and his bare hands washed all traces of himself off and out of her. Eleanor shivered in the water despite its near scalding temperature. She would have preferred to have gone home dirty from him, stained and marked by him. She was grateful for the few black bruises he'd left on her back and inner thighs and the bite marks on her neck and breasts. She knew in a day or two this strange week with him would fade like a morning dream. She needed the marks to remind her it had happened—Daniel was real and she was more than just a seven-day loan. She had belonged to him. She had.

Daniel packed her things while she dried her hair and dressed. She felt odd letting Daniel pack up her stuff but she let him without any protest. She knew that he needed to feel in control of the situation, that her departure this morning was as much his doing as hers.

Eleanor had just finished taming her hair when Daniel came for her. His voice was low and steady, his eyes quiet. "The car's here."

She nodded, not trusting her voice, and gathered her coat and gloves. Side by side they walked in silence down the hallway, down the steps and to the front door. Eleanor reached for the door handle but Daniel stopped her with a hand on tops of hers.

"Daniel, I have—"

"Call me 'sir.' One more time at least."

Eleanor met his eyes and saw them stricken. She felt something hard in the back of her throat. She tried to swallow it but couldn't.

"Yes, sir," she whispered.

Daniel closed his eyes and opened them again slowly.

"I won't ask you to stay," he said. Eleanor could barely look at him although there was nothing more she wanted to do than memorize every line and angle of his face. "But I want to."

She inhaled sharply and forced a smile.

"I won't say 'yes' if you do ask…but I want to."

Daniel smiled back and that smile broke her heart more than any tears ever could.

"Go. Go back to him before I change my mind and keep you here forever."

"He'd come for me, you know."

"I do know. That's the only reason I won't try."

Daniel took his hand away from hers and let her open the door. The driver got out and put her bags in the trunk. He held the door open for her and she slipped inside. The driver got behind the wheel as Eleanor rolled the tinted window down.

"I won't ever see you again, will I?" she asked.

"Not unless you leave him."

"I won't," she said with merciless certainty. "But maybe," she glanced up at the great house looming behind him, "maybe someday you'll leave her."

Daniel nodded. "Maybe…Goodbye, Eleanor. Be good."

She gave him her most wicked grin.

"Yes, sir."

The car pulled away and headed slowly down the drive. Eleanor closed her eyes and leaned her head against the cold glass of the window. She would not look back at him. She knew he would still be there on the steps of the house watching her leave him, watching despite the cold, watching until every sign of her had shrunk into the distance and disappeared. That's where he was. She didn't have to look back. She just knew it.

Eyes still closed, she felt the car turn left out of the driveway and slam to a sudden stop.

"What the—" Eleanor threw open her eyes and leaned forward. Standing in front of the car in the middle of the road and completely off his property was Daniel. She wrenched the car door open and ran to him.

"Daniel…oh my god…you're—"

"I lied," he said reaching for her. "I will ask you to stay. I will and I am. I'm begging you to stay. I need you."

He kissed and she kissed back, too startled to move, too moved to speak.

She finally pulled away from him.

"Daniel, you did it. You left your house, the property. I can't believe it."

Daniel looked at the house in the near distance and laughed as if just now realizing what he'd done.

"This just shows how much I need you. I haven't stepped foot off the property in over three years but for you…here I am."

Eleanor held him just a moment longer, pressed her face to his neck and inhaled that scent that was him and only him. And in that one moment longer she saw their life together—the days among books, the nights wrapped around each other, the mornings for anything they wanted…and they would never have to be apart and there would never be another second of waiting for a door to open just enough for her to slip inside without anyone knowing…she could be Daniel's and Daniel could be hers and all she had to do was say 'yes.'

"No," she said and let him go.

"What? No what?" Daniel looked utterly stricken.

"If you were still in there, in your fortress, then I would know how much you needed me. That you're here, you're free...it's proof that you don't need me at all."

"Eleanor. Please."

"I'm so sorry," she said backing away to return to the car. "I know it won't help anything but you should know...only leaving him would ever hurt more than this."

She looked at him one last time before slipping back into the car and saying one terrible word—"Drive."

The car started forward again and this time nothing and no one tried to stop it.

Three months later...

She was seeing him tonight, all night. The knowledge of twelve uninterrupted hours with him left her dancing through her day. She danced home from work at eight and dropped her bag full of library books on her kitchen table. She would shower and change and in one hour, nine on the dot, she would be his, completely his all night long.

"Ellie?" her mother's voice called out from behind a closed bedroom door. "You've got mail. On your bed."

"Thanks!" she called back and danced to her room, not curious in the least what bit of junk mail was waiting for her. She glanced at the bed and saw a postcard on the corner of her quilt. She picked it up. On the front was a photo of mountains, snow-tipped and verdant. Now curious enough to care she flipped the card over and read…

Tierra del Fuego is actually quite lovely this time of year. Say hello to Astor and Lenox for me. Love.

It wasn't signed. Only "Love" and nothing else. But it didn't need a signature. Daniel…she couldn't believe he'd actually gone and left his home—gone even to the ends of the earth. The lingering guilt at leaving him so abruptly disappeared at last. He was fine and even more he was free.

Eleanor slid the postcard into a book she'd just finished reading and danced to her shower.

She knew what love was. And it was expecting her at nine.

Taste of Pleasure

By Lisa Renee Jones

In 2003, award winning author **Lisa Renee Jones** sold her Austin, Texas based multi-state staffing agency and has since published over thirty novels and novellas across several genres. Booklist says about Jones' suspense: "…truly sizzles with an energy similar to FBI tales with a paranormal twist by Julie Garwood or Suzanne Brockmann. Alpha, military, and paranormal romance readers will want Jones' entire series." Lisa is active on Facebook and Twitter, and you can find her at www.lisareneejones.com. Lisa enjoys receiving e-mails from her readers! Email her at LisaR…@att.net (LisaRenJones @ gmail.com - w/o the spaces). Please note that while Lisa reads all of her e-mails, it may take some time before you receive a response due to deadlines and other commitments. She'll respond as soon as possible. If you like to receive information about Lisa Renee Jones' latest books and news about contest giveaways, as well as any other information that might be fun or interesting to you, sign up for Lisa's Newsletter.

PROLOGUE

"Silk" was the name swirled in fancy, curly writing on the edged-glass, double doors of the entrance to the club. Inside, skin, sin and satisfaction dominated more than the menu—it dominated private cubbyholes with sheer curtains, the open areas as their centerpieces. Velvety couches sat in these showcased areas, all well adorned with naked bodies indulging in sublime delights.

This was a place Sarah Michaels would never in a million years have dared to enter had she known what to expect. Her close friend Carrie had dared her to be "wild and crazy," in celebration of her acceptance into UCLA's law school. And since lately, "wild and crazy" meant a burger and fries without the take-out bag and library decor, the idea held appeal. She yearned to let her long raven hair out of its tightly braided confines as much as she hungered for a little male companionship. She'd worked hard these past few years to build a future outside her family's business, to create her own identity. To stand on her own. She deserved some fun, to play a little.

But the bodies melting into bodies, the sighs and moans, were far more than she had bargained for. Sex surrounded her. Disturbingly, despite the illicitness of it all, a part of her that she didn't recognize as herself was aroused, excited. She felt young, inexperienced, afraid, but yet she was effortlessly *seduced*. Deny it as she might wish to, she reveled, with an uncomfortable certainty, in the hedonistic indulgence of watching. This was not her—she was prim, proper, all about business. The dampness clinging to her panties defiantly contradicted her silent claim.

Sarah crossed her arms in front of her body and clung to any form of cover, a shell to hide beneath. She found it in her slinky black dress and a silent vow that it would not be removed despite everyone else's state of undress.

Everyone included Carrie, who she'd just left in a private room attended by the companionship of two other females. The facade of sweet, little-girl and Goldilocks innocence that often clung to Carrie had vanished almost instantly upon entering the club. From Sarah's witness, Carrie was more like the wolf with her prey—in control, hungry for respect and pleasure.

Unwilling to consider how easily her study buddy might have become something far different and irreversible, Sarah had quickly left Carrie's presence. She had no idea where she was going, but she didn't want, nor did she need, to face her own potential actions tomorrow through Carrie's eyes. Deep down, she recognized a desperate craving for anonymity, for the freedom it offered.

Sarah inhaled, finding herself at the bottom of a winding metal stairwell. Hesitating a mere moment, she raced upward, away from her friend but not from this place—reluctantly admitting her attraction to its forbidden allure. Had Carrie seen this side of her? Seen things Sarah wasn't willing to see in herself?

At the top of the stairs she found more couches, more curtains. A heavily shadowed corner offered the impression of invisibility, and Sarah pressed tightly into its hollow. It somehow granted her permission to remain. To allow the music, soft and sultry, to ripple through her body as surely as did the lusty heat of arousal as she watched one sensual act after another.

How long she stood there, she did not know. How long until *he* appeared—far too long. Tall, powerfully muscled, with longish, light blond hair, he stood before a half-moon-shaped couch, a light spraying him in a dim glow, as if he commanded its attention. Certainly, he commanded hers, and that of the two voluptuous, naked females who stood before him, offering their bodies for his enjoyment, receiving a noncommittal inspection in return. He was arrogant, dominant in his demand for attention by way of sheer existence. She was instantly submissive to that demand, instantly seduced. He wasn't even naked, but then, he didn't have to be—he was that ruggedly beautiful. His presence exuded an elixir of leather-clad man rippling with delicious muscle and erotic promises.

Heaviness expanded in her chest, her nipples tingled and tightened. Her eyes traveled his body with frenzied hunger. Never before had she drunk of a man's presence as she did this one. Never before had every pore of her body cried out in explosion at the mere sight of masculinity. She wanted to know why, wanted to know "more."

She studied him, inspected his physique with the thoroughness of an artist inspecting a masterpiece. She blinked as he removed his shirt. Wet her lips at the sight of his bare chest, his skin glistening golden-brown beneath the glowing lights. Broad shoulders complemented a defined chest sprinkled with just the right amount of hair. Her eyes dropped to his ripped abdominals where a tattoo circled his belly button. She couldn't make it out, wanted to make it out, wanted to see it up close, touch it…lick it. Her hand went to her stomach. God. What was this man doing to her?

Suddenly, his chin snapped upward, attention diverted from the females at his feet, gaze snapping to Sarah's corner. She froze, heart skipping a beat. Could he see her? Panicked for reasons she couldn't explain, she searched his face. But that question was shoved aside as her stomach fluttered violently. She knew him.

She knew those eyes, knew them well enough to know what she could not see at this distance—that they were baby-blue, sparked with flecks of amber that made them look like ocean water twinkling at sunrise. Knew him because their families were enemies, a friendship flawed through the corporate anger that had arced between two fathers—his and her own.

Seconds passed, pregnant silence surrounding her, blocking out the music, the surroundings. There was just her and him. Tension stretched, and so did the warmth in her body, so did the arousal heavy in her limbs. His lips twitched, lifted—a smile but not a smile. Awareness. That word came to mind. He knew she was there, that she watched, that she longed to do more than watch. Perhaps he knew who she was. Perhaps he did not. If he did, he gave no indication of that knowledge. His eyes lingered, held her paralyzed. An invisible hand seemed to stretch across that couch, across the space, and caress her with promises of forbidden pleasures she would not soon forget.

She should have moved. She should have left. She felt traitorous to her family, to her roots and to herself. Rebellion and desire flared out of nowhere and pressed her against the corner wall, not away from it. Sarah wasn't going anywhere, she realized. She was staying. She was watching. She was celebrating.

CHAPTER ONE

Eight years later

If not for the weight of the four long weeks as interim CEO at Chocolate Delights, Sarah suspected she would have known he was there. Suspected she would have recognized the tingling awareness trickling down her spine as more than the warm splash of water in the Olympic-size pool of the Houston, Texas, country club. Instead, she dismissed the sensation as the edginess created from hours of boardroom brawls, an edginess she'd hoped to dispose of in a dozen laps. And since her swim appeared to be failing miserably, she had every intention of pulling out the big gun—a pint of Ben & Jerry's cookie dough ice cream. Of course, she'd have to run by the store. Unlike her Austin home, her corporate apartment wasn't well stocked with critical necessities like her favorite frozen treat.

Her mouth was watering with anticipation of the cookie dough flavor she adored, when she brought herself upright, her fingers curling around the concrete ledge of the pool, and blinked a pair of dusty cow-boy boots into view. Boots that could have belonged to any one of the hundreds of club members, but the late hour, near nine o'clock in the evening, coupled with the instinctive thunder of her heart, said they did not. Those boots were going to be trouble, like everything else that had been thrown her way since her father's diagnosis a month before.

Slowly, Sarah's gaze lifted, taking in long, muscu-lar, jean-clad thighs and lean hips before jerking to his face—Ryan White, aka the CEO of Delight's rival, Deluxe Sweets, for the past five, highly successful years. Ryan White, who was also the star of most of her midnight fantasies. She didn't think for a minute that his appearance poolside was a coincidence. Nor was his choice of faded jeans, rather than one of those designer suits he'd worn to grace the covers of numerous busi-ness magazines.

Deceptively casual. Calculated. As was his showing up when she was darn near naked. Well, she wasn't a young college kid anymore, easily intimidated. She was a corporate attorney with years of experience. Granted, only a few of those years were actually with Delights before she and her father bumped heads over the direc-tion of the company's future and she'd departed. But that made no difference. She'd met plenty of men like Ryan White, men who were after success at all costs. Okay, maybe not *exactly* like him. A flash of him standing over those naked women in that club years before had her swallowing hard. Regardless, he was after something—and she knew what. She knew all too well. And he could forget it.

"You heard about my father," she said flatly, not playing the game of unnecessary introductions any more than she would play cat-and-mouse.

He bent down, light blond hair framing a handsome face. "How is he?" Ryan asked, his voice, his expression, actually sounding concerned.

Emotion welled in her chest, defensiveness rising in her chest. "He has cancer," she said. "Other than that, he's great." *And he's ready to quit fighting*, she added silently. The certainty that he would lose the company was eating him alive as rapidly as his cancer. And with good reason. It was in financial ruin. No doubt, Ryan thought to take advantage of the weakness. He could think again.

Sarah lifted herself out of the pool and directly into his path, giving him no chance to avoid the splash of water. She expected him to back away. He didn't. His hands went to her waist, over the simple, navy, one-piece suit that had felt conservative before it was wet and clinging to her every curve. Sarah froze, heat rushing over her, awareness like she hadn't felt, well…ever.

"Hello to you too, Sarah," he said, his eyes latching onto hers, simmering with heat, his voice a confident, sexy drawl that dripped arrogance and sex. His gaze melted into hers a moment, and then, with intentional directness, he let his eyes slide downward, over her nipples pebbling through the material. Lingering, touching her without touching her.

How long had she wanted this with this man? How long had she known what she knew now? That he was the definition of forbidden fruit. She wanted to shove him away; she wanted to stay close. But she held her ground, refusing to be intimidated. Seconds ticked by like hours, before crystal-blue eyes the color of the pool lifted back to hers, heat simmering in their depths. Then he said, "It's been a long time."

A long time. In three words, the intimidation rolled through her. In three words, he had successfully zapped her customary control—hit her with the dreaded memory, too soon after the wave of emotion over her father—and melted her into a rare moment of weakness. Heat and embarrassment flooded her system, weakening her knees. They had not seen each other since they were children except once in that club so many years before. The idea of him using that night against her to gain an upper hand didn't sit well. Not well at all.

Her teeth ground together, her words intentionally prim and perfect. Controlled. Something she had mastered in the courtroom. In her life. "Please let go of me." She smiled. "Or you might slip and fall into the pool. In some mysterious way I'd have nothing to do with, of course."

His lips hinted at a smile, and his light blond hair accented the baby-blue eyes, alight with mischief. "You should remember our childhood games enough to know I never back down."

Their childhood. He'd been talking about their childhood. Not the club. Relief washed over her, and so did the recovery of her courtroom-honed sparring skills. "Because back then," she said, "I wouldn't have made you back down. But this is now, not then." She lifted her chin. "I've changed."

He chuckled and stepped backward, hands up in mock surrender. "You wouldn't have won so many cases in the courtroom if that wasn't true." And before she could process his admission that he'd followed her legal career, he added, "Other things can change too, Sarah. Family feuds begin and they end. We could start that ball rolling with a cup of coffee."

Or with a bedroom brawl. She shoved aside the naughty thought with a sharp reply. Too sharp, she realized too late. It showed her hand, showed he'd gotten to her. "Save your dollar and your sweet-talking conversation." She hugged the small towel around her a bit tighter, discreetly, not about to let him see her squirm. "Chocolate Delights isn't for sale."

His eyes narrowed almost imperceptibly so that only her practiced courtroom skill allowed her to notice.

"You intend to try and turn the company around then," he said. "Good." He smiled. "And you aren't about to have coffee with me, are you?"

"Not a chance," she agreed quickly.

He smiled. "Not even if I promise not to talk business?"

"Not even."

"I've done the whole take-over-for-my-father bit," he said. "You might be surprised at what I could do to help."

"Me or you?" she asked tightly, convinced he was a problem, no, more than a problem—dangerous, lethal—because she actually wanted to say yes to coffee. Yes to a "bedroom brawl." Yes to anything that involved this man.

"If I say both?" he asked. "Will I be sent for execution?"

"Both would indicate you have a self-serving purpose in mind, thus making a date with Ben & Jerry's cookie dough ice cream my best offer of the night." The flippant retort held a well-intended bite. Ben & Jerry competed with the new ice cream line he'd just released at Deluxe. And it was darn good ice cream. Better than her previous favourite, but she'd never admit that to anyone. Ever. Especially not to Ryan. Nor would she admit she occasionally sneaked a pint of Deluxe's bestselling Cake Batter Deluxe ice cream into her freezer.

Unexpectedly, Ryan laughed, a deep, throaty masculine sound that rumbled in her ears and shimmered across her skin with electric delight. "Damn, Ben & Jerry are always keeping me on my toes." He took a step backward. "I'll leave you to them then." He winked. "For now." He started to turn and stopped, his tone shifting to solemn, his expression with it. "Delights has been in trouble a long time, Sarah. If your father could have fixed what's broken, he would have. If you want to save it, don't question yourself. Don't worry about what your father will think when he returns. Own your role." His tone softened. "And if you change your mind about that coffee, you know where to find me."

He turned and sauntered away, a sexy swagger to his hips, her heart racing with his every step. He reached for the door, and glanced over at her. "You should live a little dangerously tonight," he said. "Try the Cake Batter Deluxe."

And then he was gone, tempting her in all kinds of dangerous ways.

CHAPTER TWO

It was Saturday, nearly a week after her Ryan encounter, and Sarah was at her home away from home—her father's desk at the Delight's corporate office. Long hours were necessary if she intended to turn the company around. She wasn't going to let a week of discouraging financial reports get her down. Though the fantasies of Ryan, which were hot, wet, melting fantasies she could conjure both in her bedroom and in the boardroom, were becoming a serious problem. The company was in trouble and she, its only hope of survival, kept fantasizing about her biggest competitor. Naked. She kept imagining Ryan naked. With her. But then, her fantasies of Ryan were easier to forgive than her inability to change the reality of a company that needed a miracle. No amount of spending limits, staff cuts she didn't want to make, or creative cash flow would change that fact.

The company had needed a good makeover a long time ago—new product lines, creative distribution, things she'd brought up even before she'd left the company years before. Ice cream shops in the airports and malls to promote their brand and bring in new users. Movie theater distribution for packaged candies. These things could work. They *would have* worked. But now…now, good ideas weren't enough. She'd need cash. "He should have sold out years ago," Sarah mumbled, tapping her pencil on the desk. Now she wasn't sure that was an option. The minute she opened the books for review, a buyer—even Ryan, especially Ryan—would run for the hills.

Sarah's chest tightened, her eyes prickling. "Damn it," she mumbled, and tossed the latest financial reports on her fancy mahogany desk, or rather her father's fancy mahogany desk, in his fancy corner office in downtown Austin. "Crying won't get you anywhere, Sarah." The problem was, she'd seen her father that morning, seen how frail and weak he was, and worst of all, she'd seen the light in his eyes when she'd vowed the company would survive. A vow she feared she couldn't keep.

The phone rang and she jumped, her hand going to the navy silk blouse she'd paired with navy pants. Dressing like a CEO on the weekend had been a last-minute choice springing from a need to feel in control. A refined, prepared executive-in-charge, in case she ran into anyone. She felt she had to be ready, yet she so wasn't ready. The company was crumbling and even the phone set her on edge.

Her gaze touched the console and the blinking private line that said she was about to speak to her father. She drew a calming breath and grabbed the receiver, forcing a smile and praying it reached to her voice. She didn't have time to test the strategy. Before she could speak, a deep, familiar voice resonated through the phone. "The ever dedicated CEO working through her weekend."

Ryan. Momentarily stunned, the name vibrated through her body. It was like a cool blast of air on a hot Texas day, chillingly unexpected, pleasurable, and oh so powerful. "How did you get this number?"

"I'm resourceful," he assured her, and then, with a rasp of seduction lacing his voice, added, "In all kinds of ways."

She didn't miss the innuendo. Of course, he didn't mean for her to. Which wasn't the problem. That she *liked* it was. "I assume…" she said drily, sounding remarkably unaffected by him, considering she was anything but, "that since you put those resources to use to get my direct line, you have a reason."

"Come downstairs and I'll tell you," he said.

She blinked and shook her head a little. She was tired, clearly not hearing well. "Downstairs? What?"

"I'd come to you," he said. "But Big Mike didn't think that was a good idea."

Big Mike. The security guard. In *her* building. Ryan

was in the building. Heart racing, Sarah slammed the phone down, pushed to her feet and charged toward the elevator. If people saw Ryan in her building they'd think…well, most likely that she was selling the company, or merging it with the competition. People would fear the future, fear for their jobs. Assume the worse. Jump ship. She'd never hold things together then.

In a mad dash, she was in the hallway repeatedly punching the elevator button, as if that would actually make it appear on the twentieth floor faster. The ride was slow, the fluttering of her pulse erratic. Big Mike had been working his post for ten years. He knew everyone. He'd talk. *People talked*. It was human. But Mike did his job and did it by the book. How Ryan had managed to get Big Mike to let him call her private line, she didn't know. At six four, with broad shoulders and an expressionless face, Mike was the biggest, baddest, most intimidating black man in the building, and probably all of downtown—at least to newcomers who didn't know his teddy bear side.

The difference between Ryan and Mike was physical versus intellectual muscle. Big Mike intimidated by size alone. Ryan was calculating, a man with a cobra-sharp tongue he used proficiently with acid, wit or charm, or any combination of the three.

The minute Sarah exited the elevator into the lobby, she heard the rumble of Ryan's voice saying something about a quarterback who'd been sacked three times in his last game. She rolled her eyes and had her answer as to how he'd managed to wrangle her private line from Mike. Ryan must have done his homework, and known that Mike was a former University of Texas linebacker, which, regardless of the past tense or the Houston location, made him a local celebrity. Ryan had reeled Mike in, hook, line, and sinker, with football talk. An assessment validated when she rounded the corner and rolled her eyes at what she found. Ryan was standing across from Big Mike, who sat behind the extra long, black-glass security desk, dressed in a burnt-orange University of Texas football T-shirt.

Stiffening her spine, she marched forward, her heels clicking on the glossy twelve-by-twelve white tiles of the lobby. Both men glanced in her direction, and Ryan leaned an elbow on the desk, watching her approach, deceptively casual, like a tiger lying in wait for his prey. A rush of awareness, spun with a mixture of heat and arousal, pulsed through her limbs at the idea of being that man's prey. It also ticked her off. She *would not* be aroused by her competitor.

Upon arriving at the desk, she stopped at a respectable distance from Ryan and, with an intentional snub, settled her attention on Big Mike. "I see you share a love of orange with Mr. White."

"Seems that way, Ms. Michaels," he said. She glanced at Ryan, intending to offer a cordial greeting, but noting the sparkle in his sea-blue eyes, she forgot what she'd intended to say. "Funny that," she said. "Since you went to UCLA."

"I regret that choice," he said. "Which is why that was the last time I ever allowed my father to tell me what to do."

He arched a challenging brow with the silent question—*Can you say the same?*—that was too damn clear with Mike standing there.

"Can we talk?" she asked tightly. "In *private*?"

He pushed off the desk. "Sure," he said, motioning toward the elevator. "Lead the way."

She countered with a wave in the direction of the exit door. "Let's step outside."

His lips twitched and he eyed Mike. Mike grinned. "Told you she'd never let you upstairs."

Sarah's gaze flashed approvingly to Mike. "Good work, Mike."

Instantly, Mike straightened, his shoulders broadened in a prideful gesture. "Never let the offense get to the quarterback, which is you, Ms. Michaels."

Though his remark was meant to be supportive, Sarah's stomach fell to her toes, because even Mike, who knew nothing of the inner workings of the company, understood that Ryan was in offensive mode with a touchdown in sight, while she was playing a poor version of defense, with a loss in sight. She couldn't afford to have anyone believing the doom and gloom of certain failure. Not her staff, not Mike, and especially not Ryan.

Resolve stiffened her spine, and this time Sarah pulled *her* shoulders back. "Give me a few more weeks," she said, her gaze shifting to Ryan. "Ryan will be the one on the defense, not me. You can take that to Vegas and bet on it."

Sarah started walking to the exit, her intention to force Ryan to follow. His deep, sexy taunt of laughter followed in her wake.

"I do believe I just got a smack-down, Mike," Ryan said, his voice steady, unmoving. He wasn't following.

"Actually, sir," Mike replied. "That's what we call an interception."

"And my chances of getting the ball back?" Ryan asked coolly, amusement lacing his tone.

Too coolly to suit Sarah. She whirled around to face Ryan to find him, once again, leaning on the security desk, even as Mike replied, "About as good as making it through a tornado without a basement." His eyes widened on Sarah, and he rephrased, "Correction. You're a broken-down Volkswagen driving straight into that tornado and you're about to be crushed."

Ryan laughed and pushed off the counter. "I've never been compared to a Volkswagen before, but somehow I bet Ms. Michaels has been called a tornado." He sauntered toward Sarah, all loose legged and confident, faded denim hugging powerful thighs.

Sarah wanted to smack him. Or get naked with him. Or both. In that order. Or maybe the order didn't matter at all. Years of fantasizing about this man were clearly having an inconvenient impact, because now was not the time to be thinking of sex, most certainly not with Ryan. She told herself to play this cool, regardless of how hot he made her feel. She knew how to do that. She'd done so in the courtroom plenty of times, under turbulent, uncomfortable circumstances. And the dull throb of awareness settling in the lower region of her body was most definitely uncomfortable.

Calling on her inner Ice Princess persona, which she'd used for certain "uncomfortable" legal battles, she prepared for confrontation. But when Ryan stopped in front of her, toe to toe, close enough to be considered intimate, close enough to smell the spicy male scent of man, and his undoubtedly expensive, delicious cologne, her wall of ice melted under the scorching heat of his presence. Good Lord, she could feel the heat radiating off his big, gorgeous body. She blinked into the predatory gleam alight in his blue eyes that said he wanted to gobble her up. When she might have turned into one big puddle of melting female, she reminded herself, he'd gobble Chocolate Delights up right along with her.

Her chin lifted, her gaze narrowed. "I know what you're trying to do, and I won't let you. You can't have Delights."

Seconds ticked by at a crawl, his expression unreadable, his body too near. "I didn't come here today for Delights," he said, his voice low, sandpaper rough. "I came for you, Sarah."

CHAPTER THREE

Ryan watched the flicker of uncertainty touch Sarah's naturally warm amber gaze, before she quickly masked it behind anger. "I don't know what game you're playing."

"No game," he said. "Just here to collect that coffee date."

She stepped closer, lowering her voice. "I'm not buying you being so calculated for a cup of coffee."

He laughed, amusement impossible to contain. "Did you really just accuse me of seducing your security guard?"

With a sharp nod, she crossed her arms in front of her chest, glaring up at him without any inkling of intimidation and seemingly oblivious to how, at six foot two, he towered over her a good eight inches.

"If the shoe fits, buddy," she said. "And I'd say it's just the right size."

His lips twitched, his zipper expanded. "What happens at six tonight, Mike?" he called over his shoulder.

"UT kicks the Aggies' butts, sir."

Ryan arched a brow. "Satisfied?"

"Like I said, you had a plan, which I assume is to start rumors about my private meetings with the competition, and shake up my staff."

"If I wanted Delights," he said, lowering his voice, "I'd go after Delights in a far more aggressive way than starting a few rumors. And just so we get this behind us once and for all, I couldn't buy Delights even if I did want it, not with its present balance sheet, and not without my stockholders having me shot."

Her eyes widened. "What do you know about our balance sheet?"

Compliments of their many legal issues with unpaid vendors—plenty. "This isn't a conversation for the lobby," he said. "Invite me upstairs."

She inhaled a sharp breath, her gaze probing, assessing his resolve, before she accurately determined that he wasn't going away without some one-on-one time. "Not upstairs," she said. "Outside." She turned on her heels and marched toward the door.

Holding his ground, he tracked her retreat with what he knew was a hot, hungry gaze, enjoying the sway of her hips and picturing the moment he'd hold that tight little swimmer's butt in his hands. It was true there was a business element to his visiting Sarah, but not one she would ever expect, and not one he'd even determined he was willing to pursue. But he'd been curious about the little girl who'd become a beautiful woman with erotic tastes. Curious if she'd ever pursued those tastes beyond a secret corner. The answer was no, she had not. He could see it in her eyes, feel it in her presence.

And so he let her run for now, let her have a few seconds to compose herself, knowing he had her on edge, when his real intention was to *take her to the edge*. That meant being gentle, giving her the safety and security to explore and let go, with him, through trust. And she *was* most definitely *running*—from him, from what she was going to have to do to save her family business, and from the secret they'd shared so many years ago, But most of all, she was running from herself, and while he'd be easy with her, while he'd protect her, he wasn't going to let her hide.

When he finally joined her outside, as expected, she'd recovered any lost composure, and her gaze flashed hotter than the high Texas sun. He'd already surmised her anger and sharp wit were her shields, her protective walls, and they would have to go, quickly.

"I've told you," she said. "Chocolate Delights—"

"Isn't for sale," he said. "I know." He stepped toward her and gently but forcefully guided her by the elbow. "Over here." He maneuvered them inside the intimate enclave created by the side of the entryway and a large round pillar, and he settled her against the wall, cornering her with his big body, but dropped his hand, didn't touch her. Anticipation had value, it excited and intensified pleasure. "I also know how protective you feel about the company and your father right now. But we are not our fathers. And I'm not your enemy. Even if Delights was thriving right now, it's gone a different direction than Deluxe. We aren't even direct competitors anymore."

Her eyes flashed. "And if I change that?"

"I hope you do," he teased. "Then I really could buy you out."

"Maybe I'll buy *you* out."

"Let the challenge begin," he said, smiling, and then sobered quickly. "Sarah. I saw my father's face when he heard about your father's cancer. He cares about him. I'm not even sure either of them really even remembers why they're fighting. If mine does, he refuses to talk about it. They're just old and stubborn, and just won't get over it, whatever *it* may be."

"They fought about how fast to grow the company," she said.

"Did they?" he asked. "I'm not sure my father would be so secretive if that were all there was to it. But either way, you're in the same boat I was. And let me tell you, taking over for my hardheaded father was no walk in the park." Ryan hadn't had the guilt of a cancer diagnosis either, like she did now. "I bet you didn't know we were near bankruptcy when I took the reins, now did you?"

Her eyes went wide. "No. You...I had no idea."

He nodded. "My father was a great visionary, not a great leader. So when I said I know what you're going through with the company, I do. You can talk to me, Sarah."

"I can't talk to you, Ryan," she said. "I can't just forget who you are."

"Why?"

"Because," she said. "I just…can't."

"Even though you know you want to?" A welcome cool breeze slipped past the pillar, and a wayward strand of Sarah's rich brunette hair fell over her brow. Ryan reached up and brushed it from her eyes, the touch hissing with an instant, intense charge of electricity. Her eyes were warm with awareness, and he wondered what they'd looked like when she'd watched him in the shadows of that club. "Do you ever secretly wish you could let go of control, Sarah?"

"Never," she said, her mouth a lush pink, her eyes telling a different story.

"Liar," he accused, letting his hand drop.

"Do you?"

"Pleasure is my form of control," he said. "I do believe it's your personal hell."

"You couldn't be more wrong." She laughed, but there was an edge of bitterness to it, an edge of discomfort. "Not having control is my hell."

"You're afraid of thinking you have control and then finding out you don't."

"Which never happens to you, I assume, oh master of the great balance sheets?"

"Master, Sarah?" he asked softly. "I wonder what made you choose that specific title?"

Her eyes went wide, her face paling with the realization of what she'd said, of what he'd said, of what they now had out in the open. "I'm done talking." She tried to sidestep him.

He maneuvered slightly, so she'd have to touch him to pass, successfully stalling her retreat. "What we shared that night is nothing to be ashamed of."

Her eyes widened farther, her cheeks flushed. "We didn't share anything."

"Didn't we?"

Panic flared in her eyes. "Let me pass."

"I give the orders," he said. "That's how it works."

"Not with me." Yet she held her ground, didn't try to pass again. She wanted to know more of what he could show her, and he was frankly shocked that she'd clearly never explored the world she'd visited inside Silk beyond that one night. Shocked that she'd suppressed her obvious desires so completely, yet he was undeniably pleased she could be his to teach, his to pleasure.

"You're afraid."

"I'm not afraid."

"Then why did you hide from me that night in Silk? Why not walk right up to me and take part in the experience?"

"I was dragged there by a friend," she said. "I didn't even want to be there. And we weren't exactly friendly. The strife between our fathers was at its worst back then."

"Which would have added a sense of the forbidden we would have enjoyed," he said. "Knowing yourself, Sarah, facing your fears, knowing what pleases you, what *controls you*, what turns you inside out, makes you stronger. Gives you control. And you will have control. We set boundaries and limits. You do nothing you don't want to do. But you need to know that neither do you get to hide from what you want to do. I won't let you."

Desire and fear, a hint of panic, flickered in her eyes. "I don't want—I can't…no."

"You can," he said. "And you want to." He studied her a moment and then stepped backward. "But obviously you aren't ready. When you are—and I believe you will be—you know where I am." He said nothing more, leaving her there to face the decision, and herself, alone. Until the time when she faced it with him.

CHAPTER FOUR

At nearly nine o'clock, a month after her encounter with Ryan, Sarah sat at her desk, her fourteen-hour workday still well under way. She had a million plates spinning in the air, and she was terrified one of them was going to tumble and break, with devastating results. She reached in her drawer and pulled out the note Ryan had sent her the morning after his visit. *When you're ready—Ryan*, the plain white note read, along with several phone numbers.

Sarah stared at it, as she had innumerable times, as she'd tried to deny she wanted what Ryan offered her, that she, the ultimate control freak, could actually want to be controlled. But the fantasies of Ryan doing just that were far too many and far too frequent. Still so very easily, the image of him at that nightclub so many years ago—naked, powerful, commanding, and wholly masculine. The ring of her cell phone had her setting the note back in the drawer, and cringing at the caller ID. It was her mother, again. This made three times in the past hour, and from the prior two messages, Sarah was well aware of why she was calling. Despite Sarah's best efforts to keep it from happening, her mother had found out about one of the toughest changes Sarah had made at Delights these past few weeks.

With a sigh, she knew she had to answer. Sarah grabbed the phone and punched the send button. "Hi Mom."

"You can't stop production of the Delights Peppermint Patties," she said, not bothering with hello. "Do you know what your father will do when he finds out? That's his favorite product, our first product. It's the staple of the company."

"It doesn't sell, Mom," she said. "It's—"

"Your father's favorite product. Don't take *that* from him. He's lost his hair, his health. Let him keep his damn Peppermint Patties."

Sarah squeezed her eyes shut, aware of the fear and grief motivating her mother's illogical demand. "Mom," she said softly. "I know this is hard. It's hard for me too, but I made Dad a promise I'd save the company. And I'm going to save it. I have to attract investors to the company, and that means making tough choices."

"What am I supposed to tell your father?"

"Tell him I'm not going to let him down, and I love him." She hesitated, dreading what she had to confess, but knowing it would avoid another panicked phone call. "I'm shutting a dozen retail stores too. I'm making the announcement Monday." And considering it was Friday, it was going to be a long weekend. And a long phone call. It took thirty minutes for Sarah to calm her mother down, to explain some of the innovative partnerships she was pitching, to assure her things would be better. When Sarah finally hung up, ending the call with a heartfelt promise to visit her father the next day, she had to check and see if her hands were shaking. Who was she kidding? She was barely hanging on to control.

She yanked open her desk, grabbed the note from Ryan and, before she could stop herself, dialed. He answered on the second ring. "Hello."

His voice was deep and sexy, and….

"Sarah?"

"Yes," she said, leaning back in her chair. "It's me."

"How's your father?"

It wasn't what she expected, though she wasn't sure what she'd expected. "The doctor says he's where he should be at this stage of treatment, but he's having a tough time."

"And you?" he asked. "How are you?"

"I just hung up with my mother," she said. "She found out I killed the Peppermint Patti product line, and she was upset."

"We had a Peppermint Patti line, you know," he said. "I killed it too. They don't sell. You did the right thing."

"I know," she said, "but hearing you say it is comforting. Though it shouldn't be. I mean, you're—"

"A friend, Sarah," he said softly. "Let me come and pick you up. We can—"

"No," she said quickly, her heart exploding in her chest. "No. I have work to do. I just, well, I needed to talk to someone who understands."

Silence lingered a moment before he said, "Nothing happens that you don't want to have happen with me, Sarah. If we never do more than talk—"

"I know," she said. "Honestly, I really do know. And thank you, Ryan, for being a friend. And if you really aren't a friend and I find out I am the biggest fool on the planet… I'm going to kick your butt."

He laughed. "I'm not using you. In fact, I believe I've invited you to use *me*."

A flutter of butterflies touched her stomach, heat rushing through her limbs, before she dared to say, "Right now, I'm not prepared to reach beyond my own imagination."

"Are you telling me you've been fantasizing about me, Sarah?" he asked, his voice low and whisky rough.

"Maybe it's that forbidden-fruit appeal you mentioned the other day," she said, barely believing what was coming out of her mouth. "Or maybe I want…."

"Want what, Sarah?"

To be brave enough to act on those fantasies. But instead, she said, "I remember that night in Silk like it was yesterday. It was my first time, my only time, in a place like that. Is that the kind of place you frequent?"

"My tastes are far more refined and exclusive now than they were then," he said softly. "I'm a member of a highly elite club, where discretion is as valued as pleasure."

"I see."

"What else do you want to know, Sarah?"

"You don't mind me asking questions?"

"You *should* ask questions," he said. "Choices should be educated."

She liked that answer. "Okay then. What if I didn't want to go to this club you are a part of?"

"Then we wouldn't go," he said. "But just so you know, we would have a private suite for play, where it's just you and me."

For play. Her stomach fluttered again at what that might mean.

"We don't venture beyond that room unless I know you're in your comfort zone," he continued, "I push you, yes, but I protect you too, Sarah."

She absorbed it all, aroused, interested—terrified—needing to back away to think. A sense of desperateness rose inside her, and she quickly and without any semblance of smoothness changed the subject. "I'm closing twelve stores Monday."

And to her utter shock, he shifted right along with her, asking all the right questions and offering some solid advice. They ended the call a quick hour later, and Sarah sat at her desk with his parting words replaying in her head.

When you're ready, Sarah.

But she wasn't sure she'd ever be ready to give up control, especially not to a man like Ryan, who might not ever give it back.

CHAPTER FIVE

By the time Thursday evening rolled around, Delights'
first ever layoff had become a special news report on
a local station. Sarah's staff had panicked. Then, her
mother had panicked. In turn, Sarah had rushed from
work to the hospital, where her father was staying for
several intense treatments. She hadn't even taken time
to change from her black suit dress and high heels. And
now, sitting in the recliner beside his bed, she watched
him staring at the late edition of the news, certain he'd
be the next to panic.

Instead, when it was over, he hit the remote button
to turn off the television with a grimace on his pale,
thin face. Sarah held her breath, waiting for the explosion that didn't come. Instead, he set the remote on the
nightstand. "These news people will do anything for a
story, honey. Don't let them get to you. Once you land
these big new accounts you're working on, we'll rattle
cages until they tell the good news just as vividly as the
bad. I have faith in you."

Sarah blinked in surprise. "I'm sorry, am I in the

wrong room? Because my father is the man with a stubborn side who loves to argue with me and curse out those who tick him off, even if they are on the television."

He smiled weakly, looking far older than the fifty-two years he'd always appeared to be, and running a hand that shook ever so slightly over his head. "Your father also used to have thick brown hair that wasn't falling out or turning gray. Things change. I've read over your marketing plans and your bank proposal, and I already know the dismal truth about our bottom line. I should have listened to you years ago."

"Dad," she said, taking his hand, her heart in her throat.

He squeezed her fingers. "Cancer has made me see the light. I've spent too much time blinded by what is familiar rather than seeing what there is to learn. I just hope I survive it long enough to show you. I meant what I said. I believe in you. I know you have things under control."

Fighting the pinch in the back of her eyes, Sarah smiled at him. "I'll welcome the day you are back at the office giving me attitude and making me fight you tooth and nail to prove my decisions are sound."

Sarah spent the next hour with her father, trying to forget the cancer, the work on her desk, and the fear of letting him down. She just wanted to be with him, to enjoy every second with him. They were watching

Indiana Jones when her mother arrived with the doctor in tow. There was good news. Sarah listened to what sounded like the first real breakthrough in her father's treatment, and felt the doctor's words like a cool breeze on a hot day, washing her with relief. They weren't out of the darkness yet, but they had a night-light, and it was a beacon of hope.

The doctor left and her mother flipped the television back to *Indiana Jones,* settling into the chair beside the bed in Sarah's place. Despite it being nearly eight o'clock, Sarah was invigorated, ready to head back to the office and get to work.

"Everyone says your father looks like Harrison Ford," her mother said, looking tired but at peace for the first time since Sarah's return home.

"But better looking," her father joked.

Sarah smiled at their familiar, loving banter, and said her goodbyes for the evening, leaving her parents alone. But as she walked down the hall, her black high heels clicking on the tiled floor, her mood grew heavier with each step, her father's words playing in her head. *I believe in you. You have things under control.* What if she didn't have things under control? *I do*, she told herself. *I have a brilliant marketing plan. I have a great staff, ready to take things to a new level.* Right. She had things under control.

Forcing herself to repeat those words the rest of the way to the parking lot, but breaking her mantra when she neared her car, Sarah dug in her purse for her keys and couldn't find them. She dug harder, deeper. She emptied her purse on the hood, thankful for the parking spot near the door and the streetlight. With a bad feeling in her stomach, she pressed her face to the tinted window and squinted. Sure enough, her keys were on the seat. She closed her eyes in complete frustration, hearing her father's words. *I believe in you. You have things under control.* And what did she do? She lost control of the most basic of life's responsibilities. She'd locked her keys in her car.

She didn't know how much time had passed when she finally lifted her head, but there were tears on her cheeks and she swiped at them angrily. She hadn't cried before now, not with the cancer diagnosis, not with the grim news week after week, and not through the upheaval of racing home to take over the company. She was too tired, both mentally and physically, and she knew this. She was scared of failing. Of making wrong choices. But none of this was a good enough excuse. She didn't have cancer. She wasn't dying. It was time to get a grip on herself and do something other than sit here and act like a wimp.

She snatched her phone from her purse and tried to figure out who to call, because she wasn't going inside and upsetting her parents. Calling for roadside service seemed logical. That made sense. Instead, without consciously doing so, she thumbed through her numbers and stared at Ryan's number. She punched the recall button and dialed Ryan. "I can't believe I'm doing this," she whispered.

"Hello," his deep, sexy, deliciously male voice said after only one ring, and absolutely no time to change her mind and back out.

Sarah sucked in a breath. He could be at work, or with a woman, at his club. She had to hang up.

"Sarah?"

Damn. Of course, he had caller ID. "Yes…I…my car," she swallowed hard. "I lost my keys and—"

"Where are you?" he asked, not seeming to need more than her cryptic nonsense, also as out of character as locking her keys in her car and then dialing his number.

"The hospital," she said, and glanced around. "Row One-A at the front, by the door."

"I'll be there in a few minutes."

He hung up. Sarah sank against her car and waited for her own panic rather than her father's, panic created by what she'd just done. But instead, she replayed, not her father's words this time, but Ryan's. *By facing your fears, you grow stronger. It gives you control.*

And when Ryan's sleek 911 black Porsche pulled up beside her, and the passenger door popped open, Sarah wasted no time climbing inside. She pulled the door shut, closing herself inside the intimacy of the sports car, the masculine, spicy, powerful scent of him insinuated into her nostrils, into her bloodstream. The car idled as they stared at each other, shadows wrapping them in intimacy but not invisibility. She could see he was dressed in a dark suit, a light shirt, his tie still in place. She could see the light stubble of a newly formed beard. "I hope I didn't interrupt anything," she finally said.

"I would have come even if you had," he said. "Do you have extra keys somewhere we can pick them up?"

He'd come here fully prepared to offer her aid without any physical connection. Knowing this made her more certain than ever she wanted him. "I don't really care about my keys right now."

He put the car in Park and turned to her, his eyes dark, lost in the shadows. "What does that mean, Sarah?"

She wanted him to touch her, but he did not. She wanted to touch him, but somehow, she knew she should not. "You know what it means."

"Say it," he ordered.

Anything to get him to touch her, anything to finally know the escape this man could give her. Yes, she wanted the escape. She wanted it with him. "I'm ready, Ryan."

CHAPTER SIX

The car was dark, the engine all but silent as it idled in place, the air heavy with anticipation, with a sexual charge. Ryan had never wanted a woman's submission the way he wanted Sarah's, but true submission was given freely. It was a choice, not a reaction.

"What makes tonight the night?" Ryan asked. "What happened in the hospital?"

She stared at him a moment and then started to turn away. He captured her hand, held her in place. "Talk to me, Sarah. Is something wrong with your father?"

"No," she said. "I mean yes, but not his health. He had good news on his treatments. But he's changed. He's not questioning my decisions. He's not yelling about what went right or wrong. I know how to deal with my father who rants and yells and demands. But he said he believes in me. He said he should have listened to me sooner. Ryan, he said I have things *under control*."

He narrowed his gaze. "And you're afraid you don't."

"No," she said. "I know I have control now…it's more the pressure to stay in control I'm suddenly feeling more than ever, and it's freaking me out. It's just…it's intense." She sighed. "Tonight…I don't want that pressure. I don't want to make the decisions. I don't want to be the one in charge." This was the answer he wanted, the right answer. Ryan studied her a long moment, the pulse of arousal pumping through his veins, into his cock. He slid his hand up her arm, over her shoulder, and gently let his fingers settle on the delicate skin of her neck. He could feel the quickening of her pulse beneath them, almost taste her as his lips lowered a breath from hers, and lingered.

He inhaled the scent of her, vanilla, honeysuckle, and innocence, the kind of innocence a woman had when she hadn't discovered her true self, her true desires. His lips brushed hers, his teeth nipping roughly, before he licked the delicate flesh. "Take off your panties, Sarah."

Her lips parted in shock, a delicate sound, as delicate as her sensibilities appeared to all those who didn't know her secret desires. Proved to him by the way she showed no other resistance until voices sounded nearby, and she feared discovery, and that someone but he would know those secrets. She jerked back as if to pull away, to look for the visitors' location. He held her steady. He'd known they were there. He was testing her limits, testing her trust in him.

"You let me worry about the rest of the world." He

made the statement an order. "You focus on what I tell you to do." He leaned back, studied her, allowed his hand to fall from her neck when he really wanted to drag her to his lap and fuck her right here. But that was too much for her now, too much too soon, so instead he said, "Unless you want to stop here, stop now?"

Seconds ticked by, the voices growing closer, her teeth worrying her bottom lip. "No," she whispered. "No, I don't want to stop." She turned and eased her skirt upward, flashing the lacy trim of her thigh-highs as she lifted her hips and tugged a strip of black lace down her thighs and over her high heels.

She turned back to him and dangled them off one finger. "Do they please you, *Master*?"

The words rolled off her lips, as if practiced in those fantasies she'd shared with him, and his cock thickening in response, his zipper stretched. A slow smile slid to his mouth before one of his hands closed around the panties and the other wove into her hair and pulled her mouth to his. Sliding his tongue past her lips, he kissed her deeply, passionately, drinking the sweet nectar that was Sarah—a forbidden fruit for far too long. "Yes Sarah," he said when he tore his lips from hers. "You please me very much." Pleased him in ways unique to her.

Thirty minutes later, Ryan pulled the car to a halt inside the security gates of the sprawling, three-story, twelve-thousand-square-foot white mansion that sat on twenty acres and was their destination. He'd tried to take Sarah to his home, where they could be alone, intending to slowly ease her into his world. Sarah had quickly rejected his well-intended plan, though, insisting that "ready" meant "ready," which had spoken volumes as far as Ryan was concerned. It had told him that, indeed, she *was* ready—and not just ready, but also that she wouldn't give herself an escape from facing her most intimate fears and desires. Ready to discover what she was capable of by allowing herself the freedom of destroying boundaries, ready to take on the new challenges in her life. And so Ryan had brought her here, to the society, where a night of discovery and pleasure awaited them both.

"So this is the Alexander Quarters you spoke of?" she asked.

"Named for the owner, and the society's president, Marcus Alexander," he confirmed, having encouraged her to ask questions on the ride here, knowing trust between them would soon be paramount.

"It's magnificent," she said, her voice quavering slightly in what seemed to be a combination of awe and nerves.

He followed her gaze, seeing what she was seeing. The mansion was alight with delicate spotlights, and framed by a massive green lawn and a circular driveway leading to a mountainous ivory stairwell with huge white pillars. Inside the curve of the driveway, a rock waterfall was aglow in a pale blue haze. Various structures, all fetish fantasy lands, sat at locations spread across the property.

Ryan hit the remote control on his visor, and a garage door off the side of the house, used exclusively by the six Round Table Masters in the society, began a slow upward glide. The Round Table was a group of six masters who were the elite of the elite, a court of law for the society, with Marcus as judge. Ryan was one of those six.

By the time the garage was resealed with them inside the building, he was already opening Sarah's door, watching as her skirt rode high on her long legs, a sight all the more tantalizing with the absence of her panties. Seeming to understand where his thoughts were, she stood, her gaze avoiding his, then quickly, primly inched her skirt downward, as if he wasn't about to take it off her anyway. "You're nervous," he observed.

She glanced at him from under long, dark lashes. "I…it's just…."

He shut the door and pulled her close to him. "If you're nervous, say you're nervous."

She blinked up at him, the surprise in her expression at the sudden contact turning to warmth as she melted into him, all soft, willing woman, her fingers tentatively splaying across his chest. She was petite, delicate, a sweet flower with an exotic undertone that was part innocence, part princess and part wanton concubine. His cock thickened, tension coiling in his gut, hot tension, born of desire. The kind of tension and arousal that a recent bout of boredom had declared unattainable, with no solution to be found, no matter how daring the society game he'd tried. Yet, this inexperienced, sensual woman had him on the edge, had him hungry. He wanted her more than he remembered wanting anyone in a very long time, which only made the urgency to set the parameters for the night more imperative. Once the play began, it was critical he know where their boundaries were, and how far he could push them.

"Are you nervous, Sarah?" he repeated, when she still hadn't replied.

"Yes," she admitted. "But—"

"No buts," he said. "If I ask you what you feel, you tell me. You don't own your inhibitions tonight Sarah— I do. Just like I own your pleasure." His hand slid over her backside, and he began inching her skirt upward. "Nervous can be good, even arousing, when it's created by the anticipation and excitement of what's to come next." The hemline rose higher, exposing her backside, and he watched her swallow hard, knew she was feeling some of that anticipation now. He palmed her check and caressed downward, lifting her leg to his waist. "Are you still nervous?"

She gasped, her fingers curling around his shirt, and he slid his fingers up her thigh, where she was bare to him, no panties to stop him from sliding right into all the wet heat of her arousal.

She laughed, and those nerves of hers were etched in the sound. Then she buried her face in his shoulder, her spine arched. She whispered, "I can't believe I'm doing this."

"Don't hide from me, Sarah," he ordered, still teasing her intimately, sliding a finger over the slick, wet folds of her core that told him above all else how much she wanted this. He heard her intake of breath as he slid a finger inside her, felt her shiver, but still she didn't look at him. "Sarah. Look. At. Me."

Slowly, she lifted her head, focusing a heavy-lidded, aroused stare at him. "I'm trying, Ryan."

"Do you like what I'm doing to you?" he demanded, knowing she did but needing to hear it. There were rules and boundaries that had to be set before they were inside the society.

"Yes," she whispered.

"But yet you hid your face from me, and you claim you can't believe you are doing this," he stated. "That doesn't sound like a woman who's ready to go inside the society."

Her fingers tightened on his shirt. "No...I mean, yes I am...I...."

Her hesitation set off alarm bells, telling him she was either having cold feet or too shy to tell him what she wanted or didn't want. Whichever it was, he needed to know, and he needed it remedied if they were going further into sexual exploration.

He lowered her leg, dragged the material of her dress down her legs, and then trapped her body against the car. He broke their physical connection, his hands on the roof, body framing but not touching her. "We're going to keep this simple, since this is your first, and perhaps, only time inside the society," he said. "If you don't like something, you simply say 'stop,' and I'll stop. If I ask you if you want me to keep doing something or if you like something, and you don't answer, I will stop as well. Understood?"

She blinked at him. "Yes." Her chin lifted. "And I'm not afraid to say what I want or don't want. I'm just new at this. I...I didn't want you to stop what you were doing, but I need to make sure we have one thing clear. Tonight, I'm yours. Tomorrow, I belong to myself. And I'm darn sure no one's submissive in the boardroom. This changes none of that."

"We have an agreement," he said, and he meant it. Her ability to be both submissive and dominant drew him to her. Not that she was the first women he'd known with such a trait, but the first who had held his interest. Sarah appealed to him in all kinds of colorful, arousing ways that few others ever had. "That is, as long as you, Sarah, know that tonight, I own more than your pleasure. I own *you*."

CHAPTER SEVEN

Ryan had been right when he'd said anticipation equaled arousal, because as Sarah followed him out of the garage and into the house, with her hand tucked into his, her pulse was jumping, and her body, wet and hot in all the right places. Her high heels clicked on expensive tiles, and her gaze brushed even more expensive paintings on the walls. But her surroundings were mere decoration since it was the man who captivated her.

Sarah watched Ryan as he walked, claiming every molecule of the room with his presence, her gaze riveted on the confident way he carried himself, on the killer way his custom suit was molded to his broad shoulders, accentuating his athletic build. He was a gorgeous man who exuded power and masculinity in ways few others did. Sarah wanted the fantasy she'd lived all these years since her visit to Silk. The fantasy wasn't just about being a submissive; it was about being a submissive to Ryan. Yes. Ryan was her fantasy.

Though admittedly, she'd endured a moment of

panic back by the car with the first moment of feeling out of control—sleeping with the enemy wasn't what most people would consider smart, while willingly playing sex games with said enemy, which required her to be submissive, would most likely be called border-line insane. And perhaps, the illicit, forbidden aspect of being with Ryan was all a part of the enticement. All her life she'd been good, she'd been in control. Tonight, she wanted to escape.

They paused in a foyer, where a winding stairwell, covered in red carpet, led to a high balcony and made her think of old elegance, *Gone with the Wind* style.

"Where is everyone?" she asked, realizing that this place was nothing like Silk. They were alone, not a voice to be heard or a person to be seen. There was no music, no moaning, no naked bodies. Somehow, the calmness, the lack of what she'd assumed would be an obvious display of sex and seduction, as had been the case in Silk so many years before, set her on edge. There was no place to hide here, no place to disappear in the midst of everyone else's pleasure.

"The mansion is the master's quarters I mentioned in the car," Ryan explained. "It's an exclusive section of the society that isn't open to the general member-ship, just as a nonmember isn't allowed inside the soci-ety domains without formal application for member-ship."

She remembered what he'd said, yes, but hadn't

computed then, as she did now, that Ryan was one of the controlling masters of the society. The realization sent a wild flutter through her stomach, and a rush of heat across her skin. Of course, he was a controlling master. He was a leader in everything he did, dominant in every way, in control. Soon to be in control of her, too. Their eyes locked and held, electricity crackling in the air, and she knew he was thinking the same thing.

"Welcome to my world, Sarah," he said softly. He started to walk backward, leading her by the hand he still held, toward a double door to the left of the stairwell, when a male voice called out from the stairwell.

"Ryan."

Sarah and Ryan turned toward the unexpected voice, and Sarah found a tall, dark-haired man, in his mid-thirties, headed their way, a man who could be described as nothing shy of magnificent.

"I wasn't aware we had a guest tonight," the man said, nearly at the bottom of the stairs now, and Sarah noted that his black slacks and black button-down shirt were tailored to perfection, and clung to the long, lean lines of a body honed to magnificence. This was the kind of man who made the clothes, not the opposite. The kind of man who claimed everything he touched.

Ryan's hand slid to Sarah's back, closing the distance between them, as if *he* were claiming her, as if he sensed what she was feeling. She could feel the heat of his hand, the possessiveness burning through her thin dress. And she liked it. She liked it probably far more than she should. What was it about Ryan that made an independent businesswoman want to be possessed? She didn't know. No other man had evoked such primitive arousal in her.

The newcomer cleared the stairwell and stopped in front of Sarah and Ryan, towering above her, but eye level with Ryan. The men shook hands before Ryan did the introductions.

"Sarah," he said. "This is Marcus Alexander, the controlling partner in the society and the owner of the property." He glanced at Marcus. "And Marcus, this is Sarah Michaels. The acting CEO of Chocolate Delights."

Marcus arched a dark brow, a pair of piercing blue eyes registering understanding and interest. "An interesting pairing if I ever saw one." He offered her his hand. "Nice to meet you, Sarah."

Sarah accepted his hand, and she felt the touch clear to her toes, as if she was ultrasensitized, as if he oozed sex and it was seeping clear to her bones. She actually felt her cheeks warm, not to mention her thighs burn. Good gosh, she was an attorney, a CEO now too, and she was blushing. *In a sex club*. Something she was pretty sure was a sign she was in over her head here. "Nice to meet you as well," she managed to choke out, thinking how insane the formality was under the circumstances. Actually, the formality was etched in the very walls of this place. No. It wasn't formality, she realized. It was ultimate, complete control, that one could not, would not, be allowed to hide from.

As if driving her thoughts home, letting her know he did, indeed, believe he owned her while she was in his home, Marcus held her hand several drawn-out seconds, his stare resting on her face, assessing, probing, like an attorney with a witness on the stand, before finally he released her, his gaze lifting to Ryan's. "We have a new membership test beginning at the top of the hour. I'll arrange to have Sarah included."

Sarah's heart jumped right into her throat. New membership test? Oh no. She didn't like the sound of that one bit, but before she could fully reach the point of panic all over again, Ryan said, "Not tonight."

It was all Sarah could do to contain a sigh of relief, which she construed as yet another indicator that she was in over her head with this society. So *very* over her head. Part of her screamed with the loss of her fantasy, wanted to cling to it, while another part just wanted to run—and run fast and far.

Marcus considered Ryan a moment longer, with what appeared to be a hint of surprise, before he gave a short nod. "Understood." He then shifted his dark, heavy gaze to Sarah. "I hope to see more of you very soon, Sarah." He turned and headed to the front door.

Sarah stared after him, repeating his words in her head, no doubt the meaning meant *naked* and *at his mercy.* No. No. No. Not happening. This man might be sexy, but he had a ruthless quality to him. He'd take her control and never give it back. And it was then she realized that her ability to explore herself, her wants, desires, her fears, was only possible because of the unexplainable trust she had in Ryan, something that remarkably defied their families' rivalry.

"Sarah," Ryan said, urging her to turn to him.

Sarah whirled around. "Ryan—"

"I have no intention of sharing you, Sarah," he said, his hands settling warmly, firmly on her arms. His touch sent a deep shiver down her spine, searing her with possessiveness, with command, which somehow managed to comfort and arouse rather than intimidate as Marcus had done. "I never intended to share you," he continued. "You're off-limits and Marcus knows that now. You don't belong to him, or the society. Any play we take part in tonight will be behind closed doors. Exactly why we're going to my private chambers now where we will be alone. Where you can watch and explore, under the safety of seclusion."

Seclusion. Yes. She wanted seclusion. She'd thought the society would be like Silk, a wild festival of sex games, where she'd simply blend in, where the sheer volume of sex acts would consume her inhibitions. Maybe even, if she was honest, a way to hide from what Ryan made her feel. She wanted to keep this about sex, when she feared she was starting to feel more for him.

But it was clear now that this place wouldn't let her hide. Ryan wouldn't let her hide. But he'd also promised her protection, and he'd given it to her with the offer of privacy. He'd known what she needed more than she did. Maybe she'd sensed that, maybe that was why he was safe.

His hand slid down her arm, goose bumps gathering in its wake, her nipples pebbling and aching, until he drew her fingers inside his. Again, he walked backward, holding her stare even as he led her toward those same double mahogany doors they'd been approaching before Marcus appeared, where she assumed his private quarters were. And she followed willingly, watching him with more of that nervous anticipation, as he punched a security code into a panel, shoved a door open and turned to face her again. He stepped close, his big body touching her, claiming her.

"Before you go inside," he said, his hands framing her face, "let's be one hundred percent clear about something, Sarah. Tonight has nothing to do with Delights or Deluxe or any family dispute or competition created by that dispute. This is about you and me. You do this for you, no other reason. You have nothing to prove to me."

"I know," she agreed, surprised yet pleased with both his declaration, and the gentleness of his touch, knowing the primal male beneath such tenderness. It stroked her confidence, stroked the ache between her thighs to create a thrumming need. "But you have something to prove to me."

His lips lifted, his eyes alight with a hint of amusement. "I have something to prove to you?"

"That's right," she assured him. "You said giving away control would give me control." Though right now she was thinking more about him giving her pleasure than about control. "Prove it."

She watched his expression instantly darken, his eyes heat, before he maneuvered her to stand in front of him, her back to his chest. His hands once again settled on her shoulders, his hips framed her backside, and her body tingled everywhere he touched, everywhere she *wanted him to touch*.

"All you have to do now is step past the threshold, and I'll show you what you want to know. You will be mine for the night. I will be *your master*."

Sarah felt his words in the wet heat between her thighs, in the pebbling ache of her nipples, in the nervous anticipation that, most definitely, was arousal. She wanted this, she wanted him. She entered his private chambers, and his world became hers.

CHAPTER EIGHT

The door shut softly behind Sarah as she entered Ryan's private chambers, a moment before dim lighting illuminated the ceiling, leaving the rest of the room, and the erotic secrets it might hold, in the cover of shadows. A large room with several doors, a living area and a bedroom, she thought, as she tried to gain some sense of location, of control. Or perhaps distract herself from the uncertainty of what was to come.

Ryan stepped behind her, his arms closing around her, his lips brushing her ear. His breath trickled seductively along her neck. "Finally alone," he whispered, one of his hands flattening intimately on her stomach. "Are you scared, Sarah?"

Oh yeah, she thought. And excited, and aroused, and impossibly turned-on. "A little," she replied, and then barely contained a moan as he molded his hands to her breasts.

"Tell me what scares you," he replied, his thumbs stroking her nipples, kneading her with a hard, erotic touch. She bit her lip, holding back the need to moan again. Already he commanded her body; already she was embarrassingly wet, embarrassingly capable of orgasm.

"You," she replied, her head falling back to his shoulders, the pleasure of having this man finally touching her almost too much to bear. How long had she wanted this? How long had she been tantalizingly aware of the dark desires this man awakened in her? How long had she blamed him for those desires, and avoided him, avoided those temptations, when the truth was, she was doing exactly what he said he wouldn't let her do—hide from herself?

"I don't scare you," he said, as if reading her mind. He tugged her dress up her hips as he had in the garage and then pressed her bare bottom against the thick bulge of his erection. Acting on instinct, she arched into him, even as he squeezed her breasts and rolled her nipples with a tight pinch of each that she felt all the way to the ache in between her thighs.

"I own you during our play session, Sarah," he said, turning her to face him, his hand sliding to her face. "And if I want to know what scares you, you tell me what scares you." His tone was demanding, his touch firm as his palm slid to her backside. "There is a price for disobedience." He caressed one cheek of her backside, and then lightly but solidly smacked her there.

Sarah sucked in a breath, feeling no pain, but plenty of surprise and, yes, pleasure. A thrilling sting that started at the spot of the connection and traveled like a flame along a fuse, spread through every inch of her body.

"What scares you, Sarah?" he demanded, sliding his hand over her backside with the promise that he would spank her again, harder this time. And Lord help her, she actually wanted him to. Adrenaline set her blood coursing, her heart racing. This was a side of herself she'd never seen, never known, a side Ryan brought out in her.

"You do—you scare me," Sarah hissed.

"Wrong answer," he said, a sharp note of disapproval in his voice. "We both know I'm not what scares you. The first rule of play, Sarah, is trust, and there is a price for violating that trust." He released her, leaving her skirt at her hips. "Take everything off but your shoes."

Stunned by both the absence of his touch, and the order, Sarah stood immobile a moment. Undress. He wanted her to undress while he watched, while he judged her and her body. While he remained fully clothed. Of course, she was standing there with her skirt at her waist anyway, which had to look ridiculous.

"Undress, Sarah," he repeated, his voice low with warning yet somehow gently prodding.

It was the way he managed to both soothe and demand, she realized, that had drawn her to him, drawn her here tonight. Made her feel safe to explore this side of herself, a side she knew existed but had for so long suppressed. With a deeply inhaled breath, Sarah slid her skirt into place down her hips, then tugged the zipper at her side down as well. She shrugged the material off her shoulders. Her dress fell to her feet, and she stepped away from it, her gaze riveted to Ryan, looking for some reaction.

He stared at her, his gaze hooded, his arms crossed, his jaw set. "All but the shoes," he reminded her.

Sarah reached behind her, nervous and fumbling with the bra hook, then helplessly glanced in his direction. He moved around her, unhooking the bra and caressing it off her shoulders. His touch was again gentle, yet the crackle in the air still sang with the promise of something darker, of reprimand.

She tossed the bra aside, not sure what to expect now, anticipation thrumming through her veins, sensitizing her body.

"Put your hands on the door," he ordered.

"What?" She started to turn, but his hands settled on her waist and stopped the action.

"You heard me," he said. "Put your hands on the door."

Sarah's lashes lowered, her breath lodged in her throat. She was really going to do this. She needed to do this, could feel her body hum just thinking about fully submitting her will to him. Sarah took the short steps forward that allowed her to press her hands to the doorway, could feel his attention on her, goose bumps rising all over her flesh with his hot stare scorching her.

"Spread your legs wider," he said, still not touching her. Why wasn't he touching her?

Sarah tried to look over her shoulder. "Ryan?"

His hands came down on her hips, his body framing hers, his cheek pressed to hers. "I'm here," he said, his hands sliding to her breasts, caressing and teasing. "Does that feel good, Sarah?"

"Yes," she murmured, and tried to cover his hands with hers.

He pressed them back against the wall. "Leave them." His hands covered hers, his body stretched over hers. "Do I feel good, Sarah?"

"Yes," she said. So good. Too good.

He slid his hands over her arms, over her back, over her hips, and then inched her legs apart, spreading her wide. His finger slid along the crevice of her backside, even as his other hand slid low on her stomach.

Sarah gasped as both of his hands pressed into the aching sensitive heat of her core, an assault of pleasure from both front and rear, even as his teeth nipped her shoulder. "So wet and hot," he murmured, nipping again, one of his fingers penetrating her. "Do you want me to keep touching you?"

"Yes."

"Do you want me inside you?"

"Yes."

His hands moved to her hips. "Then tell me what scares you, Sarah."

She squeezed her eyes shut, wanting to beg him to touch her again, to stop pushing for an answer she didn't want to give. Because he scared her, and she knew he didn't like that answer. She didn't know what to say. "Ryan—"

His hand slid into her hair and gently but firmly pulled her head back to his shoulder, her lips an inch from his. "I don't scare you or you wouldn't be here." He kissed her, a long, deep, hot kiss that had her panting with need, and when he released her mouth, he said, "You don't kiss me like I scare you." He released her hair, slid one hand down to her backside. "What scares you, Sarah?"

"You do," she said. "Damn it, you do, Ryan."

He smacked her backside, a short stingy slap that had her gasping for air, and her sex clenching with ache. And then he smacked her again, and once more. She was panting when he finished, preparing for another smack, wanting another connection. His hand slid to her breast, fingers tugging roughly at her nipples. "You like being spanked," he said. "You like the idea of me controlling you, and that's what scares you. You're afraid of yourself, of what you want…what you need."

Her head fell forward as she struggled with an admission that made her feel vulnerable. "Yes."

"Do you want more?"

"Yes."

"Yes what?"

Yes what? "Please."

He smacked her backside three times, not hard, just stingingly erotic and oh so pleasurable, then he turned her to face him, pressed her against the door, his hands doing delicious things to her body—touching her breast, sliding to her sex, fingers pressing inside her until she was riding his hand like a wanton wench, and spasming in release. She was panting and, at the beginning of embarrassment creeping over her, he said, "Don't. Don't even think about regretting what just happened. I forbid it. And I am the one in control here."

"I wish it were that easy."

He gently stroked her hair from her face. "It *is* that easy. While you're here with me, you just let me make all the decisions. The weight of making them yourself lies just outside that door. And you're beautiful and sexy when you let yourself go, Sarah." She warmed at the words as he added, "And I will never do anything to hurt you."

"I know," she said, meaning it. "I know or I wouldn't be here. And I…want to be here." Nerves fluttered in her stomach, but they were good nerves, so good. The kind that was accompanied by yearning for what came next, knowing it would be unexpected and perfect, in the same moment. "What's my next lesson, *Master*?

And please tell me it includes you naked or I'm going to leave really disappointed."

"Naked and buried deep inside you," he assured her, and picked her up, carrying her toward a massive, four-poster bed, which he proceeded to show her he owned as much as he did her pleasure.

CHAPTER NINE

Six weeks after the first of many "play" dates with Ryan, Sarah sat at her desk, chatting with her father on the phone. "I'm thinking I'll retire," he said, "let you run the company."

"Retire," Sarah repeated, certain she'd heard him wrong. "You live for the company."

"I used to live for the company," he said. "But you've proved you're the one who can give it life."

She knew he meant the huge new contract Delights had managed to land with a bookstore to provide various products in a large test region. "The contract only matters if I get our credit line extended at the bank, to manufacture and distribute the product. The meeting is this afternoon."

"You will," he said. "I have complete faith in you, Sarah. You have more of a vision for Delights than I have had for years. I was just too stubborn to see it. I am so very proud of you, Sarah."

"Dad," she said softly, her heart squeezing with the pride in his voice. "Thank you."

They chatted a few more minutes before Sarah hung up the phone. Almost instantly the warmth of the call turned to a knot in her stomach. She *had* to get the credit line approved.

Her mind went to Ryan, to the escape he gave her, to how addictive that escape had become. Though he'd yet to introduce her to the society, assuring her that day would only come *when she was ready*. But they'd watched the play in the club, exploring her limits, exploring each other.

The jangle of her phone jerked Sarah into a frenzy of disaster fighting, a frenzy that ended not long before she had to leave for her meeting at the bank. She was packing up when the call came in and, without looking at the ID, she quickly answered.

"Are you alone?" Ryan asked.

A shiver raced down her spine at his deep baritone voice, her gaze flickering to the closed door. "I am," she said. "I'm about to leave for my meeting."

"Look inside your briefcase," he said. "Side pocket."

She reached down to where it sat by her feet and opened the side pocket where he'd apparently stuffed two envelopes, one white and one red, sometime the night before when they'd been together.

"Open the white one first," he instructed.

She did as he said and found a business card. "The President of National Bank?" she asked, reading it.

"He's my banker and a close personal friend," Ryan

said. "Someone very eager to keep my business. In other words, he'll give you your credit line."

She sucked in a breath, her mind racing with the pros and cons of this offer. Ryan owning her in play was one thing, but owning her in business was another.

"Use this," he said. "Tell your banker if he won't extend your credit line, National Bank is willing to step forward."

"They haven't seen my financial reports," she said. "So how can they—?"

"I told them I'd sign a note if I had to," he said. "And I will. I also know you won't let me, but then you won't have to. You'll use my connection for leverage as you should, and you'll get your credit line."

"And you get?"

"You, Sarah," he said thickly. "I get you."

The possessiveness lacing the words sent a rush of heat through Sarah's body, and a rush of erotic memories with it. Memories that reminded her just how delicious being possessed by this man really was.

"Open the second envelope, Sarah."

Sarah crossed her legs, amazed at how a phone conversation with Ryan, especially minutes before her big meeting, could have her aching with need. She tore open the flap to the envelope and pulled out a delicately taped square of tissue, which she opened. Her heart squeezed when she saw the heart-shaped necklace with a shackle attached.

"The story of O," she whispered, recognizing the BDSM emblem he'd shown her on a previous occasion, and its relevance.

"Symbolic of your journey into submissiveness with me, and me alone, Sarah. A journey that has only just begun, if you choose to wear that necklace. It's easily tucked into your blouse and hidden. We wouldn't want anyone to know you're sleeping with the enemy."

She smiled into the phone. "I stopped thinking of you as the enemy sometime…oh, maybe a week ago."

He chuckled. "That's not what you said last night."

"Ah well," she said. "You were making me mad and words were all I had to fight back with." Because he'd had her tied to the bedpost.

"Because I wouldn't let you come," he supplied.

"Exactly," she said, laughing then quickly turning somber, remembering Ryan talking about the BDSM jewelry, how some took it lightly, how he did not. He was a society master, a rule maker, a protector of those in the community. His chosen submissive was a reflection on the entire community, and no one had ever been worthy. The necklace said she was, though. It said he was reaching out to her, claiming her in a way that reached beyond a few erotic encounters. And he'd given it to her now, as a show of support before her meeting. Her fingers closed around the necklace. She had no idea where their relationship was going, how it could work out with the rivalry between families and companies, but she knew she had to find out. "The next time you see me, I'll be wearing the necklace."

"Tonight," he said. "After you go get that credit line."

"Yes," she agreed, with a smile. "Tonight."

Taking Her Boss

By Alegra Verde

Alegra Verde lives, writes, and teaches literature at a college in Detroit. Virgin Blacklace published her first erotic short stories "The Student" and "The Judge" in the anthologies *Misbehaviour* and *The Affair,* in 2009. In 2010, "The Pub Owner's Daughter" was featured in *Fairy Tale Lust* and "Things I Used to Do" was published in *Too Much Boogie*. Her e-book series *Taking Her Boss* (April, 2011) and *Tempting the New Guy* (December, 2011) were published by Mills & Boon® Spice. "The Brother" will be published by Strebor Press in an anthology edited by Zane in August of 2012.

My boss, Bruce Davies, CEO of Davies and Birch Advertising, stood there in the doorway with his mouth open in surprise. I didn't say anything. I couldn't. Alex had me bent over my desk, my short black pencil skirt shoved up to my waist, my breasts spilling out of its matching jacket, nipples trailing against the desk blotter, and his big cock shoved so far up my cunt that I felt like singing opera. Alex was breathing hard behind me, a death grip on my hips. "Don't move," he barked as he increased his speed. My ass twitched against his groin as he filled me again. His shirttails tickled my lower back. "Oh, Glory." His voice was a harsh whisper as his cock grew and hardened inside me. I squirmed to get closer, feel more of him. "I can't stop, babe. I can't." I flexed my muscles, stroking his cock to let him know it was okay to keep going, that I wanted him to continue, that I was feeling him. His hands, slippery now, slid along my ass as he tried to maintain his grip. And then he was coming, his body jerking against my ass as he spewed his seed. I was glad I'd remembered to make him wear the condom. It felt like he had uncapped a fire hydrant and couldn't get the cover back on. Finally, he trembled a bit and went still, his hands coming to rest on my waist and lower back.

"When you're done here, Ms. James, I'd like to see you in my office," Mr. Davies said before he backed out of the doorway and pulled the door closed.

"Sorry about that," Alex said as he pulled out, tugged my skirt over my exposed ass, and set about repairing his clothing.

"Hey, what can you say?" I said, not just to soothe him, but because there wasn't anything to say. I'm Glory James, Junior Account Rep, but mostly I am, or was, assistant to Mr. Davies. I don't file or type his correspondence or anything like that. He has another assistant for those things. I handle the things he doesn't have time for like preliminary research, clients' back-grounds and sales or production figures that he needs right away, or tweak contracts before Legal finalizes them. Sometimes I pick a client up from the airport and make sure he or she is settled in, and occasionally I take them to dinner or for drinks when Mr. Davies has an emergency. That was the case with Alex here. Alex and his ex-wife design and manufacture shoes mostly, but they do fashion and have recently developed a line of furniture. They've been scouting ad agencies. That's where I come in. There's a pun in there somewhere, but fucking Alex was not intentional. I mean, it isn't in my job description. I just liked him. He's a big man who takes care of his body and he's smart, reads books, not just trade magazines and newspapers.

"Will you be okay?" he asked after we'd both straightened our clothes and exhausted the container of wet wipes I kept in my desk drawer. "Do you want me to talk to him?"

"No, I'm good," I said, smiling at him 'cause what the fuck. I've been working for Davies for two years with no complaint. I've always done everything he asked and he has continued to give me more responsibility. That must mean he likes the way I do things. If he can't forgive this one indiscretion then he's in the wrong business. Besides, it's after hours, and the client is none the worse for wear.

Alex pulled me close, offering me comfort. He kissed the top of my head. "I don't think he will, but if he fires you, you can come work for me and I'll take my business elsewhere."

I leaned my face into the crisp baby-blue of his shirt taking in his masculine scent and the heat that radiated from his chest.

"And don't let him bully you into doing anything you don't want to do." He pulled me back a bit from his chest so that he could see my face, and I could see the meaning in his eyes. I nodded.

"I'll wait here," he said, turning me toward the door.

"No," I said. "You go on back to the hotel. I'll call you later."

He stood there, unmoving.

"Really," I assured him, "I can handle this."

"Glory," he began.

"I got this, Alex, really," I said, and picked up the file we'd come up here for. "And take this with you. Read it over and tell me what you think. I'll call you. Tomorrow midmorning at the latest." I was shoving him and the folder out the door.

"I can wait, and you could come back to the hotel with me," he coaxed.

I laughed. "Thanks, but really, I need to deal with this and I need a minute. I *want* you to go, okay?" You have to be firm and clear with some guys. Alex is nice, but I wasn't looking for a relationship. You have to give him credit, though. He isn't like some of these jerks who get theirs then skitter off like the rats they are at the first sign of difficulty.

I stood on my tiptoes and pressed my lips against his. I could feel his soften and meld with mine. "It was good," I said against his lips, and it was, too, even though I didn't come off. That probably had more to do with being interrupted by Davies. "*You* are good," I said, and slid the tip of my tongue between his lips. He cupped my ass and squeezed.

"Now go," I said firmly, and pushed him out the door.

I watched for a minute to make sure he headed to the elevators and didn't detour to Davies's office. When I heard the ding of the elevator, I closed the door to my office and leaned against its hard surface to catch my breath and steel my nerves. Then I headed to the side door of my office, the one that led directly into Davies's.

I knocked once. "Come in." He voice was muffled by the closed door, but it was clear. Uncertain how these matters were usually handled, I stood in the doorway contemplating my next move. "Sit," he said, and waved toward one of the three leather armchairs positioned in a half circle in front of his desk. I took the center one, seating myself directly in front of him as he sat behind his massive desk leaning forward, his elbows just at the edge supporting his weight. He studied me for a minute letting the silence speak as he clasped his hands together. One finger strayed from the steeple to toy with his lips.

"Alex Rodriquez?" he said, or was it a question.

"Sir?" Mine was a question.

"Why?"

"I like him." The bare truth. He nodded.

"Why here?"

"It just happened. We came back here for the prospectus. He didn't want to wait until tomorrow."

"Is he the only one?"

"Sir?" What was he asking?

"Of our clients?"

"Yes."

"I must say—" he leaned back in his chair "—I was surprised by your…actions."

I waited.

"Of course, I've always known that you were a very sexual person. Anyone can see that, but you've always been so…so…well behaved."

I couldn't help it. I laughed at that. Well behaved, where did that come from?

"No." He reddened a bit. "I mean, you've always been businesslike in your dealings with me."

What does one say to that? I nodded, and I'm sure my eyebrows rose and furrowed like they do sometimes when someone says something obvious or irritating.

"I mean, I've always found you appealing." His fingers were rubbing his chin thoughtfully like he does when we brainstorm about clients and contracts and plot the best strategies to lure and secure them.

Oh, no, I thought, and I really liked this job. I liked Davies. He was a good boss, good at what he did and he trusted me to do my job, no second-guessing. He seemed to know my strengths and made sure that I had input on the accounts that could benefit by them. Further, he kept his hands to himself. We'd been out drinking with clients many a late night and he'd never even allowed a hand to accidentally brush my breast, and if a client got too friendly, he never failed to divert the client's attention, and on one memorable occasion let the client know in bold words that my favors were not on the menu. I respected Bruce Davies. The little girl in me wanted to cover her ears and click her heels.

"And you're quite capable," he went on.

Of what, I wanted to ask.

"I like a capable woman," he said.

My eyebrows did their thing. Two years, I was thinking, two years of prepping, planning and hard work. I thought that I could make a home here, that I could grow. I sat up and scooted to the edge of the chair preparing to leave. I'm good at my job; I do not have to fuck the boss or anyone else to keep a job.

He tensed. "Wait," he said, holding a hand out as if he could hold me in place with the gesture.

"Glory, I'm not making any demands on you. We can continue on as we have been. It's just that when I saw you with Rodriquez…"

"You figured I was fair game," I finished for him.

"No," he said, and looked directly at me, as if he wanted me to see the truth, "I realized how much I wanted you."

The baldness of his statement stopped me for a moment.

"Do you have someone special?" he asked.

I shook my head. It was difficult to look at him because his eyes were searing into me.

"Me neither," he said. "Since the divorce, there has been no one I can trust. And without trust, I'd rather go without."

I looked at him now, trying to understand.

"I like to be told what to do," he said simply.

I nodded as though I understood, but I didn't really, not entirely. I was seeing another side of this man, a side that he rarely shared with others. He sat there in his dark immaculately tailored suit, the tie a little loose, but still in place. His hair was thinning slightly, but his close cut made no excuses and gave the impression that he was solid, reliable. The cut was flattering because its sparseness gave full rein to his sharp cheekbones and gray eyes. At forty something to my twenty-seven, he could have been…well at least an uncle, but there was still a draw there. I could feel the pull. He was telling me that he needed me, but he didn't move. He sat and waited silently for me to issue a verdict.

"I'll think about it," I said finally.

He nodded, his finger rubbing his lower lip as he studied me.

I stood up.

"Glory," he said my name softly, "only if you want to. No strings."

"See you tomorrow," I said as I made my way back through the door to my office.

After a few days, everything went back to normal,

more or less. Alex signed with us. He called a couple
of times and I went out with him, usually to dinner
with dessert in his hotel room, but I was glad when he
went home. Nice guy, but I knew he had a girlfriend
back home in Madison, Wisconsin, and I wasn't interested in taking her place. Mr. Davies was the same. He
didn't look at me strangely and he didn't slack up on the
work. He had a smile for me when I greeted him in the
morning, and treated me with the usual courtesy when
we lunched with a client or if we were having a bite
alone in his office while discussing a campaign. That's
why I was so surprised when one evening about three
weeks later, I turned to see him standing in the doorway
that connected our offices. For one, he never used that
entrance, and for another, he looked uncertain, almost
pained.

"Did you think about it, Glory?" he asked.

I wanted to say, "What?" A part of me wanted to pretend I didn't know what he was talking about, because
things had been going along so nicely.

"Yes," I said because he wanted me to, and I had
been thinking about it. I had been thinking more about
what he might want. I got that he wanted me to make
demands, *to tell him what to do*, but I was afraid of
how far it could go. However, if I were being truthful
with myself, I'd have to admit the prospect was both
frightening and alluring.

"What would you do?" I asked.

"Anything," he said. His voice was a whisper, confiding.

"What are your limits?" I needed more information.

He thought a moment. "I won't hurt anyone. I wouldn't hurt you." He stopped, and then added, "You may…hurt me, punish me if I misbehave."

I nodded.

"It must be between us," he reminded me.

"I know," I said. "You can trust me, Bruce."

He smiled, a brilliant one, one that I had never seen before.

I went to the door of my office and turned the lock. He waited, hands at his sides, loose.

"What I'd like," I said as I stood behind my desk and eased my bottom onto the smooth surface of the blotter, "is you, on your knees before me."

He moved woodenly at first. "Close the door," I said as he neared. "Lock it," I ordered. He did as he was told and then he was kneeling before me, still in his jacket and tie. A hot hand grazed my thigh, a nose pressed close to my sex, rubbed against the moisture on my panties.

"No," I said. "Not yet."

He stopped and sat back on his knees.

"Remove my panties."

His hands slid under my skirt, up my thighs, and pulled at the elastic band drawing the bit of silk along my legs and off. Then he sat back on his legs, head bowed, my panties scrunched up in his hands.

"I want your mouth on me, your tongue sliding over my clitoris, slipping between the lips of my sex," I said as I sat back on the desk.

He, with the utmost care and gentleness, pushed my skirt further up around my hips, rested my legs on his shoulders, and pressed his mouth to my center. I was glad that I had gotten a wax this morning, and that Bruce was faced with a thin, pleasing line rather than the sometimes-unruly bush.

Pressing his nose through the slit, he held it there breathing in as though it truly was a rose, all soft petals and sweet scent. And then he lapped along the slit, nipped, bit and nuzzled until I was pulling his hair and pushing at his forehead. But he kept at it until I was trembling, batting myself against his mouth, and biting my lip to keep from keening.

He pressed his face into my inner thigh, and then held his cheek there until the trembling subsided. "May I…"

"No," I said.

"I just want to feel you."

"No." I don't know where it came from, but I suddenly needed to get away. I lifted my leg over his head and slid off the desk. "I have to go." I fixed my skirt, picked up my purse, and without another word, I walked around him. He fell back onto his bottom sending my chair skating back against the wall. He was looking down at his hands and the bit of pink silk that they held as I walked through the door.

The next morning, it was as though nothing had happened between us. There was a general staff meeting with breakfast in the boardroom. Trays of hot buttered croissants, iced Danish, spiced as well as regular coffee, cranberry and orange juice, and slices of mango, pineapple, melon, and fat strawberries.

"Somebody's upgraded the fare," one of the account execs said to a colleague as he loaded his plate. "Where'd they bury the doughnuts and bagels?" The statement elicited a burst of chuckles from the growing crowd.

"You lot deserve the upgrade," Bruce said as he came into the room. "Two new clients, and the Blake cereal campaign is performing well in the test markets."

He cast me a generic smile, the same one he'd given everyone else in the room. I had expected him to be angry or sullen, but he wasn't. He was jovial, spirited even as he took his seat at the head of the table. I sat in a corner to his right nibbling at a piece of melon and sipping coffee. I figured it was a good place because I was nearby if he needed me, but out of his immediate vision. The table filled quickly followed by the seats that lined the walls. By the time the graphics guys made it up from the basement, there was standing room only and the fruit was running thin. They stocked up on coffee, rolls, iced Danish, and found spaces to lean on the wall.

Davies was in rare form. He listened intently to reports, offered suggestions and praise where warranted, solved disputes with the Wisdom of Solomon and delivered quips like a seasoned stand-up comic. Birch who sat at the other end of the table chimed in only occasionally. He, too, recognized the high that Davies was on and was more than willing to take full advantage of it. Everyone filed out of the meeting full and happy, and when they were all nearly gone, he turned to me with a beatific smile before gathering his notepad and file folder and following the crowd.

I stood there stunned for a full five minutes before I found my way back to my office. Our little interlude the night before had pleased him. I had to think what to do with this revelation. I had to think whether or not I would proceed. It was clear that he saw it as a beginning, but I wasn't sure it was something I could do or even wanted to do. I got my purse and told Claire, Davies's assistant cum secretary, that I wasn't feeling well and was going home for the afternoon.

Davies called, but I didn't answer the phone so he left a message on my machine expressing his concern and wishing me well. The next morning I'd made up my mind. I handed Bruce a key card to a room I'd rented at a Super 8 off I-75 south. It was clean and catered to families on road trips to Six Flags or Disneyland.

I'd stayed there the night before and watched the mothers sit under umbrella-covered tables and sip soda from cans while their kids splashed around in the tiny kidney-shaped pool just off the parking lot. The fathers spent their time loading and unloading SUVs and Volvo station wagons.

He held the key in the palm of his hand as though he wasn't sure what it was. The hooded look he cast me seemed uncertain for a moment, but it disappeared quickly and turned blank. I told him to go there at nine, to shower well and wear a polo shirt, jeans and sandals, nothing else. He nodded and tucked the key into an inside pocket. He asked no questions and we continued our day as though we hadn't spoken of the coming evening. We sat through a brainstorming session with the team assigned to Alex's new furniture line, had lunch with a potential client, met with another client who was less than pleased with the cost of production for a series of thirty-second spots. The day ended just before five after the two of us met with Claire to update our schedules and give Claire instructions regarding letters and contracts that needed to be generated. Through all of this, he never touched me or gave me a look that was out of the ordinary. I followed his lead, but I must admit that I was a bit nervous and suffered from inattentiveness from time to time, but no one seemed to notice.

***

When I heard the door click and then open, I was finishing up in the bathroom. "Glory," he called in an almost whisper.

"Here," I replied. "Take a seat on the bed. I'm almost done." I heard the door close, the click of the security lock, followed by the soft swish of the mattress as he sat down. I'd slipped on the thigh high stockings, the black thong and the thigh length black silk robe with the pink dragon embroidered on the back. I'd already done my eyes, shading and lining them with dark colors and brushed out my hair so that it was full and wild. I finished the makeup bit with a smudge of blush, lipstick and a smear of rouge on my nipples as an afterthought. OK. I was ready. All I needed now was courage. He could wait. The wait would be good for him. I slipped my hand deep into my thong and stroked my clitoris and the lips of my vagina until I was moist. The blood rushed into the little nub causing it to jut out between the lips. I held on to the rim of the washbasin to steady my legs. A flush stained my face and my eyes were dark and bright, I moistened my lips with my tongue and smiled at the hot girl in the mirror. Tugging my thong back into place, I stood up, dabbed a quick towel under my breasts to remove any dampness and decided that I was ready to play.

I opened the door and stood in the tiny space between the closet and the beds. His eyes had apparently been trained on that spot. My rouged breasts and the flat of stomach that ended where the slim black triangle began burned and tingled as his eyes, like fingers, trailed over them. At first, it was difficult not to cover the expanse of exposed skin, to tug the black silk kimono closed, to hide from the hunger in his eyes, but it was exciting, too. It was exciting to let his eyes scorch my skin, to know that he wanted me like that, to see the rawness of it in his face, the way he held his lips.

I walked to him and stood in front of him, a hairbreadth from his lips, letting him smell me and feel my heat. When he closed his eyes in order to master his control, I moved forward a notch and rubbed my nipples across his lips. His lips and tongue sought my nipples like a new, still blind puppy sucking and lapping, but his hands did not touch me. I let him suckle for a while and then I pulled away.

"I want you to make me come with your mouth and your hands," I said as I moved over to the other bed and sat down across from him. Arms straight, I leaned back and opened my legs. In seconds, he was kneeling between them, his mouth on my breasts again making the nipples long and hard and wet, his hands gripping and massaging my ass. He slipped the thong down my thighs and bent to run his tongue down the slight arrow of hair there. I opened wider to him and he began to rasp his tongue against the lips of my pussy as his fingers continued to tug and coax my nipples. I squirmed beneath his assault and his tongue slipped deeper into the moist lips and bumped into the jutting nub. A jolt passed through my body and my legs closed around his head. He rasped his tongue over the nub, nudging it back and forth, as he inserted two wide fingers into my already dripping passage. His fingers created a rhythm counter point to his tongue, and my body began trembling, jerking as I came, but he held me down with his mouth, and he continued to kiss and suck at the continuously tingling lips of my pussy. I had to push his head away before I screamed and startled the families on the other side of the walls. I pushed at his head, but he resisted.

"I want…" he began as he clutched at my thighs. "May I…?" he was asking, his cheek to my inner thigh as though he was afraid to look up at me.

"No," I said, and pushed hard, then harder. "No," I said louder, and kneed him in the chest. He fell back and landed sprawled on the carpet.

"No," I said as I pulled my thong back on and stood. "Don't touch me unless I give you permission," I reprimanded as I ground a spiked heel into his jean-clad thigh. Something in me wanted to laugh and say "bad dog" and smack him with a newspaper, but I didn't have a newspaper and I was glad because I was afraid that it would be too much and that I'd end up breaking character.

"Get up," I instructed. "Sit on the bed."

He did as he was told. I stood in front of him, my

pussy level with his face. He leaned forward. "Don't touch me."

He sat back and waited.

"Have you ever been fucked in the ass?" I asked.

He looked away. I grabbed him by the chin and tilted his face upward, rough. His eyes evaded mine. "I asked you a question."

He didn't say anything. I released his chin and slapped him, hard across the face. My fingers left a burning red mark. He flinched and for a moment, his eyes flashed anger. My stomach jumped. *Had I overstepped? Hey, you learn by doing.*

I tilted his chin up again and claimed his eyes with mine, making sure that mine were hard, unrelenting. He nodded. I smiled. "Are you a fag?" I asked. He shook his head no. "What do you call it when you let men fuck you?"

"It was only the one time." His words were barely audible. "I was curious."

"Did you like it?"

"It hurt at first," he confessed.

I stepped back and looked him over.

"Take off your pants," I ordered. "I want to fuck you."

He stood and slowly, almost reluctantly, unzipped and removed his pants while I went to unpack the strap-on dildo I had bought for the occasion. When I turned to him, his cock was full-on and straining upward. He was well-endowed, thick and long, and for a moment I regretted the limitations I had placed on tonight's festivities.

"Come here," I ordered. "Secure this for me."

He came to me and dropped down to his knees in order to reach between my legs to secure the straps, a set of buckles and Velcro with an underside of something soft and cushiony that allowed it to lay and hang comfortably around my hips. His fingers and hands lingered on my inner thighs leaving trails of tingles wherever they touched. I let it go. When he was done, he sat back on his haunches and looked up at me, his thick member straining against the cotton of his polo. My own penis jutted out just where my clitoris sprouted. It was a snub-nosed hard rubber piece, about five inches or so. I didn't want to hurt him.

"I want you on the floor between the beds, your face in the carpet, your ass in the air." I pointed.

He hesitated.

"Now," I ordered.

He did as he was told.

I knelt behind him and held the weight of his balls in my hands. Then I bent down and sucked as much of them as I could into my mouth. They were tart and salty. I slid my tongue over and under them stroking with wide wet licks. What I couldn't touch with my mouth, I fondled with my fingers. He groaned and pushed his bottom further up into the air.

I took that as my clue that he was ready for the next step.

I stuck three of my fingers into a jar of cream that I purchased along with the dildo. The boy behind the counter said it was great for novices, "makes anything go in with ease and it tastes good," he'd said grinning at me as he took my money. I slid my fingers down the length of his ass, over his balls, and up and through the crevice. His ass trembled. He whimpered. I slid one, then two fingers into the puckered hole and he groaned. I slid another and he whimpered and shivered like a big dog. I pressed my lips to the fleshy part of his ass and took a little bite, then nipped the other side. He pressed himself closer to my face. I reached under him to tug and stroke him, my hands running the length of his rod. It was hot and tight and dripping. He was breathing hard, and I could feel his anticipation. I gripped my own penis with a well-oiled palm, tugging it with a fist a few times to ease the cream over its surface, adding an extra dab for the tip.

I rose up behind him, pressed my cock to the puckered hole, and pushed, slow at first, but he pushed back against me and I slid in farther. There was a slight protrusion built into the dildo harness that pressed against my clitoris every time I pressed my cock into Bruce. It was addictive. Before long I was banging my cock into Bruce's tight little ass and every hit sent a series of surges and shivers back to my tight little nub.

It seemed to tighten and grow with each thrust. I tensed the muscles of my ass to get a harder, firmer thrust. I held on to his hips and let the rush and lighting surge through my body; it was a clean rush of power and pleasure, but I didn't surrender to it completely. Bruce groaned, a loud surrender, and nearly rose up. I reached under him, gripped, and tugged the length of sex with my slippery fingers. His body jerked and released a spray of semen saturating the carpet. I pulled out and he fell forward covering his mess.

I left him there, a puddle of sated man, and slipped into the bathroom, packed all of my toys in my overnight kit and slipped back into my jeans and T-shirt. When I came out of the bathroom, he was sitting on the bed, still pantless, his cock docile and quiet between a set of well-toned thighs. I picked up my purse from the dresser and headed to the door.

"Clean up this mess before you leave," I decreed as I stood near the door. He nodded without looking at me. I stepped out into the night. There were still a couple of kids and their parents around the pool. I could hear the splash as someone jumped in, the lull of conversation, a woman's laugh and the clink of glasses. I pulled the door closed and made my way back to my car.

Work was hazy with cubist edges and a fluorescent glare; I wandered around on autopilot. I was no Bruce Davies; I couldn't pretend that there wasn't something

really strange going on between me and my boss.
I couldn't look at him without remembering the size
and length of him, the hardness of his thighs and the
firmness of backside. I would sit across from him as
he sat behind his desk scanning a storyboard while I
took notes, and the muscles of my sex would clinch. A
dampness would creep between my legs and I'd think
of little scenarios that we could act out right there on
his desk with my legs wrapped around his head. I was
afraid that he could sense my arousal, smell me as I
sat across from him. But he was as stoic as ever. Well,
not really stoic, his spirits were good, and he was quite
personable to everyone he encountered. But he seemed
unfazed by our episodes and impervious to my discomfort. Okay then, it was me. I had to learn to cope or
to desist. I chose the latter. Oh, it had been fun, the
intrigue, the fulfillment of fantasies, but I wasn't cut
out for the aftermath, the lingering arousal, and yes, the
guilt.

A series of cold showers and a call from Alex a week
later helped me to stick to my guns. We had dinner and
an evening of normal but very hot sex in his hotel room
followed by a stiff morning ride before he had the town
car drop me home to get dressed for work. Alex, unlike
Bruce, was not one to ignore a night of hot sex.

Claire informed me that Bruce had been looking for
me so I headed into his office as soon as I dropped my
purse and briefcase on my desk. Alex was sitting at

the circular table near the rear of Bruce's office. Bruce stood over a bottle of Dom Pérignon in a bucket of ice. He was twisting the corkscrew into the bottle as I walked in.

"We're celebrating," Bruce said to me. "Alex wanted to wait for you."

"You're pleased with the campaign?" I asked Alex.

He actually stood up, took my hand and drew me to the table to stand between the two of them.

"He's so pleased that he's giving us a crack at the shoes and clothing lines." Bruce popped the cork and poured the wine into the waiting glasses.

"It means I'll have to visit more often," he said, and leaned in to plant a kiss that ended up getting lost somewhere in my hair because I tried to dodge it under the guise of reaching for the champagne glass that Bruce held out to me.

Alex laughed, "We have nothing to hide from Bruce. He's seen us at our most vulnerable."

Bruce sipped from his glass, but said nothing.

There was logic to that, but Alex was not aware of all that had transpired between me and Bruce since that night in my office. But Bruce remained silent. Maybe it didn't matter to him. Maybe he expected a woman who orchestrated clandestine perversions to have multiple lovers. Maybe he was fine with it as long as he got his share.

"To a long and fruitful alliance." Bruce held his glass

out to ours. The glasses clinked. I drained mine and held it out for a refill. Maybe he thought this was normal for me. I drained the second glass.

"I'd better get back to work," I said, putting my glass down on the table.

"I thought we'd have breakfast," Alex said, capturing my hand again.

"I've got to see legal about the contracts," I adlibbed.

"Bruce won't mind if you come away with me for a few hours," Alex coaxed. He directed his words at Bruce, but continued to look at me.

"There are a few things pending that require Glory's touch." Bruce's words were a balm. "Maybe she could issue you a rain check."

"Tonight," Alex said, using my captured hand to draw me to him.

"I'll call you when I'm done," I said as I slipped my hand out of his, offered him a placating smile and headed back to my office. Enough already. Alex stayed another week to oversee the opening of a new store, an uptown boutique that featured his company's high-end line. It kept him busy and he didn't seem to even notice that I had been dodging him. When I showed up to represent the agency at the store's inauguration, he was affable and warm. I rewarded his nonchalance by fucking him senseless in the back of the limousine as we took a long ride along the riverfront and through the park. He was so attentive that I was sorry I had put him off all week. But I wasn't too sad when I rode with him to the airport to see him off. He held me in his arms and nuzzled my neck as the chauffeur pulled his luggage from the trunk. It felt good to bask in the shelter of his body, the heat of his chest pressed against my cheek. He is an affectionate man, a good man, and I felt sated, normal. I could go back to my life, the way it was before Mr. Davies became Bruce, before that night.

"Glory!" I could hear him through the door. I pretended not to, but his bellow was followed by the long shadow of his frame as it filled the doorway. "Why haven't you followed up on this?" He waved a folder. "You said you wanted more responsibility. I give it to you, and this is what happens." He slid the folder onto my desk and stormed back to his. I was hoping that he would slam the door behind him, but he left it open suggesting that he wasn't quite finished with his rant. I waited, expecting a follow-up, but he'd shifted his ire to Claire. I could hear him demanding that she stay after to finish the correspondence she'd failed to complete. "I wanted to sign them before I leave," he fumed. Claire apologized, explaining that he'd only given them to her an hour ago. "Be that as it may," he said, ignoring her reasoning, "I want them on my desk first thing in the morning so they can go out with the morning mail." I looked at the folder he'd given me. Just as I suspected, it was awaiting an adjusted budget. Accounting had promised to email it to me within the week. I sent Somers, the department manager, a reminder, turned off my computer, grabbed my sweater and headed out the door.

I mouthed goodbye to Claire, and she tilted her head in Davies's direction and mouthed, "What's his problem?" I shrugged and double-timed it to the elevator. I didn't want to have to ride down with him, but I wasn't fast enough. I was standing there pushing the button for the third time when he came up behind me.

"Long day," he said.

"Yeah," I agreed, and pushed the button again.

"A drink?" he asked.

"I'm tired," I offered, still with my back to him.

"Just one," he said, and then added, "I want to talk."

"Where?"

"Dottie's."

"Okay."

He followed me in silence onto the elevator. Neither of us said a word as we left the building side by side and walked the two blocks down the street to the seedy little bar that still boasted the tall oak booths that must have been Dottie's grandfather's pride and joy when it had opened in the 1940s. The bar, which according to Dottie had been named for her grandmother, was known for its burgers, and did a brisk lunch business with the office workers in the area. At night, the crowd was a bit more colorful, more Dickies and less Brooks

Brothers. When we got there, the place was almost empty. A couple of guys nursed drinks at the bar, and there was one guy eating a burger with his beer in one of the front booths. We took the booth all the way in the back. Bruce ordered burgers for both of us, beer for him, and vodka and cranberry juice for me. It was what we always had at Dottie's. "Do you want fries?" he asked. I shook my head no. The waiter disappeared with our order.

Bruce loosened his tie. "It's been over a month, Glory," he said as though we had been in the midst of a conversation.

The waiter brought our drinks. He placed the cocktail napkins in front of us then sat the drinks on them. I thanked him and he was gone. I removed the tiny straw and sipped my drink.

"Is it Alex?" he asked.

"No," I said, and took another sip.

"I don't like it," he said as though I hadn't spoken, "but I can live with it. I just don't like being shut out."

"It's not Alex. It just makes me uncomfortable."

He didn't say anything for a while. He drank from his glass, and finally asked, "What makes you uncomfortable?"

"It's just not me." I looked at him, into his eyes so he could see how I felt.

"But you're so good at it." I wasn't sure whether he

was trying to cover up his apprehension or whether he was trying to blow it off.

"I'm serious."

"So am I." He stroked his glass as he watched me. After a moment of silence, he reached over and touched the back of my hand. I let him. "We don't have to play the games all the time," he offered.

I must have looked as if I was considering it because he added, "We could take turns. You could tell me what you need."

The waiter came with our food. We sat back and let him slide our plates onto the table. The young man asked the cursory, "Do you need anything else," but scurried away when Bruce shook his head and turned his attention back to me.

I doctored my burger, mustard, ketchup, relish, and passed the condiments to Bruce who began the process. It was good. I chewed and smiled at Bruce. He bit his and smiled back. We ate in silence, using our napkins liberally and sipping our drinks between bites. When we finished, Bruce handed the waiter our empty plates and ordered more drinks. I sat back feeling comfortably full and relaxed.

"Come home with me tonight," Bruce suggested.

I sat up. "I don't think so," I said, and more firmly added, "Not tonight."

"Why? It isn't as though there is someone at home waiting for you?"

"I'm just not ready."

"Okay," he said as the waiter placed our drinks in front of us.

"Okay," I said.

His head jerked up.

"No. I mean I'm glad you're okay with it."

He leaned forward. "I *can* be the aggressor. Do you want me to be the aggressor?"

I couldn't help but smile. "I thought you said okay."

"It's just that I know that sometimes women like…" He stopped as though he was afraid to finish.

"To be attacked?" I laughed outright.

"To be seduced," he corrected.

"Women are the only ones that suffer this affliction?"

"You have the advantage here because I am terribly attracted to you, and I haven't been with anyone since we were together. It's difficult —" he laughed and shook his head "—to think, with you sitting there."

"I'd better go," I said as I gathered my things. "It's getting late."

"I'm sorry if I made you uncomfortable. Stay. Finish your drink." I held my clutch in my hand. Resting both clutch and hand on the table, I began scooting out of the booth. He reached over, pulled the little purse out of my hand, and placed it on the seat next to him. *No he didn't.* The move completely deflated me. I sat back.

"Stay. Just for a while," he said again, his voice soft, placating. "Finish your drink."

"All you had to do was ask."

"Really." His smile was wry, as if he didn't believe me. I knew what he was thinking. *If that were true, you would have come home with me.* But, he didn't ask again.

"Okay," he said, and stood up, still holding my bag. "I'll walk you to your car."

I stood up. After pulling some bills from his pocket and tossing them onto the table, he took my sweater and draped it over my shoulders before handing me my purse.

We tried to make small talk about the office and new accounts, but by the time we reached the parking structure we had both sank into our own thoughts. His hand rested low on my back as we entered the structure. It would have been a chivalrous thing to do, but it felt as though he was doing it more for himself than for me, as if he was giving in to his need to touch me. His hand was large and hot and burned through the cotton of my dress. I sped up a little to relieve some of the tension, but he kept pace with me and for a minute, it was as though we were both hurrying to get somewhere.

It was late. The garage, lit intermittently with fluorescent lights, was dim. It was always darkest near my car, which was parked in a corner near the elevator. I was glad Bruce was here. He stood over me. His body a half-circle fortress around mine as we waited. We took the elevator up to the floor reserved for Davies and Birch. A concrete wall separated my car from the glass enclosure that housed the elevator, a gray slab that blocked out light and created a blind spot that hid my parking space from the protective eyes of the security camera. Bruce's and Birch's cars were parked to the right, behind the other concrete wall in the spaces reserved for the executives. Because we worked for Bruce, Claire and I were given optimum spaces next to the elevator. Birch's assistants were in the same bank, next to me and Claire. It had been a not so secret bone of contention to some of the higher earning account execs and department managers, but Bruce had dismissed their bickering and innuendoes. When one of the newer execs complained that he'd never worked for a company that gave secretaries better parking spots than the high rollers, Bruce had simply said, "They're not secretaries. They keep me functioning at my best. I need them near and on time." Since then, the guys have kept their comments to themselves.

He took my hand as we left the enclosure, and led the way to my car. "I could come home with you," he said as he pressed me back against the car door and his mouth against mine. It was good. He tasted wet like beer and hot burger and man. He leaned in and my hip nudged the door handle. I kissed him back. He groaned and pressed his luck allowing a hand to stray behind my back and down to cup my bottom. The hard notch of him pushed into my waist and belly. I shoved at him.

His hand was under the skirt of my dress. I shoved him again, but not with much force. His hand moved to the elastic waist of my panties and stopped. His mouth still claimed mine, his tongue a comfortable weight hovering at the entrance and teasing the inside of my lips.

"I just want to feel you."

I shook my head and he deepened the kiss.

"Just a little," he whispered, and kissed my cheek.

He tugged at my panties again, pulling them down my thighs. I let him, lifting first one, then the other foot so that he could slip them off and into his pocket. A breeze glanced over my newly bared skin followed by a large warm hand and fingers that burrowed into the dampness, searching and finding my center. I clutched at his shoulders, my fingers crushing the fabric of his jacket as his plucked and stroked and inflamed me. I could barely think but I could hear the clink of his belt buckle and the purr of his zipper. The subtle musk of his cologne wafted up to me as my mouth found his neck in the loosened collar of his shirt. His skin was warm and salty. The texture was slightly rough where his beard was trying to grow back. I ran my tongue over the tiny spikes and then gnawed them with my bottom teeth. He groaned and snipped my chin with his teeth. I opened my legs wider in anticipation. He lifted me up by my bottom, his hands slipping and cradling my thighs as he pressed me more firmly into the car. Only the linen of my skirt and a pair of large warm hands shielded me from the cold steel and glass. I lifted my legs to embrace his now, the rasp of his nearly naked thighs against mine in their thigh-high nylons causing a tingly friction. He slid in further, the knob of his sex already pressing against my opening. My feet, clad in a pair of burgundy strappy heels, found purchase against the cement wall a couple of feet behind him.

He leaned forward and found home, filling me completely, the width of him leaving no room as it made a slow drag deep into my center. He hit bottom, breathed a sigh, found my mouth again and pulled almost all the way out. I waited, my pussy making clutching movements, eager for his return. He came back and I scooted toward him trying to squeeze him, to hold him, but he had found his rhythm. Leaning forward, he secured me with his shoulders, chest and hands as he continued his assault, pounding into me. The fullness and the bliss of the slide in and out caused my legs to tremble against his. I closed my eyes as he began to swell inside me, the hardness pushing against my walls, the pace crazy, out of control, the rough hair of his groin setting fire to my too sensitive labia. I bit the thick cloth at his shoulder to keep from screaming, and then he was coming. His fingers clenched my nether cheeks as he tried to pull me even closer, and then I was spiraling. The muscles of my sex clenched and pulled at him milking him as I came and came, my juice making a broth with his.

When I came to my senses, he was still holding me, his sex softer, but still tucked into me.

"Okay?" he grinned.

I laughed, "Yeah, okay. But we can't keep this up like this. There has to be protection."

"Fine, as long as there is a next time."

"I want to get down."

He stepped back. His sex plopped out and fell slack between his legs. I slid my legs down and pulled at my skirt, trying to right it. Linen is an unforgiving fabric. He tucked himself and his shirt away and zipped himself. When he was done he was a bit rumpled, but the lightweight wool of his suit was much more resilient than my linen.

"Come home with me?"

"Not tonight." I shook my head. "I need my bath. I need a long soak and lavender salts."

"I have a bathtub…and salts."

"I need time."

He nodded and stepped back. His foot found my purse where it had fallen. He picked it up and handed it to me. I retrieved my keys and opened the car door.

"See you in the morning," I said as I got into the car.

He nodded, and as I pulled the door closed and started the engine, he walked to the edge of the cement wall and waited for me to drive away.

The next morning I was replete with guilt and mis-

givings. Angry at myself for being weak, for not stick-
ing to my guns. But Bruce was back in Davies mode,
very much in charge and charming the office staff and
account execs alike, bolstering them with praise for
small deeds, and letting them down easy when he didn't
like a pitch. On his way out at lunchtime, he stopped at
the door between our offices.

"Dinner at seven. That little French place on Eighth,"
he said, standing in the open door, pulling on his suit
coat.

"Who's the mark?" I asked.

"I had Claire make the reservations," he answered as
he pulled the door to him. "I'll see you there." The door
clicked closed and he was gone.

I had Cup-a-Soup for lunch, microwaved in the little
kitchen down the hall, and sipped over a desk full of
contracts.

Claire came back from lunch and I gave her the contracts with my corrections and asked her who Davies
and I were having dinner with.

"He asked me to make the reservations for two," she
said. "I didn't know you were going. Should I make it
for three?" she asked.

"No, I just thought…" And I didn't know what else
to say, how to clean it up.

"Oh, maybe it's a raise or a promotion," she said,
brightening as though she'd caught wind of something.

"I don't think…" I tried.

"Maybe he wants to surprise you. He can be so thoughtful," she gushed.

"Do you think you can finish the corrections before four? I'd like to make sure Legal got them before five," I asked, changing the subject.

"Sure," she said, and turned back to her computer.

Bruce didn't come back to the office and I wasn't sure what to do about dinner. I went home and changed. I went with my black spaghetti-strapped Audrey dress. I wanted to look nice, even if I had to put a stop to this.

Bruce was there, sitting at the table, waiting for me when I got there. He looked good in the black Prada. I've always favored it because it made him look dark and rich, and terribly powerful. His eyes welcomed me. The waiter pulled out the chair across from him; I sat. All this was accomplished in silence.

The sommelier broke the silence in a rapid, pointed French as he cradled a bottle of wine as if he was a proud daddy. Bruce smiled up at the intense little man and responded in kind. The man poured, Bruce sipped and actually grinned. The sommelier's smile got bigger and he poured generous amounts of the rich red liquid into both of our glasses before he left us alone.

"The dress—" he tilted his head towards me "—very becoming."

"Thank you," I said, taking a sip from my glass.

"Are you hungry?"

"Yeah, I guess."

"I've already ordered for both of us. I hope you don't mind."

"No, that's fine. Whatever. Bruce, what is this about?"

"I wanted quiet time with you, time unencumbered by work."

"Dottie's was nice."

"Yes," he said. "I enjoy your company."

We were quiet as we spread our napkins on our laps and the waiter sat bowls of consommé in front of us.

"Now, you say you enjoy my company," he chided me.

"I do," I said, tasting the soup. "But I don't think it's wise to see each other without the buffer of work."

"What harm could there be? This is neutral territory. Public."

"For now."

"Are you anticipating dessert?"

"There isn't going to be any dessert tonight. Is that why you ordered me here." I pushed the plate away, my appetite dwindling. I hate being manipulated.

"I didn't invite you here to seduce you."

"Then why?"

"I thought we could talk."

"About what?"

"Us."

"There's nothing more to say."

The waiter took the soup away. The heated plates that took its place held filet mignon, asparagus and light flaky potatoes au gratin. This man knew me. He kept the fare simple, well seasoned, and the filet mignon was juicy and so tender it didn't need chewing. We ate for a while, before he spoke again, but it was as though the conversation had never halted.

"I have more to say," he said after taking a sip of wine.

"Ah," I responded. I wanted to add, "what a surprise," but I filled my mouth with asparagus instead.

"What do you want, Glory? What can I do for you? Just tell me and I'll get it for you."

"I don't want anything." I lay my fork across my plate. "I was content before."

"Only content, Glory? I want to make you happy."

"This, whatever we've been doing, doesn't make me happy. It makes me uncomfortable."

"How can we make it comfortable for you?" He sounded so reasonable, like he does when he speaks to favored clients.

"We can't."

"What aspect of it makes you uncomfortable?"

"All of it," I blurted, feeling like a six-year-old.

"I don't believe that's the complete truth, Glory. Some parts of it were pleasing to you. I could feel you."

"I don't like the discomfort of going back to the office afterward, the pretense, the fear of discovery."

"We've been completely discreet. No one need ever know."

"That can't continue forever."

"For as long as you want it to."

"How can you be so unmoved. You sit at your desk or in the boardroom and you don't even see me."

"I see you." His words trembled and their heat sent a jolt to my core.

"I'm not as adept at hiding as you are," I said after letting the bolt pass through.

"What do you want, Glory?"

"I don't want anything. I want it to be like it was before."

"That can't happen. I wouldn't want it to."

"If we stop now, maybe."

"It's too late for that, Glory. I want you too much for that."

I sat back and looked at him. He sat, back straight, cool and poised.

"What can I do for you, Glory? What can I do to make you happy?"

Okay, so he was playing hardball here, and negotiations were in full swing. I don't know what I expected but it wasn't this.

"Bruce, it just isn't for me. I'm just not the type."

He didn't say anything, just sat there silently. He knew that there would be more and he was waiting for me to get it all out.

"It was exciting at first, but it's not right. Not the way things are supposed to be."

He nodded and refilled my glass. I didn't even know I'd emptied it. I wondered if his crazy sex habits were the reason he and his wife divorced. If it had escalated to a point where she couldn't take it anymore. I could see how that could happen. Bruce encouraged a kind of limitless freedom.

"I don't...think...I could..." I found myself sputtering.

"It's just the two of us," he reminded me as if he knew I was considering it, considering what I could do to him. "No one else needs to know. Unless you want to include someone else. We'd have to be discreet, but if it's something you want..." He seemed shy again, like he did in the motel. My pussy twitched and moistened.

"I like my job. I like the way we were at work before," I told him.

"This has nothing to do with us when we're there. You're good at what you do. I rely on you. What we do in our free time doesn't have to affect our work."

I knew that to be the lie it was. I remembered how his mood shifted when he got what he wanted as opposed to when he was denied. I remembered Claire's face when she realized I was having dinner with Bruce alone. He must have been reading my face because he added, "As closely as we work together, there's bound to be some speculation. It's a normal by-product of having a female assistant. But again, what others choose to speculate doesn't have to affect us."

He watched and waited. I didn't say anything. I didn't know what to say short of walking away from all of it—this man, the hot sex, my job. But, I really like my job and he was something different.

"Do you need more money? A bigger apartment?"

"Monetary inducement?" I shook my head and gave him an admonishing smile.

"I just want to make you happy."

"I'm not a whore."

"You could move in with me." He completely ignored my remark, apparently dismissing it as irrelevant, and threw a fastball that hit me square in the chest, knocking the wind out of me. "I have a big house and there's only me. It feels quite hollow sometimes. You could have a wing to yourself."

When I didn't respond he said, "Come home with me."

I shot him a look. "To see the house," he added hastily.

"I've seen it."

"Only a couple of times and then only the first floor. You couldn't have seen much. You were only there long enough to hand off a few papers."

"I saw enough."

"Come on." He was smiling now. "I'd like to show you my home."

I sat there frozen, overwhelmed. *Unfair*, he was far more skilled at this than I.

"No strings," he said, trying to capture my eyes.

He lied, and he knew I knew he was lying.

I excused myself, needing a minute of near privacy to recover. When I returned, he had settled the bill and stood to help me with my shrug before fitting his hot hand onto my lower back to guide me out of the restaurant and to his waiting car.

As I sat next to him in the backseat of the town car, I was both frightened and exhilarated because I had realized that I couldn't turn this man down. I could be myself with him—pushy, demanding, cruel or loving. He encouraged it, fed off of it. The prospect was intoxicating and I knew, as the car pulled out into traffic, this was just the beginning.

A Paris Affair

By Adelaide Cole

Adelaide Cole has lived, written, edited, and researched for an array of fiction, technical subjects and journalism on three continents. As in her fiction, she seeks a bit of the extreme, whether in the high Canadian Arctic or when crossing hostile desert borders in the low Saharan of West Africa. She speaks a few languages and holds a couple of passports, just so to keep satiating curiosity. Her Italian-born husband of 15 years says she keeps him on his toes. He appreciates Adelaide's professional wine education; she brings lovely bottles home that keep a domestic adventure interesting.

"Oh-laaa! Tu me fais chier quoi, Paris de merde! Ville des putain de lumières! Tu m'emmerdes!"

Valérie swore angrily as she tried to wipe the thick smear of soft, fetid dog shit off her shoes. "City of fucking Light! Go fuck yourself!" she muttered. The quaint Paris cobblestones, and in fact all the streets of Paris, were a landmine of dog turds. And they were a racing course of nasty little speeding four-cylinder cars, and of scooters driven by rude and careless teenagers.

She found the building. With Mathieu trailing, she entered the courtyard and tried to wipe her dirty shoe on a mat. She and her son made their way up the four flights to the medical specialist's office.

The receptionist looked at Valérie with undisguised boredom. "I'm sorry, *madame*, but there's nothing I can do for you. Your son requires *this* form—" she held one up in the same manner that a primary-school teacher would use with a pint-size pupil "—*before* he can have this appointment with the doctor."

"But I have the appointment *already*. This is *it*. It

is *now*," Valérie said, pointing to her watch for effect. "How can someone have given me an appointment that I'm not allowed to have? It makes no sense." Mathieu was whining at her side. He'd been complaining for most of their errands. "*Maman*, juice! Thirsty! Juice!" he repeated, tugging at her pant leg.

Valérie rummaged in her handbag and found a small bottle of water and handed it to him. He drank. The break in his whining felt like a release of some of the overwhelming, exhausting pressure in her head. Mathieu, her younger of two children, was almost five, and should have been speaking in complete sentences. But he wasn't, and when her veil of self-denial was finally lifted by the primary school's refusal to admit him because of language development issues, she'd unhappily begun to travel the routes of help for developmentally delayed children.

The receptionist sighed heavily. "The appointments are given six weeks ahead. *Madame, all* the families understand that they have those six weeks to have their *assessment* done before they are permitted their initial follow-up here. *Everyone* knows that before they arrive here. I'm terribly sorry you didn't understand that, *madame*, but it's commonly understood by all the doctor's patients."

Valérie had fought so many of these grinding, bureaucratic battles since they'd returned to Paris that she knew it was utterly pointless to continue any exchange with the receptionist. "*Bon. Merci, madame. Au revoir,*" she replied, with necessary courtesy.

"*Au revoir, madame!*" clipped the receptionist in return. Valérie gathered her grocery bags and stuffed the folded blank forms inside. They left the office and made their way back down the four winding flights of stairs.

Mathieu hung on her coat as they walked through the drizzling rain, dodging aggressive human and car traffic. "Watch your step for dog poop, Mathieu," she instructed. They walked back down into the Métro, where Mathieu's jacket pocket became snagged on the turnstile. He got stuck and began to wail. People behind him complained loudly and shoved their way through the next turnstiles. She unhooked his pocket and untangled him. They struggled through the crush of humanity on the platforms and trains, through six stops and two line changes. The air was stuffy and stale and the cars were crowded. Valérie fought her way to empty seats and plopped her son on them to keep him from whining for at least a few stops.

Then, back up the escalators and stairs from the Métro to the street, where she tripped over the knee of a woman sitting on the pavement, begging for money. The woman yelled at Valérie, who decided this city was a horrid little piece of hell.

After walking the four blocks to their building, they wearily climbed their own three flights. Each step up drained energy from Valerie's body. Reaching the final landing, she felt as if all her vitality had been leeched out, bit by bit, by those nasty streets, regulated offices, irritating shops, stifling Métro cars, and finally, their own never-ending stairs.

Back in the apartment, Philippe was already home from work, having picked up Mathieu's sister, Manon, from summer art camp. Though he looked wan and tired, he tried to summon a bit of enthusiasm as they pushed through the door.

Sweaty and fatigued, Valérie left her shoes, still stinking and dirty, outside the door, making a mental note to clean them after the kids were in bed. Mathieu sank onto the floor and began to cry.

Valérie dropped her bags, hung up her coat and walked directly to the bathroom. Maybe she would feel better after a hot shower, she thought. Before shutting the door, she said, "How about a nice glass of wine when I come out, dear?" Then she closed it behind her and undressed, leaving her things on the floor. The building's ancient plumbing hammered and banged as she turned it on.

By the time she finished her shower, Mathieu's tears had tapered off. His attention was caught by a piece of a toy he'd found on the floor, and he was murmuring to himself. The shower did lift some of the stress of the day, and a moderately refreshed Valérie emerged from the steamy bathroom, wrapped in a robe and towel-drying her hair. She sat down at the kitchen table and smiled at Philippe. He gave her a tired smile and handed her a glass of Bordeaux. "*Santé*," they both said joylessly in unison, clinking their glasses out of routine. *To better days,* they both thought to themselves.

Valérie took a big drink with one hand and continued toweling her damp hair with the other. She sighed deeply. "So, how was work?" she asked, instantly regretting having done so.

Philippe rolled his eyes upward and shook his head. "Politics, politics," he said wearily. She didn't ask for details, and he didn't offer them. As with so many married couples, this was a rerun of many similar conversations. They fell silent and sipped their wine.

The two had met while at university in Paris. She had grown up in the south, in Provence. He came from Bretagne, in the north. She was petite and olive-skinned, with a mass of dark, curly hair; he was blond, fair-skinned, tall and thin. She was emotional, effusive and Mediterranean, while he was cool and intellectual. Opposites attracted, and they had enjoyed the city together as a young, courting couple. They'd crossed the country together to meet and visit their respective families in the north and south. Their love was solidified in the shared fun of travel, and in the discoveries that new adventures brought. Valérie sometimes thought, lately, that their marriage felt so difficult now because those common joys had vanished with this new phase of their life.

After they married, Valérie worked as a city librarian, and Philippe secured a job in the Ministry of Foreign Affairs. He was smart and rose in the ranks, and within a year had won a junior posting in Copenhagen's French consulate. That began their international life, and two more foreign posts, in Los Angeles and Hong Kong, followed over the next several years. They enjoyed an exciting time abroad, where Valérie had little more to worry about than how they dressed and the appearance of their home. Their postings were politically calm spots, and their lives were easy. But new milestones brought new difficulties.

They started their family during their final post abroad, in the Canadian port city of Vancouver. They had both wanted children, but Valérie had difficult pregnancies and deliveries, and child rearing was a steep learning curve. She had always been emotionally and physically sensitive, and the twenty-four-hour days and mini-crises of minding babies and small children took a toll on her. Philippe was a caring husband and father, but he couldn't take the time away from work that Valérie's constitution seemed to require. He worked hard in his position, and at home felt put upon.

Philippe and Valérie had experienced a joyful bond as a childless couple, but found it difficult to make the transition to their new life with children. Their love and caring did not wane, but some of their happiness together did. Valérie often felt isolated, and those feelings only multiplied when Mathieu began showing odd behaviour as a toddler.

At the same time, Philippe was offered a desk position back in Paris. It was not a job he particularly wanted, and it paid less than the international posts did; but it was strategically important in the schema of his career. It was a stepping-stone position, so it was impossible to refuse. They left their life in green and airy Vancouver, and settled back into crowded Paris and its cramped apartment existence…this time with two young children, one of whom was showing developmental problems.

In this new life, Valérie shouldered the burden of the children's care. While their international positions had afforded a nanny and housekeeper, this Paris assignment didn't come with those luxuries. She was on her own. Philippe wasn't any help on the domestic scene, since his days were spent in a Machiavellian cauldron of colleagues jockeying for position. The couple missed the days of their foreign postings. CONSUL licenseplated SUVs conferred special status, and cocktail parties were filled with easy, empty diplomatic conversation and the champagne that advertised France's good life to the world.

Valérie missed those parties and dinners. And she missed the stylish distinction of being a Frenchwoman abroad. Being French attracted an automatic cachet she had enjoyed. "Oh, Valérie," she would hear from a new friend in a foreign country, "I couldn't pull off that look with that scarf. Only a Frenchwoman can do that. You always look so elegant." And felt so lighthearted.

But the breezy confidence that foreigners gave her turned into yet another casualty of their move back to Paris. Now she was now just another forty-something wife and mom among a million stunning French girls. She tried to maintain her standards, but the demands of two children didn't leave her with the same motivation or time that she'd had before, when a nanny helped with child care and a housekeeper with the mundane tasks that were now hers alone.

The children's needs, plus her husband's new job, also took a toll on their romantic life. They were never alone together in the tiny apartment, and sex became perfunctory, if they weren't already too tired to bother. Their love and commitment was intact, but sexual heat had dissipated, at least in these days of grocery shopping, child rearing and career challenges.

"I'll get the kids dinner," Valérie said, pushing herself up from the table. She took her glass with her.

"I'll help. I'll make a salad," Philippe said, getting up as well.

She boiled pasta for the children and recounted what had been accomplished that day along the lengthy progression of Mathieu's diagnosis and treatment. Life abroad had been deceptively easy, and they had taken it for granted. If they'd been less self-deluded in their former post, they would have noticed signs that their son wasn't developing normally, but the easy international scene had seduced them into thinking that their entire life was a carefree ride. Had they noticed, they would have sought help earlier and avoided the degree of difficulty they now faced.

The discovery that Mathieu sat somewhere on the ever-widening autism continuum brought with it despondency as they fought to regain their equilibrium as a couple, as parents and as a family. Valérie and Philippe both struggled to relegate Manon to last-in-line for care and attention as they tried not to grieve over the loss of a dream of having two perfect children. Life weighed heavily back here in Paris.

"One piece of good news," Philippe said as he drained the bottle into his wife's glass. "My parents called and said they'd like to have the kids for a few days. My vacation is already on the schedule at work, so I thought I'd take them up on the train on Wednesday and beat the rush out of the city."

They both knew that Valérie disliked his parents and wouldn't want to go, so he didn't even ask. "You can have a break from the kids and all the appointments and running around. You can stay in your pajamas all day and relax."

Valérie smiled at him, took his hand and squeezed it gently between hers, saying, "You're my angel." He leaned over and kissed her forehead.

Philippe was careful with Valérie ever since she had suffered a minor emotional breakdown in the midst of the move back to Paris and the shock of their troubles with Mathieu. Philippe made sure she took her anti-anxiety medication, and tried to ease some of her daily load.

"*Papa*! Mathieu ripped the head off Chloé!" Manon stomped into the kitchen and displayed the evidence in both hands.

"I didn't! I didn't! I didn't! I didn't…!" Mathieu yelled repeatedly from the other room. Valérie dropped her head. She so desperately needed respite from the chaos of…of just everything. She missed the big houses of international life. Here, space was a rare commodity, and although they had a roomy apartment by Paris standards, it was claustrophobic for a stressed family.

Philippe glanced at his wife, and when he saw her strained expression, jumped up and ushered Manon out in order to calm the waters.

PREPARATIONS AND DEPARTURES

The day before their departure, Valérie was packing Philippe's and the children's bags for their holiday in Bretagne. She was going through a mental checklist of what they would need for their beach days when the cell phone rang.

She walked into the hallway, found her bag and dug through it for her phone.

"Yes, hello!"

"Valérie?"

"Yes?"

"You don't recognize my voice? Of course, it's been so long. It's Oscar from New York...."

"Oscar...Nathalie's friend? Yes, of course...Oscar, how are you? It's been a long time."

"Yes, it has, but I had such a nice time at that dinner, and I've never forgotten you both. How is your husband, your children?"

"Fine, fine. Are you here in France?"

"I am. That's why I'm calling. I'm in Paris for a few days. We had such a nice dinner in New York,

so I got your number here from Nathalie. She told me
you had moved back. I was going to ask if you and
Philippe could meet me for supper while I'm in the
city."

Valérie was stunned to be getting this call. Her heart
began to pound and she started to sweat. Thank God
this was over the telephone and not in person! She
had to concentrate in order to keep her voice sounding
offhanded and light. Oscar, of all people!

During their Los Angles posting a few years back,
Philippe and Valérie had flown to New York to visit
Valérie's sister. Nathalie had married a New Yorker, and
worked as a private French tutor for firms that did business abroad. Oscar was a senior manager in an international sports federation, and needed to be multilin-
gual, since their business was done around the world.
He became one of her students, and eventually a friend,
and had been a guest at the dinner party.

Valérie was instantly attracted to him. She had been
seated across from him and they'd chatted throughout
the meal, which his wife hadn't attended. Oscar was not
a big man, maybe 5'6"—which accounted for his talent
at soccer when he was young—but she liked his size,
and beneath his sharp business suit his build seemed
compact, lithe and muscular. She'd sensed a fierce
sexuality under those executive clothes. He had light
olive skin, and his face looked toned and angular. She
even liked the shape of his neck, which made her wish

he hadn't been wearing a tie, so that she could peek at his chest.

She loved a man's fit, lean torso, and how it made her eye travel down to his sex, and she still remembered that the lines of his shirt suggested he was strong and muscular. He sat comfortably, with his legs apart and his elbows resting on his thighs, and exuded the alpha confidence of an athlete. Philippe, though very attractive, was not particularly fit, and he held himself the way intellectuals and businessmen do, with their heads somehow disconnected from their bodies. But this man was different. She had felt that he was *in* his body, and that his mind and body were a powerful team. He had an aura that seemed to knock other men out of the room.

He was several years older than Valérie, and had beautifully graying hair and an appealing, virile five o'clock shadow that brought out his square jawline. His eyes, which had held her gaze longer than normal for a casual dinner gathering, were dark green. She'd found them captivating, and more than once had looked away when she felt the intimacy overwhelming.

She still remembered how, when he spoke, he'd rested his elbow on the table and lightly stroked his lips with his thumb while holding her glance. She'd found him sexy, and a little sly. For a diplomat's spouse, dinner parties were akin to a part-time job, and she met scores of good-looking men, married or not. Valérie had never imagined being involved with a man outside her marriage, and she and Philippe had been very happy together at that point. But Oscar had left an impression on her that hadn't disappeared.

All they'd shared that evening was common dinner party conversation, but underneath the banter she'd felt a current of heat between them. Had he shared her feeling? She had always thought so, because his eyes never left hers except when they perused her hair and her shirt front. She felt as if he was carefully checking her out, and was flattered, because she found him so attractive.

But she never found out one way or another. She and her sister didn't share intimacies, so Valérie had never mentioned him to Nathalie except in completely casual terms. She'd prayed that nobody at the party had noticed the heat she had felt between them.

At one point in the evening she had spied Philippe in a conversation with him, and when they were on their way home she learned her husband had exchanged phone numbers with Oscar, who apparently traveled widely for his job and sometimes found himself in Los Angeles. She had been nonchalant about it to Philippe, but was secretly thrilled. She was disappointed that they never heard from Oscar again, but had never quite forgotten him.

Clearly, the momentary attraction had not faded, because she was as excited as a schoolgirl to have him on the phone.

"Well, Philippe is taking the children to the north

coast to his parents' for a few days, and I'll be on
my own. We could get together for a coffee tomorrow.
How's that?"

"Lovely. You're there in the sixteenth arrondisse-
ment, at the address your sister gave?"

"Yes, yes. And we have a good café at the corner,
called Café Liberté. It has a blue awning—you'll see it.
It's across from a little grocery with flowers in front."

"No problem. Is four o'clock fine for you?"

"Perfect. Tomorrow at four. See you then."

"I look forward to it! I'm so glad I'll have some company for a bit! Paris is a little harsh when you're alone."

"Oh, your wife didn't come with you?" she ventured.
What the hell am I thinking? she wondered.

"No, no, I came for work in Madrid. She has work in
New York."

"Oh, that's too bad," Valérie lied. "Well, anyway…till tomorrow then. Bye-bye."

"Tomorrow!"

They hung up simultaneously.

Valérie stood in the room with the phone in her hand.
Then she sat on the bed, in the middle of the piles of
clothes and toiletries and open suitcases. She dropped
the cell back into her bag and took out a pack of ciga-
rettes. Philippe disapproved of her smoking, but wasn't
too angry if she did it only occasionally, and when she
was alone.

She got back up, went to the window and opened

it, then lit up and took a deep drag. She looked mindlessly at the traffic below and the neighbors around her, and recalled her single meeting with Oscar. She remembered the color of his eyes and now, with the phone call, the calm of his smooth, sexy voice. She swallowed and took another drag of her cigarette, feeling something deep in her body that she hadn't felt in years. It was pure, sexual wanting. It was dormant sensation reawakened by the voice of this man she'd met for just a few hours years ago. She felt a flicker in her sex, as if it was being shaken awake, too.

She had never been unfaithful in her marriage, and had never shared more than an innocent flirtation with another man. But…then *what*, exactly? she asked herself. Things at home were so stressed, and sex was lukewarm at best. She didn't even wait for arousal anymore with her husband. She just wanted it to be done so that she could sleep. What a state!

Her discontent allowed a space to open within her. It did not open in her heart, but in her body, and she felt it through her nerve endings. She felt that a ray of daylight was piercing the dismal gray cloud of her life, and offering her something beyond her marriage. How could the timing be so *perfect*? she asked herself, careful to avoid the word *affair*. She didn't wish for any real distance from Philippe and her children; but while they were having *their* little holiday, might she have a "holiday" of her own…?

She was dying to know if Oscar was interested in her, and if he ever strayed outside his marriage; what man *wouldn't*, she wondered, if the opportunity presented itself? She felt the stirring storm of sexual anticipation that she had in New York. It had been *so* long since a man had moved her sexually. Physically, she lived in a dry desert of neutered sex, and had actually forgotten the earthquake of desire. Here it was, rumbling inside her.

She recalled the sizzling undercurrent she'd felt with Oscar, and her nerves jumped. Did he really just want a cup of coffee, or something more…? She would have to wait and see. And if *something more* meant something that could harm her marriage, the stability of the life she and Philippe had made together, or their children…these were issues too monumental for her to allow herself to consider.

Valérie wasn't a schemer or a planner, and wasn't deceptive by nature; but her circumstances and her own emotional weakness left her open to seizing a moment and hoping it would all turn out for the best. She felt such a great longing for respite from a difficult period in their lives. And unless she was very wrong, Oscar's sudden appearance felt ready-made: *prêt-à-porter*!

Looking out the window, she recalled Oscar and her sense of him. At the dinner she had imagined what he looked like under his sharp business suit—from the way his clothes fell she'd thought she could make out a taut, slim muscular build. She'd felt his raw sexuality. She remembered his green eyes gazing into hers like a cheeky dare…and she breathed hard. She put her cigarette out on the window ledge, closed the window, and turned back to packing for her family's trip.

The next day all the preparations were in place. The taxi was ordered, bags were packed, and the grandparents were expecting them at the train station. They were leaving around lunchtime, so Valérie had prepared food for the trip.

"All ready to go?" Philippe asked the children. He looked at his wife. "This will be a good change of pace for everyone, don't you think?"

Valérie smiled warmly at him and hugged him around his waist. He reciprocated with his arm around her shoulder. They stood together, looking at the children, who were stuffing last-second treasures into their bags. The apartment buzzer rang, signaling the taxi. "Let's go! Taxi's here!" Philippe said.

Ding-dang-dong… The three-tone notices hummed continuously over the loudspeaker, announcing trains coming and going. Gare de l'Est was a loom in motion. Families, singles, couples, old people, children, backpackers—they walked and ran in every direction, their paths crisscrossing in a colorful weave.

"We'll miss you, my love," Philippe said. "Mathieu,

you know *Maman* is staying home. She's not coming with us. It's just us three visiting *Mamie* and *Papie*."

Mathieu looked at his parents, then turned back to watch the crowd. He clung to his mother. "He's gonna throw a total fit the second we get on the train and he sees you're not coming," Manon said, matter-of-factly.

"Try and relax," Philippe directed, "and don't smoke too much. Remember to eat properly. I'll call you as soon as we're there."

"If I'm out, don't worry. I might go to a film or sit in a café. Just things to clear my head. Maybe I'll do some shopping for the kids. Make sure you all enjoy yourselves."

Ding-dang-dong…boarding train 631 in five minutes to Lorient on track 15…

CAFÉ LIBERTÉ

Back in the apartment in front of her bedroom mirror, Valérie thought that the pale green top gave her a flirty décolletage, but that maybe the black skirt wasn't so flattering. On the other hand, she thought as she tried on things from her closet, the pale pink linen dress showed off her waist and had décolleté as well. She chose the pink dress and stepped into it.

She was in good shape for her age, despite having had a couple of kids. Her breasts hadn't bounced back to their former glory, but were still nicely shaped. Her olive skin tone was still pretty, and she had a slim waist and nice legs. She was a petite height, and had to watch what she ate to stay slim, now that she was nearly forty-three. She still cared about her figure, but had never anticipated being *naked with another man*. It had simply never occurred to her. She looked at her body and thought that her hair was still her best feature. She had wild, glossy black curls that fell below her shoulders.

Oh, maybe it's just a coffee, after all, she thought,

hoping that it wasn't…but afraid that it was…! Conflicting notions pulled her one way and then another. On one hand she felt as if she had the right to a moment of pure joy with someone; yet on the other hand she knew she would be breaking a commitment she'd made to her husband. And then again, Oscar might be simply meeting an acquaintance for a coffee….

A police siren passing on a street snapped her out of her confused reverie. "Oh!" she said out loud to herself. She stood up straight and looked in the mirror. She glanced at the clock by the bed. She was meeting Oscar in just fifteen minutes. She fluffed out some of her curls, placing a thick mass just over one eyebrow. She tucked another clump behind one ear to reveal a dangly silver earring. She put on a bit of mascara and then sat back to look at her reflection. *Am I still pretty?* she wondered. She looked at the lines that had begun to appear around her dark, almond eyes, and at the circles underneath. *Just a coffee,* she repeated, dabbing on a bit more perfume and checking her lipstick in the mirror.

The café was half-filled. The right number of people: it was neither uncomfortably intimate, nor too busy and bustling. Oscar already had a table.

"Oscar!" She made her way through the tables. He stood.

"Valérie, my dear!" They brushed cheeks in a French greeting.

"Lovely to see you, my dear," Oscar said.

"Wonderful to see you again," Valérie said in return, instantly hoping that she wasn't giving herself away.

Oscar was exactly as she had remembered him. In a split second she sensed the same magnetic pull between them. He wore another smart business suit and looked as dashing as she'd recalled. Her stomach leaped, but she tried to act casual.

"Have you seen Nathalie recently?" she asked, starting the conversation with a subject they shared.

"Yes, few months ago," he answered, "and I called her for your new phone number. Are you close with your sister?"

"No, not so much," Valérie admitted. "We've been in different places for so many years now."

The conversation was casual, but the air between them was not. His eyes locked on hers. While they mouthed pleasantries, she gazed back into the green eyes she recalled from the first time they had met. She felt drawn to him.

"And is your family well?"

"Everyone is fine. Our kids are happy at their schools, and I hope they're working hard. How is Philippe's new post? You must all be happy to be back in France."

"Yes, of course," Valérie said. "It's always easier in your own language. And the new posting is working well. It was a good move." She lied, feeling that the truth of her life was too heavy a burden for this lighthearted meeting.

"Well then, everything fine for all of us!" Oscar said brightly. He caught the eye of the passing waiter and turned to Valérie. "Listen, how about a nice glass of wine instead of coffee? I know it's a bit early, but it's so nice to be here. I'd like to take advantage of my few days in Paris…."

"Yes, yes, why not?" Valérie answered. "A glass would be nice." She knew that a glass of wine would loosen her up, but she felt as if every step forward led toward a precipice. The feeling both excited and scared her.

Oscar scanned the café blackboard menu and ordered wine for them both. His French was smooth and fluent. The waiter left.

"Your French is excellent, you know?" Valérie said, complimenting him.

"It's easy to learn with a good teacher like Nathalie! But I didn't have a choice—I had to learn for work. And you, are you working at all?"

"Me? Oh no, I'm too busy with the children. When they're older I'll go back, but they're still small, you know."

The wine arrived and Oscar toasted to reacquaintances. "*Santé!*" they said together, touching glasses lightly. They both smiled, and their eyes met again. He gave a sly smile, and she felt a rush of warmth throughout her body. She had a fleeting image of the slim hips and tight muscles under that suit. She wanted to run her hand over a curving biceps, and suddenly thought, *I know how people do this*. She had an image of a grassy plain and a cliff's edge, and felt that a marriage was on that plain. At the cliff's edge was Oscar, and leaping off it together wourld be a daring, heart-pounding adventure. Looking into his eyes made her move closer to the cliff's edge.

"So," Valérie said, trying to be a bit flirtatious. It was a long time since she'd flirted with anyone, and she felt as if she was treading uneasily on unfamiliar, uneven ground. "How do you have time away from your work here to drink in the afternoon?"

"Oh, I don't have anything to do in Paris," Oscar answered, draining his glass. He stretched out his legs, crossed his arms and looked at her with a half smile. "I was working in Madrid and asked the company travel agent to arrange a layover. Just to relax, really. My wife is busy with work. And why didn't you go with Philippe and your children?"

Valérie rested her forearms on the table and leaned her chest toward Oscar provocatively. "Oh, Philippe had a chance to take the children to his parents', and we both agreed that it would be nice if I had the week to myself at home. I don't really get along with my in-laws, anyway." She cocked her head and answered his gaze with her eyes.

"Mmm." He nodded. "And me, I didn't want to waste all those French lessons on work! The Americans say 'All work makes Jack a dull boy.'" He laughed. Valérie laughed, too, and their smiles and their fast-disappearing wine both lightened and intensified the air between them. She felt as if a weight was lifting, and as if the cliff edge was fast approaching.

Oscar read her thoughts. "Listen, Valérie," he said, and when he leaned over the table he took her hand. He did it so swiftly and smoothly, without skipping a beat or breaking eye contact, that it took her breath away. Valérie felt her heart start to pound. *What daring!* she thought, truly shocked. *He knows I'm married!*

"Instead of another glass here, why don't you be my Paris guide and we'll have a walk along the Seine? I was going to ask you and Philippe for supper, but he's away. Maybe you'll join me for dinner tonight. Yes? No fun to eat alone, you know."

Before she could answer or remove her hand, which buzzed from his electric touch, he released it and signaled to the waiter for the check. *He's so cheeky,* she thought, attracted now not only to piercing green eyes, slim hips and strong hands, but by his daring. *He must want me, too,* she thought, feeling more confident than ever.

"I can't think of a reason to say no…." Valérie said, cocking her head slightly and holding his gaze for a few seconds. She twirled a lock of hair behind her ear and smiled at him.

"Well, there you go, then. It's decided," answered Oscar.

As they left the café and walked into the sunshine he subtly took her arm. In return, she moved closer to his body, feeling his strong, slim thigh beside her hip. She felt him beside her as they walked, and her nerves tingled. *When* was *the last time the sun shone?* she wondered.

DINNER OUT

Near evening, Oscar took Valérie to a restaurant he said he'd always wanted to try when in Paris, but hadn't had the chance. He said it was written up in the American food magazines, and its chef-owner won accolades for his North African-French fusion dishes. They drank a deep, bold Bourgogne, and toasted to "a little holiday together," as Oscar called it.

They tasted each other's adventurous plates, and at the end traded bold desserts where sweet and spicy flavors danced together. Fresh figs were gently enrobed in French *pâte feuilletée* and flavored with orange-water and cardamom. Spanish peaches were embedded in couscous spiced with vanilla and cinnamon.

"May I?" asked Oscar quietly.

Valérie put down her fork and looked at him inquisitively. She didn't know what he wanted. With his thumb and forefinger he picked up a warm, supple, deep amber fig, dripping with its honey-and-orange glaze, and lifted it to her mouth. She smiled and parted her lips. When he carefully slipped the slim brown tip inside, she closed her mouth around it and bit softly through it, its tiny seeds relenting to her teeth. Her cunt jumped with pleasure.

Oscar smiled with one corner of his mouth. He held the dripping fruit to his own lips, licked the part where her mouth had touched, and bit it off. Juice ran down his finger. They didn't speak. The intensity of their exchange blurred everything around them.

Valérie wanted him. The wine was erasing the edginess in her nerves, and she felt less confined to the imposed rules of marriage. She felt that the universe would let her love her husband and *make love* to Oscar. She *had* to feel his body around hers, she thought. But she just couldn't bring herself to tell him, to say it out loud. Would he say something? She fingered her long, silver chain and leaned toward him over the crisp linen tablecloth. She felt the wine in her body, felt her face flush and her vulva pulse.

Oscar's eyes met hers, and he finally said, quietly, "You're a beautiful woman, Valérie. You must know I think so. Is this a moment for us to share? If it isn't, maybe we should stop right here." He stroked her hand with the tips of his fingers and held her gaze. But before she could tell him how she felt, he said, "Don't answer now. I've had a wonderful time with you, but I'm going to put you in a taxi."

Valérie's eyes widened.

"Let's think about what we're doing," he added. "If

we go any further, I'd like to feel that you're sure. We've got lots to protect, both of us. Listen, I'm going to sneak in a business call to New York before bed. It's still early there," he said.

She didn't know how to reply. She wanted to tell him that she wanted to feel his skin, to touch him, but she felt conflicted between desire and giving too much away.

"You're sure I can't offer you a cognac…?" she said, hoping it was the right thing to say in a situation where the lines between them were blurred. Now they were neither friends nor lovers.

He held her hand as they left the restaurant. The valet hailed a taxi, and before Valérie knew it, Oscar was holding the door open.

"I've had a wonderful afternoon with you, my dear," he said softly. "What a nice surprise. Thank you for sharing your day. And what are you doing tomorrow?"

"I have no plans, and I'd love to make plans with you…." A mental picture flashed through her mind of an embrace with him, of them standing against a wall and him pumping his ass against her, between her legs. She snapped out of the reverie. "Uhh, I have *nothing* to do. You know, if my family's away, then I'm on holiday, too. Why don't you call me in the morning? I haven't been to the Centre Pompidou in *years*.…"

"Let's do it—let's be real tourists," Oscar said with a laugh. Then the mood shifted in an instant while they looked into each other's eyes. Oscar's hand swept into the back of her hair, and he leaned in and met her mouth with his with an urgency that sent a current of desire down her loins. The kiss was hot, deep and hungry. They both shuddered, and his hand palmed her body from between her legs, where he pressed against her, up to her breast, which he squeezed, kissing her even more passionately. Just as quickly, he let her go and held her by her shoulders, away from him. They looked at one another and breathed hard.

"I'll call you in the morning," Oscar said. He guided her into the taxi, announced Valérie's address to the cabbie and handed him some folded euros, then gestured warmly to her as the taxi moved into traffic. With the wine in her head, and the sensation of their kiss, and of their shared dessert…she simply remained in those moments. She felt the breeze from the open windows of the speeding taxi, and watched the glow of passing lights and fluorescent signs. His touch was branded on her senses, and their sexual energy hummed through her body until the taxi stopped at her building.

Valérie turned the key in the lock and entered a quiet, dark apartment. She kicked off her shoes and dropped onto a chair at the small kitchen table. She realized that she had never been in the apartment when it was empty. The silence pressed on her; she was unaccustomed to it. No din of the children. Nothing.

She turned the handle to open the window and let

in the sounds of the Paris night. She looked out at the night sky and neighboring apartments. Her head spun with the excitement of being with Oscar, and it spun with the wine. She was still slightly startled that he was…well…*gone*. Not that she had expected otherwise, she reminded herself….

She looked back into the dark apartment and noticed the red blinking light of the telephone answering machine. She sighed. She knew it was Philippe, but she wanted to remain in *this* moment.

Valérie got up, went to the bathroom, and then straight to bed. She couldn't remember when she had last felt that rush of electricity and anticipation. It was exciting and exhausting.

SIGHTSEEING

The morning was gray and rainy. She got up and showered, replaying the events of the evening with Oscar. She heaved a sigh out loud, knowing nobody could hear. After she dressed, Valérie dialed Philippe's cell phone.

"Philippe! How was the trip? How are the children?"

"We called but you weren't home! Where were you? Are you all right? Did you get the message?"

"Oh, I went out to a film and I had a sandwich in a café. I did a little shopping. And I didn't want to call and wake anyone." Her sense of guilt made her feel that even Oscar's presence in Paris was contraband, and she quickly decided to avoid his name altogether. She knew that they had crossed lines, no matter what happened now.

"Understood. We're all fine, and I think the sea air is good for the kids. After all the time at the beach and in the water, they slept like logs."

They covered the news of the trip and of the children,

chatted and soon had nothing more to say. "I love you, my darling," Philippe said.

"I love you. Kisses to the kids," she answered. And they hung up.

The buzzer rang. Their next-door neighbor, Thérèse, came by most mornings to ask Valérie to watch her baby for a minute while she ran to the bakery for her morning baguette. "Yes, Thérèse!" she called as she walked to the door and automatically opened it.

"Am I bothering you…?"

"Oscar!"

Oscar let himself in, and closed the door. "You're so surprised! Should I leave?" He held up a bag. "You have a wonderful bakery just around the corner, and of course they make the best brioches and croissants. I just couldn't help myself. If you're busy, we'll just have a bite and I'll leave. Otherwise we can share a *petit déjeuner.*"

"Oh, no, I'm not busy at all! Of course not! Come in, come in. I'll make coffee." She was grateful that she'd already dressed, but wondered at the state of her unmade face and hair. She brushed her fingers through some slept-on curls and hoped they would fall right. "I thought you'd call, but that's fine. You're a rascal, aren't you," she teased. She took the paper bag and started ahead of him toward the kitchen.

"I can be…." And she suddenly felt his hand on her arm. He took it firmly and pulled her back toward him, so she gasped in surprise. He turned her to face him and tugged her body to his. One hand moved up to her head, and he didn't hesitate before delivering a long, firm kiss. His fingers were entwined in her hair, and his other hand clasped her arm so that he held her close to him. His kiss was demanding, tantalizing and precise. She shivered. He smelled clean and yet musky. She drank him in. He stopped abruptly.

He held her shoulders and moved her away from him to look squarely in her eyes. "Let's make sure we know what we're doing here…. I *want* you, but we've got families…." He *knew* the significance of what they were heading toward, and he wanted their intimacy acknowledged, permitted. He gave her time to refuse, to have a second thought. One of his hands left her shoulder and ran through her thick, wild hair.

She met his gaze, but didn't want to face real costs. Valérie didn't care about his wife or why he was doing this; and she didn't care about her own life at this moment. She simply felt intoxicated by him, and she *wanted* him. "Let's just call it a holiday…." she whispered, putting an index finger to her lips. "From everything…and no strings attached…" And she moved swiftly to his mouth, kissing him and pulling him to her. *Finally*, she thought, running her hand over his chest.

"Oh, yes!" she murmured aloud. Nerves shot up from her deepest insides to the roof of her mouth. Her body remembered these long-dormant carnal sensations. She swiftly undid his shirt buttons and felt the hard curves of his chest muscles. "I want you!" she whispered in his ear as she gently bit his earlobe.

They connected with fierce energy. Their mouths played together, lips and tongues in a wild little dance. His hands began exploring her skin, and all roads of sensation led to her pussy, which was pulsing and throbbing with the tension of *wanting*. She felt his desire in the strength of his arms. His urgency, when he pressed her to him, made her gasp. His hard cock pushed against her. Her heart pounded and the blood rushed into her cunt.

Her moral compass spun with the gravity of what she was doing, yet she lacked any motivation to stop it. She had been drawn to Oscar from the beginning, and hadn't synchronicity put them in the right place at the right time? She hadn't felt such a pull to a man in decades. "I wanted this when I met you in New York. I wanted to touch you as soon as you looked at me," she whispered.

The precipice they'd been on last night was crumbling beneath them. His hands were exploring her skin and she felt his mouth on her neck, then on her chest…and then his tongue on a nipple made her leap and gasp with delight. His hand kneaded her breasts and clutched her to him. "Ahh!" she sighed loudly. Her knees felt as if they would melt. She hadn't felt such abandon and joy in someone's body for so long!

"Let's get comfortable," he murmured in her ear. He looked up and saw the bedroom and led her to it—to Valérie and Phillipe's marriage bed—where he both pulled and pushed her onto it. They fell together onto the still-unmade mattress. Every nerve exploded as her blouse was pushed up and away by Oscar's hands. He lightly skimmed her skin with the palm of his hand, and she strained and arched her back to meet his touch. She gasped. After so many years of lovemaking to the same man, her senses were in shock.

Oscar smelled different, a musky, sweaty scent coupled with a foreign cologne. He was firm and exigent, where Philippe was tender and tentative. Oscar *made love*, while Valérie's marriage bed had become a rote exercise. She reveled in his body as his mouth moved across her breasts and he sucked and bit her straining brown nipples. "Oh!" she cried without even realizing it.

"Baby…" he replied, pinching her other nipple between his thumb and forefinger.

For a single moment she felt a pang of self-consciousness about her body. How long had it been since a stranger felt her like this? The last time a stranger ravished her she'd had taut skin and the firm breasts and flesh of a young woman. But they were here, now, and Oscar showed no signs of stopping for dinner conversation. They explored each other like new lovers. He palmed the curves of her body everywhere; his hand slipped over her back and her ass. His fingertips trailed down the backs of her thighs and into crevices of olive flesh. She moaned with pleasure.

She pushed him away so that she could discover his sinewy form, which was as rippled and muscled as she had hoped. His cock was long and thick, and it strained while she ran her hands over his chest, down his slim hips and over his thighs. Then he growled from his throat and dragged her panties down, off her hips and down her legs. She helped by kicking them away. Finally, he flipped her over on the bed and opened her legs with his own. So fast, she felt his hands squeeze her ass, and then his finger search for her opening. She was wet and he slid his finger in.

"I've wanted to fuck you since I first saw you," he whispered in her ear, on top of her. He lifted himself and grunted with pleasure. He had his cock in his hand, and opened her legs wider to mount her. He dived deeply into her, and when he stopped for a second she felt as if his cock touched every nerve her body. He began to rock and pump. She cried out, overtaken by waves of pleasure as he moved in and out, in and out.

"Baby, baby…I want to fuck you…." he murmured, lowering his head to nip at her earlobes and tongue her ear. His deep whispers made his fierceness even hotter. She had a fleeting reflection that she had taken someone into Philippe's bed, and struggled for a moment with the reality of it.

But Oscar interrupted those fleeting thoughts. "Do you have a vibrator, honey?" he asked, breathing hard.

"Uhh…" she stammered, lifting her eyebrows in shock. Talking to this man about intimate sex toys of her marriage…?

She stared blankly, and he whispered, "Married men know what works!" Valérie laughed and pointed to her bedside table. He laughed, too, but he wasn't fooling around. He pulled out of her and went directly for the drawer, opening it so roughly that he brought the whole table crashing to the floor, with the lamp following. There, in the mess of spilled contents, was indeed her plastic, pink-hued vibrator. Oscar smirked, grabbed it and turned it on.

He flipped her onto her stomach and slid his straining cock back into her. "Honey…" he said, pumping again. He lifted her hips. He grabbed a pillow to make a cushion between her cunt and the vibrator head. Then he put the vibrating unit against her while he pumped his cock. She could feel all her nerve endings climbing. She felt her orgasm coming, and the sensation was that she was flying off that cliff that they had leaped from. The buzz of the vibrator registered like a plane engine.

And that was the end. She came with a crash that exploded deep inside, and her clit growled like a cat ready to pounce. When it did, she saw a kaleidoscope of colors so vivid that she gave an openmouthed cry. Did it last a second or an hour? She lost track of time, and came out of it sweating and heaving.

But Oscar wasn't done. He pulled out of her, sweet sex honey running everywhere, and turned her over. She had a chance to look at his cock. It was bigger and thicker than Philippe's, which accounted for its performance, she guessed. Oscar slid himself into her, face-forward, and devoured her with his mouth. His tongue explored every part of her tongue and, still pumping, he bent over to suck her nipples, first one, then the other. Finally, he emitted a grunt that began quietly, then grew to almost a shout. She felt as if she was fucking a tiger. She was thunderstruck.

It was over. His cream streamed out of her and onto the tangled mess of sheets. He flopped over onto his back and lay there, sweating and panting. Beads of sweat shone on his olive skin. She looked at him naked for the first time. His skin was darker than Philippe's, and he was hairier, but it suited him, since he was like a wild animal, she thought.

"I love your body…" she said quietly. His arms were muscular. He wasn't big, but she was right about the sexual power he held. He was hard and sinewy, his muscles taut. But she couldn't reconcile making love with him in Philippe's own bed, so she put it out of her mind.

"The timing was right," he said. "It was meant to be."

He circled the curves of her breasts with his fingers as they lay on the bed. "I forgot how lovely it is to lie together after making love," she said.

"Your hair is wild. It reminds me of an exotic queen," he replied, twirling a lock with his thumb.

She put thoughts of her husband out of her mind and instead chose to experience the moment, as if time was just stopping briefly. "I love your body...." she repeated, running her palm from his curved biceps, over his strong chest and down his stomach, where she stopped and kissed him.

"Maybe I'll make coffee...?" she asked, looking up from his chest.

He laughed and sat up, and grabbed a bedsheet to wipe some of the sweat from his brow and then his chest. "Yes, yes...and those croissants now. I'm famished. Can I jump into a shower?"

He came into the kitchen in his boxer shorts. He smelled faintly of her family soap, which confused her senses. He sat down at the kitchen table, where she had breakfast things laid out. "Please," she said, gesturing to the table.

He poured her espresso, then his own. "Sit down, sit down," he said, grabbing her hand as she moved back and forth in the small kitchen. "You're okay with this...?"

"I don't know. I've never done this before. I just wanted you...I wanted you ever since I saw you," she said, sitting down across from him. "Sometimes you meet someone, and then if you're lucky, you get a moment with them, I think…and this is my moment with *you*."

"That's how I feel," he said. "And wonderful things can happen even when you only have that moment."

He reached under the table and stroked her thigh. "No strings, just a…a short vacation from our lives? And nobody needs to know." He drank his espresso and tore a croissant.

"It's a deal. I never knew it could be so easy." They smiled at each other. "Have you done this before? Since you were married?"

"Maybe once or twice… I've been married a long time," he answered with a wink. "So it's a deal. It's between us." He extended his hand.

She took it and he pulled her toward him for a kiss. She laughed and drew away. "This won't get us far in Paris," she said.

"I don't care. *You're* what I want to see in Paris, baby," he answered, lifting her shirt to stroke her breast. "Come back to bed with me," he said, kissing her neck. He led her by the hand, and they fumbled their way back to the bedroom. They fell on the bed and he kissed her body, making his way down to her pussy.

Philippe hadn't bothered with oral sex for years. Now a soft stroke of Oscar's tongue on her inside lips made her quiver. His tongue found her clit and he sucked it gently. At the same time, he slid a finger in and out of her rhythmically, and in minutes her body rose in a tide of sensation.

Before she could come, he moved up and pushed his thick sex into her. Every nerve she possessed was now riding the white water of body bliss. "Taste your sweet honey," he whispered. "Give me your tongue." She parted her lips and he licked her tongue, and they exchanged her juices as they kissed again. He pumped her sopping wet cunt, and when she began to cry out, he let himself come, bursting into her with shivers of pleasure.

They lay together in a sticky mess of sweat and cum, and finally came apart. But it didn't last long. They began to kiss again, fondling and stroking each other's body.

"How about a shower...again?" Oscar suggested. "And this time you come with me. Then we'll get out and enjoy the city, like we planned."

"I *am* enjoying the city," Valérie said, "since *you're* in it."

He led her off the bed and into the shower. Water flowed and they soaped one another, sending bubbles running down and around and across hard and soft flesh, over breasts and taut muscles, soft curves and asses. Valérie soaped Oscar's soft penis, pumping it with her warm, wet hand, and it came to life again, hard and hungry.

"Turn around," he whispered in her ear. "I need to fuck you again…." She turned, and he entered her from behind, pumping hard while the warm water fell between them. He stroked her tits from behind and she caressed her own sex. "I want you to suck me before I come again," he urged. He pulled himself out, still hard and straining.

She went on her knees on the floor of the tub and took him in her mouth. He was bigger and wider than Philippe, and when she couldn't hold him in she sucked the purple tip of his cock, and licked it like candy. He moaned and grunted, spurting over her face. She caught some cum with her tongue and he groaned again. He dropped to his knees and kissed her deeply, tasting himself in her mouth.

"Okay," he laughed, when they had recovered from the moment. "Now let's really get out of here." They finally cleaned up, dressed and prepared to leave the apartment.

TOURISTS IN THE CITY

They decided to visit the Centre Pompidou. Valérie hadn't gone in years, and Oscar, always more interested in athletics, had toured few galleries. The diverse and modern collections gave them much to talk about, and they continued their conversation over lunch in a casual bistro where they ordered *steak frites* and a bottle of light rosé. They shared *clafoutis aux cerise* for dessert like lovers. They walked through the old neighborhoods and admired buildings that Valérie hadn't looked at in years. Who admired seventeenth-century architecture with two tired, arguing children in tow? she thought to herself. Who stopped to study the details of medieval gargoyles while hauling bags of groceries?

Oscar was a charmer, and he made her laugh with stories from his business travels in the world of pro sports. They held hands and shared ice cream. They kissed in the street. Oscar took her hand everywhere, and put his arm around her at every opportunity.

They ended the day with a stroll through the Jardin

du Luxembourg, resplendent and majestic at the height of the season, topaz-toned sand and stone bright in the summer sun. "I'd forgotten that Paris is such a fabulous city," she said, "or maybe *you* are what's fabulous?" She looked at him.

He smiled and winked. "It's the moment we have together, and it's *you*." He drew her to him and kissed her.

"There's a restaurant I want to take you to," Oscar said as they were leaving the gardens.

"You took me out last night. I'll make you something at home," Valérie replied.

"Didn't you say that this is a little holiday?" he said playfully. "And on holidays don't you eat in restaurants? Let me take you. My wife buys all those food magazines, but they just sit there, so I read them. I love to eat. I read about another new bistro." He took out his handheld and searched for the address. "Here it is. Let's go." He looked up and down the street, scouting for a taxi.

"Your wife…" Valérie started.

Oscar stopped her midsentence, putting his index finger to her lips. "'My wife,' 'your husband'—don't worry about anything. This is *our* little 'lost weekend' away from everyone. When it's over, we'll go back to our worries." He kissed her, and soon flagged a passing cab. She thought, in the taxi, as he held her hand, that he was right. There was no point in overthinking a little tryst, and she promised herself that she wouldn't mention it again. Reality, she knew, would return soon enough.

They ate in a stylish bistro that celebrated classic French cuisine done with global flavors. They fed each other grilled sardines dipped in miso-rosemary sauce from lacquered chopsticks. They drank a dry white wine, and ate French favorites—woodsy cèpes, aubergines and courgettes—in Sichuan spices. They nibbled and shared desserts of apples with burnt sugar, folded into layers of paper-thin Greek phyllo pastry. "I love to eat with you," Oscar said, brushing her cheek with his hand. "You enjoy food like you enjoy sex, and that's a very sexy thing." He reached underneath the table and caressed her thigh.

"Here's to us and our little holiday together" she replied, raising her glass. He raised his, but before they drank he took her other hand and brought it to his lips. She smiled and exclaimed, "I think I'd like a vacation in New York!"

"Why don't you come to my hotel tonight, and enjoy a four-star room? It's no fun for me all alone." He brushed a finger against her cheek again and smiled in turn. "Let's start walking, and if we get tired we can grab a cab."

They walked toward the river, stopping in front of small gallery windows to look at paintings. They passed a bookstore having an author's reading and stopped in the doorway to listen. They continued on, sharing favorite authors.

The only sour note in this symphony of romance was when Valérie realized she couldn't be away from the apartment for a night without an excuse for Philippe. She hated lying to him—hated the feeling of guilt in the pit of her stomach—but her desire for Oscar was greater than her wish to examine her life outside the confines of these few precious days.

"Listen," she said to Oscar, "I have to make a call...to Philippe.... I'll just step over there a moment," she said, gesturing to a large doorway entrance into a courtyard between two ancient buildings.

He nodded in agreement. "I'll wait here."

She flipped her cell phone open and speed-dialed. "*Mon amour*!" her husband answered brightly. "I left a message this morning. I didn't get you at home and I called your cell, but you didn't answer...."

"Oh, maybe I was in the Métro and didn't hear it. I've been out a lot, just shopping and in the stores—it's so much easier without kids, you know."

"Of course," Philippe answered. "You should be having some fun."

"Well, I am...just meeting old girlfriends I haven't seen in so long. But listen, I have to go.... I just wanted to tell you that I plan to go to bed early and get a good night's sleep with no interruptions, you know? I'll probably turn off the phone tonight, so if I don't answer, I'm just at home asleep. Are the children fine?"

"Yes, they're having a wonderful time, and they miss you and love you, like I do. I won't call tonight, and you have a good, restful sleep. *Je t'aime, mon amour*."

"You'll all be back soon—the day after tomorrow? *Je t'aime*…bye!" She hung up.

Valérie glanced up the street to find Oscar. He was standing in a doorway looking at his messages on his phone. He lifted his head and their eyes met. They both smiled. She walked to him.

"Everything fine?" he asked. "Fine. Let's go." He took her hand and they walked together. Afternoon turned into a warm evening. Streetlights blinked on and Oscar pointed to the sky. "Let's walk down to the Seine. Maybe we'll see a star or two."

At the bottom of the narrow street they arrived at Pont Neuf. They walked across and stopped to admire the Seine, its current glistening in the evening light. Boats moved along under them. Oscar tugged Valérie toward him and kissed her. He took her face in his hands and kissed her deeply and slowly. She heard other lovers whispering to each other as they crossed the bridge, and she heard bicycle wheels whirring past. She felt the night breeze brush past them, and the cool scent of the water wafted by. She felt the spirits of a thousand lovers on this ancient bridge, all having embraced and loved, as though it were a place where time stood still for passion and tenderness between souls.

"Come," Oscar said, after what felt like a kiss that flowed between time. "Let's find a taxi and go to the Tour Eiffel." They hailed a taxi and headed for the Jardin des Tuileries.

A NIGHT ON THE TOWN

Arriving close enough to the Eiffel Tower to have it looming skyward before them, Oscar said, "Let's take a detour. When was the last time you were on that big Ferris wheel?"

"La Grande Roue?" Valérie laughed, pointing to it. "You're crazy! It's been forever." In the park, tourists took photos of their children, tired from busy vacation days. The smell of popcorn filled the air around them, and they crunched kernels beneath their feet as they walked.

He took her waist and they approached the Ferris wheel, a perfect circle of twinkling lights by night. "Two, please," Oscar said to the ticket taker. They waited for the next turn, and were placed in a car. In others, young couples giggled and kissed.

Up, up, up moved the little car. The big wheel swept them up above the park trees, green in the city-lit night. Up, up and up, and they looked at the lights of Paris around them. Traffic circled endlessly around the Champs Elysée. A thousand tiny lights glittered on the

Eiffel Tower. And when Valérie looked up into the sky, she saw stars shining and planets blinking.

"The City of Lights. Beautiful, isn't it," Oscar said. At the top the Ferris wheel stopped for a few minutes, and they both registered their amazement.

"I forget that I live here…." Valérie sighed.

Oscar turned and brought her to him, and they kissed again. He stroked her cheek. "I want you," he said quietly.

When the ride ended, they made their way out of the park, hand in hand, and caught a cab to Oscar's hotel. "How is it that a lovely hotel makes you feel like you don't have a care in the world?" she said to him as they entered his room.

He drew her to him, and they fell on the bed together, their kisses a tango of tongues and eager lips. They shed each other's clothes, undoing buttons and zippers and unpeeling layers until they were naked and rolling together over crisp, white hotel linens.

He urged her head to his cock. After years spent making love to the same man, she wondered what Oscar liked. She licked the soft, purple head and heard him gasp. He held it at the base and moaned as she tongued its length. He stroked her hair while she pumped him with her wet mouth. It made her feel young and sexy and dirty, and she loved it.

She felt liberated from the dead air of her sex life. She pumped his cock and sucked hard. He gasped and groaned, shooting his white cum over her and the bed. He dropped onto the big pillows and exhaled deeply, exhausted. "Oh, baby," he said, lifting her to him to kiss her deeply. Their tongues collided passionately, and she felt a rush of not just her carnal high, but of happiness with this man and this moment.

Then he slid down her. His fingers parted the soft lips of her pussy and he carefully stroked her hard fuchsia clit with his tongue. It was confident and sure, not tentative like Philippe's. She cried out, and Oscar stroked it back the other way. He let his tongue travel outside and inside the plump, engorged lips of her vulva, and finally was too excited to continue. "I have to fuck you *now*," he growled, and mounted her in an instant like an animal. He drove his thick, rigid sex into her and they both panted like primal beasts. His hands were all over her hot flesh. She came with a cry, and he grunted, pushing himself into her harder and harder until he was empty.

They came apart, wet and sticky with sweat and cum. With his eyes closed, he left a hand roaming her skin, over her breasts and nipples. Finally, he turned toward her and kissed her. "A shower and room service? I'm famished again."

While Oscar showered, she wandered the hotel room, then stood at the window to watch the view. He came out in a thick hotel robe. "Your turn, my dear. What would you like?" he asked, picking up the room service menu. "I'm going to order a steak sandwich."

"Oh, I don't know. I'll have what you're having. And a glass of wine would be nice."

In the shower, among the little luxury hotel soaps and shampoos, Valérie looked forward to staying the night. The hotel made her feel as if her own world were truly on the other side of the globe, and with it her life of wife and mother. She showered a long time, running the hot water over herself like a summer rain. When she finally came out, body and hair swathed in thick, white hotel towels, the food had already arrived.

"I didn't want to bother you in the shower. I hope it's not rude that I started without you."

Valérie laughed. "You're kidding. Nothing could bother me right now. Restaurants, room service…" Then she lowered her voice, adding, "Making love with you…what could bother me now?" They toasted to the fun they were having together, ate and relaxed. Valérie stayed the night with him, made love and slept in the fantasy comforts of his hotel.

That night her dreams featured a whirlwind of movement. She dreamed of museums and taxis, and a place that looked like the Italian coastline where she'd once spent a week with a boyfriend when she was young. Always moving, never stopping, and making love in hotel rooms with open shutters that let in the summer air.

The next morning she and Oscar ate croissants and drank café au lait from room service. They sat in their plush white robes and looked at the newspaper together. "Well," Oscar began, "I have one more day here. What would you like to do? See some monuments? Go to one of those huge flea markets? Walk through the Marais?"

"A flea market…what a fun idea. I never go—it's impossible with the kids," she said.

They hopped in a taxi and spent the morning in one of the rambling, labyrinthine markets. They ambled through the alleyways and past the stalls. Oscar bargained with sellers just for fun, and they ate spicy little merguez sausages in baguettes for lunch, and washed them down with beer. "I don't know when I've had so much fun," Valérie told him, wrapping her arm around his waist.

Oscar said that he'd never been through any of the city's famed churches, and so they spent the afternoon exploring Notre Dame and Saint Germain des Pres. Standing on the street and looking at a map made her feel like a tourist. She felt above the bitter bustle of daily Parisian life, above it and apart from it, just like a *real* tourist.

"How about a glass of wine somewhere?" Oscar said as they left the cathedral. "Maybe we can find a nice bistro and have a bite for dinner. I don't want to be the first one to say it, but maybe this is our last evening together."

Valérie knew it, but had put it to the back of her mind. "Then let's go back to your hotel, so at least we can be alone." They flagged a cab and sat in the back with fingers entwined.

"I'm not looking forward to saying goodbye," she said.

He took her face in his hands and kissed her. "Don't talk about goodbyes. We still have a few hours…and who knows that we won't be together again sometime?"

"We'll have the Chateau Margaux 1983," Oscar ordered on the phone to room service. "A *confit foie gras de canard maison sauce poire* and an *escalope de veau*," he added, reading from the menu. "And a warm goat cheese on toasted brioches from the appetizers."

"Our last supper." Valérie smiled sadly, cocking her head.

"Listen," Oscar answered, "never say never. But let's just remind ourselves of the wonderful time we had…and let's make one more memory until we see each other again." He led her to the big bed they'd made love in. She slid out of her shoes and backed onto it as he kissed her, pulling her to him. They rolled on the bed, enjoying each other's body. "Were we meant to fit together so perfectly?" Oscar whispered.

Room service knocked. He signed for the food and closed the door again. "Let's go back to where we were," Valérie said, taking his hand and leading him back to the bed. There, they made love for the last time. They embraced tenderly and they embraced passionately. Oscar caressed Valérie's body, and tongued and sucked her nipples. When he thought she couldn't take any more, he drove his sex into her, and they rode a tide of pleasure together. They played together in bed like new lovers, enjoying and exploring, not knowing what the next moment would bring.

When it was over, Oscar opened the Chateau Margaux and brought glasses to the bed, where they lay naked in wildly rumpled sheets. "Here's to us," he said, pouring the wine. "Here's to us. Here's to little holidays from reality…and to little secrets." They put their glasses together and kissed.

EVERY VACATION ENDS

Philippe and the children came back without incident, and they were all happy to be together again. The children were tanned and rested, and Philippe seemed to have enjoyed himself despite spending a week with his parents. His family's happiness was his own. The children's tan faces reminded him of a week well spent, and he was grateful for the air of calm the week had brought to his wife.

She felt the letdown that came with the end of every vacation, but maybe it was also a small relief to return to her own surroundings. The children and their din, and Philippe, as he was, were those surroundings. She looked at his tall, thin frame and his slight paunch. She noticed that he was beginning to stoop slightly.

She didn't say much about how she had spent her days; she said that there wasn't much to tell. "Just rest and relaxation," she told Philippe "I think the Americans call it R & R."

For Your Pleasure

By Elisa Adams

Award nominated author **Elisa Adams**' short erotic fiction has been published by Ellora's Cave, Samhain, Loose ID, and in Red Sage's annual "Secrets" anthology. For Your Pleasure is her first story published with Spice Briefs. She says her stories 'aren't for the faint of heart!'

I.

The heat was almost too much to take. Humidity robbed me of a decent breath and sweat coated my brow no matter how many times I swiped it away with the back of my hand. The misery would last for three more days, according to the radio news broadcast I caught this morning on my way to work. Three more days before we got a little relief.

Birds chirped in the trees overhead. Even their songs sounded weak. Uncomfortable. Summers in New England tended to be like this. Hot and sticky for days on end. Some people loved the heat. I hated it. Hated the way my hair and clothing seemed plastered to my body. Hated the restlessness that settled into my gut and wrapped its fingers around my throat.

Even now, I shifted in my lounge chair, wishing I'd put in a pool last summer like my sister had tried to talk me into doing. The air conditioner was on the fritz. The repairman couldn't get here for two more days. I groaned. The only place to escape the heat would be the office.

A flash of movement drew my attention and a smile tickled the corners of my lips. The slight breeze wasn't the only bonus to being outside. A light in my neighbor's window reminded me of the real reason I'd come out here after dinner. He always got home from work at eight-thirty on weeknights. And changed with the lights on.

My neighbor had yet to put curtains in his bedroom windows.

I'd seen him for the first time two weeks ago, when he'd moved into the house across the yard from mine. The second-story windows were tall and narrow, spaced three in a row with only inches between them, affording me a very nice view. For days I'd been telling myself watching the guy was only wrong if I got caught, but it didn't matter. Wrong or right, I couldn't stop.

From the first moment, I'd been obsessed. I didn't know his name, didn't know anything about him, and yet all my fantasies in the past few weeks had revolved around him. Tonight was no exception. Already I could feel my pussy getting damp. Primed. I knew what would happen next. Most nights, he did more than change with the lights on.

My skin tingled with anticipation. I ran my hands up my sides, teasing my breasts until my nipples peaked, all while wishing it was his touch instead of mine. I just wanted him to fuck me. Was that too much to ask?

Apparently. A sigh born of frustration burst from my lips. Two solid weeks of watching, and he never even looked my way.

Sad, Callie. So very sad. At thirty-two, I'd been reduced to a voyeur, wanting what I could never have, logging way too many hours with my battery-operated boyfriend. I tucked a sweat-slicked lock of hair behind my ear. My sister, the psychiatrist, would have a field day with this one.

My neighbor was gorgeous, but not in a conventional way. Toned muscles. Tanned, tattooed skin. Long, dark hair and an ever-present five o'clock shadow. Ripped T-shirts and worn jeans, the kind of man every girl's mother warned her to stay away from.

The kind of man I needed over me, inside me, making me scream his name.

I wrapped my hand around the glass of iced tea sitting on the table next to me, stroking up and down like it was his cock. The condensation cooled my hand and I wiped the liquid down my neck. It did little to slow the fire raging inside me, both from the weather and the man across the yard.

He stripped off his shirt and it dropped out of sight. Next, his jeans followed and he dropped to the bed in just his boxers. He ran his hand absently over the bulge there, the muscles in his abdomen flexing and bunching as he stroked his cock through the fabric. I mimicked the motion, sliding my hand over the wet bikini bottom between my legs. Two seconds in and I was already squirming, striving for release. It came quickly when I thought about him, about that big cock and what it would feel like inside me.

I waited, breath held, muscles tense, for him to take off the boxers, but tonight it didn't happen. My neighbor got up and walked away. Somehow, his absence escalated my excitement. Was he somewhere in a darkened room, watching me out a window?

I moved aside my shorts and panties, exposing my pussy to the hot night air. I brushed my finger down my slit, wishing it was his finger instead. My skin was already slick with moisture, and the dampness increased as I stroked myself with my wet fingers. My breasts tingled, my nipples ached for his lips.

How many nights had I touched myself, thinking of him? Too many, but never like this. Never outside, in full view of anyone who happened to be looking.

In full view of my neighbor, if he chose to look.

But he hadn't seen me yet, had he? Maybe he wouldn't. To someone like him, I was invisible. I'd seen his women. Watched him fuck them in his bed while they clawed at his back and thrashed their heads from side to side. An endless parade of blondes, with the occasional redhead thrown in. My neighbor liked them tall and model thin. Two things I would never achieve. Not in this lifetime.

I wasn't bitter about that, though. Five foot four was

tall enough. I liked my curves. The men I dated liked my curves. If my neighbor didn't, that was his loss.

A car door slamming somewhere in the neighborhood made me freeze, but only for a second. The trees throughout the yard would keep most neighbors from nosing around, and his was the closest house to mine. If he saw me, I didn't care. Maybe I even wanted him to.

My lids sank closed, my mind already forming images of what he might be doing since he'd left the room. I continued to play my fingers across my flesh, slowly now, knowing I was getting too close to climax and not yet ready for it to be over.

The hair on my arms prickled. I opened my eyes and my breath caught in my throat. He'd moved back to the windows and was standing there with one palm pressed to the glass. The heat in his eyes made my pulse skitter. I swallowed hard. Oh, God. *Not my imagination.* He was watching me. My movements stilled. What was I supposed to do now? I started to pull my fingers away from my body, but he shook his head. One word mouthed from those full lips had me shaking in my chair.

More.

I swallowed hard. This couldn't be happening, and yet, I couldn't deny it. He didn't want me to stop.

When I didn't move, a sexy smile spread over his face and a spark of challenge lit his eyes. My whole body quivered, my pussy growing even damper. "Come on," he mouthed now, and even though a pane of glass separated us I could almost feel his deep voice slide over me like cool silk. Helpless to stop myself, I obeyed the command in his eyes, slipping my hand back between my legs to finger my pussy again.

I slipped two fingers inside my channel, stroking in and out. My thumb on my clit, I pressed down and cried out at the jolt of pleasure. It was too much. I wasn't this bold. I wasn't sure I could masturbate with him watching me, but I didn't want to stop. I squeezed my eyes shut, blocking out everything but the feeling of my own fingers. He still watched. I could feel his gaze all over my skin. The idea of putting on a show should have turned me off, but it didn't. All this time I'd wanted him to notice me, and now he had.

A minute or so later, strong hands moved my legs apart and my eyes flew open. He knelt between my legs, his mouth inches from my pussy. His gaze met mine and locked. The heat I found there made a wisp of arousal curl in my belly.

My face flaming, I pulled my fingers out of my pussy and started to readjust my bikini bottom, but he didn't let me finish. He grabbed my hand and brought it to his lips, sucking my fingers into his mouth. He laved them with his tongue before he let me go. I whimpered.

"What's your name?" he asked in a deep whisper.

"Callie." I didn't ask his, because I didn't want to know. It was more exciting this way, lying here so completely open to a stranger. I could barely breathe, barely move.

"Callie." He wrapped his voice around the word, dragging out each syllable. "I've been dying to taste you."

And then he did. His mouth closed over my clit and he drew the tight bud inside. His tongue flicked over me again and again, the small movement enough to drive me right to the brink of orgasm. My back arched. Seconds after his lips touched my body, I was ready to beg him to fuck me.

"Please." The word slipped from my lips, not much more than a whisper of breath on the summer breeze.

In answer, he chuckled against my skin. The thrust of his fingers inside my pussy took me by surprise, making me cant my hips toward him for more. The masterful swirls of his tongue and thrust of those thick fingers had me squirming on the chair. I threaded my hands through his hair, holding his head close while he continued to eat me out. His fingers dug into my thighs, holding me open to him.

The man was a master. Like an explosion, the orgasm took me by surprise, rocking the very foundation of my world. It tightened my grip in his hair, my head dropping back as a silent scream tore from my lips. He didn't let up right away, and tremor after tremor raced through me until all my muscles felt weak. Liquid and useless. And then he backed up and stood, leaving me cold.

Spent and trembling, I could do nothing but lie there and watch him work the buckle on his belt, his gaze never leaving mine. The heat in his eyes made me tremble all over again. My juices glistened on his chin. Once his pants were unbuttoned, he freed his cock and I licked my lips. It had been way too long since I'd had a man inside me. I wouldn't have to wait much longer. I shifted, reaching my hands toward him, but he shook his head.

"Not tonight. It's getting late, and I'm sure you have an early morning."

A little sound of protest whispered past my lips, but he said nothing. Instead, he took the length of his erection in his hand and stroked it from base to tip. His head dropped back, his eyes closing and his lips parting. It didn't take him long to get off, and he came in heavy spurts over my stomach. His lips drifted open and, gracing me with that sexy smile, he leaned down and rubbed his come into my skin.

"Another time, Callie." He pressed a quick kiss to my forehead before he turned and walked away.

A long time later, I was finally able to make myself get up and go into the house. This was one night of fantasy I would never forget.

2.

Three days had passed since my backyard encounter with my neighbor. I hadn't seen him since, but then again, I hadn't really been looking. Part of my reasoning could be attributed to mortification, but another, larger part relished the idea of what I'd done. What I'd let him do to me. Seeing him again might taint my memories of what had happened. Even now, as I walked up the front steps toward my door, a frisson of heat shot down my spine, settling between my legs.

I tried to brush the feeling off as I walked up the path toward my front porch. It had been a long day in an even longer week. Thank God it was the weekend. I needed time to rest. To sleep in and recharge before I had to do it all again on Monday. Funny thing was, as much as I wanted some time alone, away from people, I had to wonder what it would be like to be with my neighbor again. This time, completely with him. I didn't want his mouth, amazing as he'd made me feel with it. I wanted his dick.

An involuntary sound escaped from my lips, followed by a giggle. Being a bad girl had never really appealed to me, but I liked the way it felt. It was a heady rush of power that made me smile.

I reached the top step, keys in hand, and headed for the door, when a movement from the shadows in the corner of the porch caught my attention. I froze, the hair on my arms standing on end. "Who's there?"

"Do you always stay so late at work?"

The voice—*his* voice—made me drop my keys. They clattered to the porch, glinting in the light from the dim bulb overhead. I swallowed, bending down to pick up the ring. "You scared me. I have a project. A deadline."

"It isn't good for you. You need some downtime. Relaxation."

Easy for him to say. "Why are you here? Surely it's not to chastise me for my work habits, since you don't know me well enough to know what they are. Actually, you don't even know me at all, do you?"

He laughed. "I know what your pussy tastes like. I know what sounds you make when you come."

Already my pussy was wet, and growing wetter by the second. I'd been needing to feel his cock inside me for days now. No, longer. Much longer. Since the second I'd seen him in that upstairs window not long after he'd moved in, stroking his cock with such abandon.

"You know why I'm here," he continued, stepping

closer but still clinging to the shadows. "You want me here. Want what's bound to happen between us."

"No." The denial was automatic, but untrue. He had to know it. There was no strength behind the single word. I tried to turn toward him, needing to see his expression, but his palm between my shoulder blades stopped me.

"Don't. Stay right where you are."

The command should have annoyed me, maybe even offended me, but instead, it made me even wetter. My pussy muscles contracted, softening. Readying for him.

He dropped his hand lower until it rested on the small of my back, just above my ass. He rubbed his fingertips into the hollow there and I whimpered.

"Bend forward and put your hands on the door, Miss Jenkins."

A chill washed down my spine. I ignored his command, still trying to process what he'd said. "How do you know my last name?"

He pressed on my back, arching me forward. Fingers on my wrists, he brought my hands up to rest on the cool metal surface of the door. "I was curious, so I found out. Surprised?"

I could only nod. He moved his hands to my hips, bunching my skirt until he had the material gathered at my waist. He fit his knee between mine and nudged my legs apart. The excitement inside me threatened to bubble over, but this was wrong. Even more wrong than what had happened in my backyard. I couldn't let it continue. "Don't. We're out front, right under a light. Someone might see."

His soft laugh washed over me. "I thought you liked that. Liked to be watched. You like to watch me, too."

I went cold. No way. It wasn't possible. "You knew?"

"Oh, yeah. And I loved every second."

I licked my lips. All that time, he'd been performing. Putting on a show, the way he'd urged me to outside. I should have been upset, but then again, he should have been offended that I'd watched in the first place. The fact that he wasn't turned me on even more.

"Those other women…"

"They had no idea. But I knew. You liked watching me fuck them, didn't you?"

I shook my head, my denial emphatic. "No."

"Why not? Tell me the truth."

"Because I wanted it to be me." Every single, goddamn time, I wanted it to be me.

His fingers crept up my hip, tickling, teasing. "Do you still want that?"

"Yes."

"Good. I want it, too. Have for way too long." He slid aside my panties and ran his fingers along the length of my slit. I was so slick, so wet, that I felt hypersensitive.

He stroked my clit. Tingles spread from my pussy out to my limbs. My legs shook. I cried out, wriggled back, but every time I managed to get his fingers right where I needed them, he shifted, keeping me on edge but not letting me topple over. The tips of his fingers were callused, as if he spent his days working outside. Such a contrast from the executives I usually brought into my bed. They were all polish and class, where my neighbor was not. I hadn't realized until now that I liked it rough. Raw and sexy.

He pressed a kiss between my shoulder blades. The rich, clean scent of his cologne surrounded me. "I've been thinking about you. I shouldn't have walked away that night."

"Why did you?"

"I knew it would be better this time if I did. So much hotter."

I was on the verge of begging him to fuck me…when his other hand came down on my ass. The resounding smack echoed through the silence. Shock stole my breath. Even the crickets stopped chirping. My ass cheek burned and blood pounded in my ears. That had to have been a mistake.

A mistake that had felt so damn good. "What do you think you're doing?"

He caressed the spot he'd just spanked. "Following my instinct. You've been a bad girl, haven't you, Callie? Spying on the neighbors. Peeking into their bedrooms." Another smack, another sharp sting. Another wave of pleasure flooding my pussy. "Watching me with other women. Watching me by myself. Do you know what I was thinking about every time I jerked off?"

His raw choice of words made me shudder. My nipples rubbed against the lace cups of my bra, sending little jolts straight to my pussy. "No."

"You. I was thinking about you. About sinking my dick into your hot pussy. Making you scream my name as you begged for more."

"I don't even know your name."

Another smack, this one harder than the first two. My body pitched forward, toward the door, and I had to brace myself. I let out a gasp. *Oh, my God.* I'd never been so turned on in my life.

He pressed a kiss to my ass, right where I ached. "Actually, you do. You know more about me than you realize."

I wanted to question him, but he chose that moment to thrust two fingers into my pussy. All rational thought fled from my mind. I moaned, no longer caring if the neighbors heard. Not caring if they saw what we were doing. I was beyond embarrassment, beyond asking him to stop. I wanted him inside me, but so far, all he'd done was tease.

"Tell me what you want, Callie," he whispered, my name almost like a physical caress. His touch feathered across my hip where the skin lay exposed.

I arched my back, pushing my ass toward him. "Just…please."

"Cat got your tongue?"

I would have laughed, had I not been so needy, so ready for him. At this point, I was willing to let him do whatever he wanted to me as long as I found a little bit of relief. I reached my hand between my legs, but he stopped me with a pinch on my hip.

"Don't. I promise this will be worth the wait."

After last time, I didn't doubt it. A sexy man doing scandalous things to me outside, in public, was one of the fantasies I'd never dared confess to anyone. It felt almost shameful, but even that added to the pleasure. My senses were heightened, my skin hypersensitive as he thrust those thick, rough fingers deep into my sheath. He pushed a third finger inside, stroking them as high as they could go.

"Fuck," I muttered, my head coming close to hitting the door again. There was nothing polished about this guy, and that was exactly the way I needed it.

"Is that what you want?" His words were clipped, his voice a little breathless. I loved knowing I could affect him as much as he affected me.

"You know it is."

He pulled his fingers out of me and backed away. My body felt cold, bereft, like all the heat had been sucked out of the air.

I gritted my teeth. "What are you doing?"

"Looking at you. I've wanted you in this position for so long."

I squirmed just knowing his gaze was focused on me. My pussy was so wet by now I was sure my cream was running down my thighs. He had to know, and still, he did nothing.

After what seemed like an eternity of waiting, I glanced over my shoulder and found him leaning on the porch railing, arms crossed over his chest. I swallowed hard. "Please."

In answer, he pushed off the railing and walked over to the door, grabbing the keys from the porch floor and inserting my house key into the lock. I stood just before he turned the knob and led me inside. My legs were shaking so hard I could barely walk. My ass still stung, but it was a good kind of pain. The kind that made me want to tear off his clothes and have my way with him, right then and there. I didn't touch him, though. Instead, I waited, high on anticipation, to see what he would do next.

He didn't make me wait long. Once he'd closed the door behind us, he pushed me against it and pressed his body to mine. He kissed me then, a commanding attack of a kiss, his tongue forcing its way into my mouth as he took what he wanted. Amazingly, I let him. Whatever he wanted to do to me, I was his for the night. For once, I was just along for the ride rather than trying to control the situation. I wrapped my arms around his neck and hung on.

He trailed his mouth down my throat, alternating between openmouthed kisses and soft bites. Every move served to ratchet the tension inside me higher until I couldn't take any more. I ground my hips against his, desperate, needy and willing to do anything it took for him to let me come.

Seeming to sense my need, he broke the kiss and moved out of reach.

I groaned. Reached for him, even though I knew it was a lost cause. "Why are you teasing me?"

The intensity in his gaze sent a shudder through my pussy. He glanced down to where my lower half lay exposed, my skirt still bunched at the waist. A half smile lifted one corner of his mouth. "All those times you were watching me, *you* were teasing me."

"So this is payback?"

He laughed as he started unbuttoning my shirt. "No, sweetheart. Not revenge of any kind. This is all for your pleasure."

"I never really was into torture."

He laughed again, pushing my shirt down my arms until the material gathered at my elbows, keeping me from raising my arms. "You didn't seem to mind when I spanked you."

The reminder got me hot all over again. I closed my eyes and let my head drop back against the door, licking my lips. Minded? I'd fucking loved it, though I'd never imagined having a man spank me would turn me on.

I'd never known, until he moved into the neighborhood, that voyeurism did it for me, either. Surprising what a woman could learn about herself when she opened her mind to the possibilities.

His fingers traced my bra straps, sliding to the lacy edges of the cups. Instead of undoing the front clasp, he pulled the cups down until my breasts popped free.

"You have the most amazing tits," he whispered. "I knew they would be gorgeous."

With that, he leaned in and sucked one of my nipples into his mouth. My back bowed, a moan caught in my throat.

"Damn. I love how sensitive you are."

His teeth clamped down on my nipple, not hard, but enough for me to feel the pressure of his bite. He rolled the sensitive peak around, making me squirm. By the time he moved on to the other nipple, I couldn't hold still. It was all too much, too many sensations at once, and he was barely touching me.

I wasn't a prude. I loved sex, but I'd never experienced it like this. So raw, so urgent. Maybe it was wrong to want him so much, but I couldn't help it. He tugged on my nipple and I moaned. With one last swirl of his tongue over my flesh, he stood, but didn't back away this time. Instead, he wrapped one of my legs around his hip, grinding against me. Even through the fabric of his jeans, I could feel how hard his cock was. How hot.

It felt decadent to have him touching me, teasing me while I still wore my work clothes. My heels put me closer to his height, so that every grind sent a shock through me. I undulated, sucking in every drop of pleasure.

His chest pressed against mine, his breath sawing in and out of his lungs. It wasn't long before he stopped moving, leaning in to brush his lips across my throat. "I can't wait much longer."

I laughed. He hadn't really been waiting for permission, had he? All this time, he'd taken without asking, and I hadn't been complaining. "Who's asking you to?"

His laugh rumbled against my neck before he let me go and stepped away.

I'd wanted to undress him slowly, to touch and taste him like he'd done with me, but there wasn't time. Not now. Neither of us could wait. With frenzied movements, he stripped me out of my clothes, leaving me standing there in nothing but heels and thigh-high stockings. He didn't even bother with his own clothes, just unzipped his pants to free his cock. Once he sheathed himself in a condom he'd pulled from his pocket, he was back on me, wrapping both my legs around his hips. A fast kiss and then he pushed inside me.

The width of his erection stretched me full, and the position made each of his hard thrusts feel like they might tear me apart. I grabbed his shoulders, bracing myself as he pounded into me. His gaze never left mine, and the intensity I found there made me squirm. Tension hung thick between us, like an electric entity, snapping and popping, driving both of us higher.

My pussy muscles trembled around him as my body sped toward release. My fingernails dug into his shoulders, and the groan told me he felt the pain even through the soft fabric of his shirt. His teeth clamped down on the spot where my neck met my shoulder, biting hard enough for me to feel the pinch. I was so close, so ready. A few more thrusts and I'd find my release.

Frantic, I ground my hips against his, meeting each thrust. His breathing had long since gone jagged, his eyes closed and his forehead sweaty with the strain. He bent his knees a little, changing the angle of his thrusts, and I was done for. Stars exploded behind my eyes, every muscle in my body shaking as pleasure like I'd never experienced shot through me, from my pussy straight out to my limbs. The orgasm seemed to go on forever, wringing every last drop of sensation from me until I felt liquid. Floating. I went lax, unable to do anything but cling to him.

Not long after, he followed me into release, a shout on his lips. He pulled out and set my feet on the ground. Whispering an unintelligible sound, he pressed his palms to the door on either side of my head. "I think it's going to be a little while before I can walk."

I had to laugh. "Me, too."

"Think we could just camp out here for the night, or at least until we recover?"

As appealing to my tired body as the thought was, I shook my head. "I think I need to lie down. Why don't we take this upstairs to my bedroom instead."

A little after dawn, I finally stirred, opening my eyes to find my neighbor staring at me. His lids drooped a little, but he smiled when he saw me looking.

I cupped his cheek in my hand. "You do look familiar to me. Where do I know you from?"

"High school."

As soon as the words left his mouth, I knew. I'd seen him before. So many times, though he'd changed. He wasn't the scrawny outcast I remembered, but his features were the same. His eyes, identical to the ones I remembered trying to avoid so long ago. I should have noticed. "Shawn Richardson."

A blush crept up his cheeks and he shrugged a little. "Yeah. Upset?"

He'd known who I was the whole time, and he hadn't bothered to tell me. I tried to muster up the proper irritation, but after the pleasure he'd just given me, I couldn't. I'd wanted sex with a stranger, and in reality, I'd come pretty damn close. I'd never really gotten to know him back in school. Hadn't even given him or his slacker buddies a second glance.

There had been a good reason for that, or at least I'd convinced myself there'd been. Looking into that intense gaze had set my nerves on edge. Not anymore.

I wanted to know him now. Everything about him. I'd start by learning how his skin tasted, and what sounds he made when I wrapped my lips around his cock.

"You look different than you did back then. Bulkier."

He laughed. "Yeah, outside work will do that to a guy. I'm a landscaper. I...ah, have to work in a few hours. I really should go home and shower."

He stood, gathering the clothes he'd stripped before we'd climbed into bed and pulling on his jeans. "Will you be around later?"

I rolled onto my back and stretched my arms over my head. "That depends. What do you have in mind?"

"I dunno. I'll think of something. I can be very creative, you know."

I chuckled at the exaggerated way he waggled his brows while he zipped his jeans. "I do know."

"Sweetheart, you don't even know the half of it. I'll meet you back here around seven?"

I couldn't help myself. I got hot all over again. I licked my lips. Did he really expect me to turn him down? No way was I that stupid. "Sounds like a plan."

Chance of a Lifetime

By Portia Da Costa

Award-winning author **Portia Da Costa**'s first published story appeared in 1991. Since then, she's gone on to write well over a hundred stories for magazines and anthologies, and has penned almost thirty novels across a variety of genres. She's best known for her sizzling-hot romances, including short erotic fiction for Mills & Boon. Portia lives in a typically Yorkshire town with her husband and the three beautiful cats they both adore. Visit her at www.Portia DaCosta.com.

Rain. Perpetual rain. I'm certainly not going to miss the British weather. I'll miss a lot of other things, but not this, not this.

I stare out of the window, down the gravel drive and out across the park of Blaystock Manor. I'm here filling in with some temp work, while I wait to take up my dream job, my chance of a lifetime working in the Caribbean at a luxury resort as a junior manager. This gig is just cleaning and helping with renovations, donkey work really, but it's all extra money to pay for my new tropical wardrobe.

Actually, it's a free day today. The marquis is pretty good about that. We get plenty of time off, plenty of breaks and other perks, and despite the fact he's strapped for cash and putting everything into this project, we're pretty well paid for our labors. Everyone else has gone off in a minibus to visit a local monastery where they brew apple brandy and make luxury biscuits and stuff, but me, I've got my own diversions here.

I'm alone in the house. Even the marquis drove off a

short while ago in his decrepit gray Jag. And I'm free to indulge my wicked secret vice.

I discovered this little sitting room a couple days ago, when I was a bit lost and searching for the Blue Salon, where I was supposed to be polishing the floor. I stumbled in here and found a room that was homely and pretty lived in, and sort of cozy. And, being irredeemably nosy, when I saw an old VCR and a bunch of tapes, I had to investigate.

Boy oh boy oh boy! What a shock I got.

And now, while the house is empty, I slip another tape into the machine and settle down in a battered old leather armchair to watch it.

It's a home movie. Filmed, I think, in this very room. And it stars my latest crush, the marquis himself, and a woman who must have been his girlfriend at the time. Obviously it was taped many years ago, because His Lordship had short hair then, and now it's long, down to his shoulders.

Here he is, possibly sitting in this very chair. His knees are set wide apart and his girlfriend is facedown across them.

He's spanking her.

He's really laying it on with his long, powerful hand, and she's squirming and patently loving it!

And I'm loving it too, and I don't really know why. Okay, I knew people played spanking games for sexual kicks, and I'd sort of hinted to various boyfriends that

I'd like to try it. But it's never happened and I've never really worried about that.

But now. Now I've seen it. I bloody well want it!

I'm so turned on now I can barely see straight. And I certainly can't stay still in my chair. I'm sweating and my skin feels like it's already been spanked, all over. And between my legs, I'm drenched, my panties sopping with intense, almost inexplicable arousal. My sex is aching, tight and hungry, as if I want to be fucked right now, but at the same time have my bottom thrashed, just like the woman in the video.

The marquis really seems to be enjoying her pleasure, even though his cool, handsome face is exquisitely impassive. It's an old, well-worn tape, but I can still see the mask of stern, beautiful composure that he affects…and the wicked dark twinkle in his eyes.

It's no good, I've got to play with myself. I can't help it and I can't bear it if I don't. My sex is so heavy and so tense, I've just got to do it.

As the woman on the screen writhes and wriggles and shrieks as His Lordship's hand comes down, I unzip my jeans and shuffle them down to my knees, dragging my soggy panties with them. There's something wickedly lewd about sitting here with my clothes at half-mast like this, and the forbidden exposure only excites me more and makes my need to touch my body ever more urgent.

"Oh God…" I murmur vaguely as I slip my fingers

between my legs and find my clit. It's swollen and ready for my touch like a throbbing button. I flick it lightly and my vagina flutters dangerously. On the screen, the spanked girl tries to touch her own sex, wriggling her hand beneath her belly as she squirms and cries, but the marquis pauses mid-spank and gently remonstrates with her.

"Come, come, Sylvia, you know you mustn't do that. No pleasure until you've been a good girl and taken your punishment."

His voice is soft, even, but shot through with sweet steel and authority. It pushes me closer to coming just as powerfully as the spanking show does. I suddenly wish I could get to know him better, and make this all real.

"Oh, my lord…" I whisper this time, closing my eyes and turning on an inner video. This time it's me across those strong thighs. Me who's writhing and moaning, with my bottom flaming.

Oh, the picture is so clear. And it's the marquis of today who's doing the business, not the one in the video.

He's wearing his usual outfit of black jeans and black shirt, and his beautiful hair is loose on his shoulders like sheets of silk. There's a sly, slight smile on his pale, chiseled face, and his long, cultured hand comes down with metronomic regularity.

I'm rubbing myself hard now, beating at my clit, but not stroking the very apex of it. I daren't; I'm so excited and I don't want to come yet. In my fantasy, he allows me to touch myself while he's smacking me.

I writhe and wriggle, both fighting the pleasure and savoring its gathering at the same time. I throw my thighs wide, rubbing my bottom against the seat of the creaky old armchair. The sensation of the smooth surface against my skin is even more pervy. I press down harder, squashing my anus against the leather. I imagine him spanking me there, and even though I've no idea what it would really feel like, I groan, wanting it more and more and more.

"Oh my lord...do it...do it..." I burble, eyes tightly closed and half out of my mind with desire and longing.

"Actually, my dear, I think you're 'doing it' quite well enough on your own. Do continue."

What?

It's like I'm falling, dropping through reality into a parallel universe. I know what's happened but somehow I can't stop rubbing myself.

My eyes fly open though, and here he is.

The marquis.

Somehow he's walked into the room without me realizing it, moving softly on the rubber soles of his black running shoes.

In a few split seconds, I take in his glorious appearance.

So tall, so male, so mysterious. Long dark hair, pale

smiling face, long fit body. Dressed in his customary black shirt and jeans, his elegant hands flexing as if preparing to copy the actions of his image on the screen.

I snatch my hand from my crotch and make as if to struggle back into my jeans. My face is scarlet, puce, flaming…. I'm almost peeing myself.

"No, please…continue."

His voice is low and quiet, almost humming with amusement and intense interest. It's impossible to disobey him. Despite the fact that I think the aristocracy is an outdated nonsense, he's nobility to his fingertips and I'm just a pleb, bound to obey.

Unable to tear my eyes away from him, I watch as he settles his long frame down into the other chair, across from mine. He gives me a little nod, making his black hair sway, and then turns his attention to the images on the screen.

So do I, but with reluctance.

But I do as he wishes and begin to stroke my clit again.

Oh God, the woman on the screen is really protesting now. Oh God, in my mind, that woman is me, and I'm laid across the marquis's magnificent thighs with my bottom all pink and sizzling and my crotch wetting his jeans with seeping arousal.

I imagine the blows I've never experienced, and just the dream of them makes my clit flutter wildly and my vagina clench and pulse. I seem to see the carpet as I writhe and wiggle and moan, and at the same time his beautiful face, rather grave, but secretly smiling.

As his eyes twinkle, in my imagination, I come.

It's a hard, wrenching orgasm. Shocking and intense. I've never come like that before in my life. It goes on and on, so extreme it's almost pain, and afterward I feel tears fill my eyes.

Talk about *le petit mort* and post-coital *tristesse*. I've got *tristesse* by the bucketful, but without any coitus.

My face as crimson as the buttocks of the spanked woman in the video, I drag my panties and jeans back into place and lie gasping in the chair. I scrabble for a tissue. I'm going to cry properly now, not just a few teardrops, and I know I should just run from the room, but somehow I just can't seem to move.

Something soft and folded is put gently into my hand, and as I steal a glance at it, I discover it's the marquis's immaculately laundered handkerchief. Still gulping and sniffing, I rub my face with it, breathing in the faint, mouthwatering fragrance of his cologne.

Shit, I fancy this man something rotten, and I've been fantasizing about him fancying me back, and falling for me, and now this has happened. I'm so embarrassed, I wish I could burrow into the leather upholstery and disappear out of sight.

A strong arm settles around my shoulders, and the great chair creaks as he sits down on the arm beside me.

"Hey, there's no harm done," the marquis says softly.

272   PORTIA DA COSTA

"Now we both know each other's dirty little secrets."
He squeezes my shoulders. "I get off spanking girls'
bottoms and having them wriggling on my lap. And you
get off watching videos of it and playing with yourself."
He pauses, and I sense him smiling that slow, wicked
smile again. "And quite beautifully, I must admit. Quite
exquisitely...."

I beg your pardon?

Hell, I must have looked awful. Crude. Ungainly.
Like a complete slapper.

I try to wriggle free, but he holds me. He even puts
up a hand to gently stroke my hair. I still can't look at
him, even though part of me really wants to.

"I'm so embarrassed. I'm so sorry. I had no business
coming in here and prying into your private things."

One long finger strokes down the side of my face,
slips under my chin and gently lifts it. Nervously, I open
my eyes and look into his. They're large and dark and
brown and merry, and I feel as if I'm drowning, but suddenly that's a good thing.

All the embarrassment and mortification disappears,
just as if it were the rain puddles outside evaporating in
the sun. Indeed, beyond the window, the sky outside is
brightening.

Suddenly I see mischief and sex and a sense of
adventure in those fabulous eyes, and I feel turned on
again, and somehow scared, but not in a way that has
anything to do with an awkward situation with my

employer. It's a new feeling, and it's erotic, but so much more.

"Indeed you didn't. That was rather naughty of you." His face is perfectly impassive, almost stern, but those eyes, oh those eyes—they're mad with dangerous fun. "Do you think we should do something about that?"

I feel as if I'm about to cross a line. Jump off a cliff. Ford some peculiar kind of Rubicon. This is the chance of a lifetime, and I'm a perfect novice in the world portrayed in his video, but I understand him completely without any further hint or education.

"Um…yes, my lord."

Should I stand? Then kneel? Or curtsy or something? He's still sitting on the arm of the chair, a huge masculine presence because he's tall and broad-shouldered. Everything a man and a master should be.

I'm just about to stand, and I feel him just about to reach for me, when suddenly and shockingly his mobile rings, and he lets out a lurid curse.

"Ack, I must take this. Money stuff," he growls, and nods to me to mute the television as he flips open his phone.

I make as if to leave, but he catches me by the arm and makes me stand in front of him. With almost serpentine grace, he slides into the armchair and pulls me across his lap. Then, as he has a terse conversation that I don't think he's enjoying much, he explores the shape of my bottom through my jeans.

He doesn't slap or smack or hit. He just cruises his fingertips over the denim-clad surface, assessing my contours and the resilience of my flesh.

Slowly, slowly, as he gets slightly cross with someone on the other end of the line, he examines my cheeks, my thighs and then, without warning, squeezes my crotch. I let out a little yelp, and that's when he *does* hit!

It's just the softest warning tap…but it's electrifying. I almost come on the spot and I have to bite down on my lip to stifle my groans.

I start to wriggle and he cups my sex harder, from behind, pressing with his fingers. Pleasure flares again as my jeans seam rubs my aching clit.

I'm biting the upholstery, squirming and kicking my legs and grabbing at his legs and his muscular thighs through his jeans. He rides my unruliness, his hand firm between my legs as he owns my sex like the lord and master he truly is.

Eventually his call is over, and I'm a wrung-out rag. He flings aside his phone and turns me over, then kisses me.

I expect domineering hunger and passion, but it's soft, light and sweet, almost a zephyr.

He wants me. He's hard, I can feel it beneath my bottom. But as if his own erection means nothing to him, he sets me on my feet then stands up beside me.

"Much as it pains me to leave so much undone and unsaid at this moment, Rose, I have to go." His eyes are dark. Is it lust? Regret? Something more complex? "I need to go to London, and I'm going to have to get a bloody taxi because I've just left my car at the garage." He pauses, then leans down to kiss me on the lips again, a little harder this time. "But when I get back, we'll reconvene. If that's agreeable?" He tilts his head to one side as he looks down on me, and his exquisite hair slides sideways like silk.

I nod and mutter something incomprehensible that doesn't make sense even to me, and then he pats me on the bottom again and strides away across the room.

At the door, he gives me a wink, his dark eyes twinkling with mischief.

"Enjoy the rest of the video," he says, then suddenly he's gone.

* * *

But I don't watch it. After he's gone, I just shoot off to my room, tucked up in the eyrie of the old servants' quarters, feeling strange and weird and disoriented, as if I've been in a really vivid dream, and I've just woken up. Then I sort of snivel a bit, not sure of my emotions.

The marquis is our boss, and up until now, he's been a sort of admire/adore from afar type man. I'm not into all this hero worship or celebs and aristos for the sake of it, but he's got genuine charisma and blue-blood charm. He's also got some weird history. Apparently in the army at some time, then a dropout, and now getting his act together and sorting out the manor on behalf of his father, the duke. The whole family is strapped for cash, but Blaystock Manor is just the right size for a deluxe, high-end hotel or conference center, and the marquis has thrown just about every penny he possesses, and some he doesn't, into restoring it and bringing it up to standard.

And somewhere along the line in this convoluted story of his, he was married, but she died and now he's alone. No doubt his dad is pressuring him for progeny, to continue the family line, but so far it seems he's resisted, and there's no marchioness.

Some very silly thoughts drift into my mind as I get ready for bed and I push them smartly back out again. I've got my dream job waiting for me in the Caribbean. I won't be here all that long.

Although I would love to see what the manor looks like when it's finished.

I suppose all this pondering is to avoid thinking about the fact that the marquis has seen me masturbate, and almost, but not quite, spanked me.

Do I really want to be spanked, though?

In the video, he was doing it for real, and that woman—whoever she was, surely not his wife—was squealing and crying out. So obviously it hurt like hell. Lying in bed later, I tug down my pajama bottom and give myself a slap on the thigh. It's a pretty halfhearted effort but it makes me squawk and rub the place to take the sting away.

Immediately though, I'm drifting into fantasy.

In my mind I'm back in the little sitting room, and this time the phone stays silent. And the marquis bares my bottom and starts to caress, caress, caress it, then lands a blow.

I slap myself again, trying to recreate the feeling. It bloody hurts, but I do it again, moaning, "My lord…"

I slap and slap and moan and moan, and suddenly I just have to play with my clitoris. I'm so turned on imagining him spanking me that my wet sex aches.

Within a few seconds I come, softly crying his name, seeing his face.

* * *

The next day, I worry. What's going to happen? Is anything going to happen? Or has the marquis quite sensibly decided to dismiss our stolen interlude as an aberration. Something of no consequence. It must be bred in his blue English blood to dally with underlings for his pleasure without a second thought.

I certainly don't see him for the next couple of days, and the cleaning, dusting and polishing goes on without incident. I work cheerfully with the rest of the team, as if nothing has happened.

But then, after a long day, when the others are all off

to the pub, I slip back to my room to change, and find a little note upon my mat.

I'm sorry we were so rudely interrupted, it says in a fine, almost copperplate handwriting. *Would you care to join me in the small sitting room, at seven o'clock this evening? I feel that there's much we could explore there in the furtherance of your education and the pursuit of mutual pleasure.*

It's finished off with a single word.

Christian.

Christian? Who's "Christian"?

Then it dawns on me. Duh! The marquis is just like a normal person in that at least.

He has a first name.

I wonder if he'll want me to call him "Christian"? Somehow it doesn't seem right, or respectful. Especially in view of what we're almost certain to be doing. It'll definitely be "My lord" or "Your lordship," or just sobs and moans of pain and pleasure in equal amounts.

* * *

At seven o'clock, I'm staring at the door to the little sitting room. It was half in my mind not to turn up, to try and pretend that what happened beyond that slab of oak never happened. But doing that would be to miss…well…miss the chance of a lifetime. I might never meet a man again who's into the things that the marquis is, and I might go through life having perfectly ordinary, perfectly satisfactory sex, but still wondering what it would have been like to try the extraordinary kind with spanking and strange mind games.

I knock as firmly as I can on the door, and immediately that deep, clear voice calls out, "Enter!" from within. Crikey, he already sounds like a stern schoolmaster summoning his tardy pupil.

I tremble.

But there's nothing fearsome or intimidating when I step into the room and close the door behind me. It's cozy and welcoming, with a nice little fire burning in the grate to ward off the unseasonal damp chill. The thick curtains are drawn, and soft lamps emit a friendly golden glow that flatters the fine old furniture and makes it gleam.

It flatters the marquis too, not that he needs it. He looks stunning.

He's all in black again, as ever. Tight black jeans embrace his long legs, and the splendid lean musculature of his thighs and his backside. As he rises to his feet from the depths of one of the armchairs, I imagine, for a fleeting second, spanking him!

Blood fills my cheeks in a raging blush, and I falter and hang back. A huge waft of guilt rushes through me at even thinking that. I open my mouth, but I can't speak, and he smiles at me.

"Come on in, Rose. Would you like a drink?" I notice

that he has a glass with something clear and icy set on a little table beside his chair. Vodka? Water? Gin? Who knows....

"Um...er...yes." I flick my glance to the sideboard and a few bottles, but I can't seem to compute what's there so I just say, "Whatever you're having...please."

"Good choice...and do sit down." He gestures like a Renaissance courtier toward a free chair by the fire, and watches me as I make my way there; I'm terrified I'll trip or something, despite the fact my heels aren't high or spindly.

I take my seat, and watch him mix my drink, swiftly combining clear spirit, ice, mixer and a sliver of lemon. He prepares the concoction perfectly, despite the fact that he's studying me intently almost all the time.

I've dressed carefully.

Jeans are awkward to wriggle out of, especially if you've got a curvy bottom like mine, so I've chosen a soft, full summer skirt that almost sweeps the floor. A miniskirt would be too obvious, not ladylike, and as I'm here with an aristocrat, I'm compelled to make an effort to be worthy of him.

On my top half I've got a little buttoned camisole, pink to match the skirt, and a light cotton cardigan over that, to keep out the chills. My shoes are low-heeled and quite pretty, and underneath I'm wearing my best and sexiest underwear.

I aim to please....

The marquis comes across and hands me my drink, then retreats to his own chair. There's a moment of silence, tense for me, but apparently totally relaxed for him, and I snatch the opportunity to feast my eyes on his gorgeousness.

He sits so elegantly, even though he's totally at ease. Long legs out in front of him, booted feet crossed.

Boots? Hell, yes! They do something visceral inside me. They make me shudder and my sex clench and seem to twist and flutter with their connotations of masterfulness. They're old and soft and well polished and not all that tall, but all the same, I almost feel faint just looking at them.

And I get mostly the same feeling from the rest of him.

He's got the most exquisite black silk shirt on, full of sleeve and so fluid it seems to float on his body. The collar's fastened up for the moment, but I have the most intense urge to crawl on my hands and knees across the room and rip it open so I can kiss his throat and his chest and suck his nipples.

And not just his nipples.

His thick black hair is shiny with a fresh-washed satin sheen and his fine-boned face has the delicious gleam of a recent shave.

Bless him, he's made as much of an effort for me as I have for him. Another reason to worship and adore him.

I take a mouthful of my drink. It is gin, as I mostly

suspected, and it's a strong one with very little tonic. The balsamic kick of the uncompromising spirit almost makes me cough, but I'm glad of its heat as the first hit settles in my stomach.

"So...here we are," the marquis says pleasantly, eyeing me over the rim of his own glass. As he takes a long swallow, his throat undulates, pale and sensuous.

"Yes...er...here we are," is all I can manage in reply. The gathering tension in my gut renders me all but speechless.

"Have you been thinking about what happened here the other day?"

I nod, dumbstruck now with intense lust. I don't know whether I want him to spank me or fuck me...probably both. But I want whatever's on offer as soon as I can get it.

"So how do you feel about being spanked a little? Does that interest you?" His lips are sculpted but somehow also soft and sensual, and when they curve into a little smile, the way they are doing now, they make me want to wriggle and touch my sex to soothe its aching. So much for wearing my best knickers. They must already be saturated with juice, I'm so turned on.

"I think we could enjoy ourselves together, you and I," he continues. "I'm not offering eternal love and devotion, but we can share a little pleasure and perhaps expand your horizons in a way that doesn't involve flying thousands of miles."

Those crazy notions caper around my mind again, taunting me with the prospect of what he *isn't* offering rather than what he is.

"Rose?" he queries, swirling his glass in the face of my continued, dumbstruck silence.

I want it. Oh, how I want it. And even just the mutual pleasure if I can't have the other thing. But I'm scared. I feel as if I'm stuck between reality and some kind of weird dream. I still can't speak, but I take another swig of my gin.

The marquis frowns. It's not a cross frown, just a sad little frown, sort of regretful. "I'm sorry. I've come on too strong, haven't I?" He tips his head to one side, his dark hair sliding across his shoulders as he lets out a sigh. "Look, don't worry about it. Don't think any more about it. Just finish your gin and we'll say no more about it. It was wrong of me to ask."

I don't know whether I'm relieved or disappointed. I felt so close to him for a moment, and God, I wanted it all so much. My heart thudding, I swig down my gin and get to my feet on wobbly legs.

The marquis rises immediately, perfect manners second nature to him. He comes forward as if to escort me to the door, and does so as I make my way toward it, my heart sinking at my own craven lack of daring.

With one hand on the door handle, he touches my face. The contact is so gentle yet so meaningful, I feel quite faint.

"Don't worry, Rose, there'll be no hard feelings. It's just a might have been." He sounds so kind, so ineffably kind that it's almost like a knife in my heart. "I may have lost all my money and be a poor excuse for an aristocrat, but I do try to behave like a gentleman. We'll speak no more of this and just go back to a friendly working relationship."

"No!"

He stares at me. The frown is a puzzled one now.

"No…I mean…yes, I am interested. Definitely. It's just something that's completely out of my experience…. Yes," I repeat, aware that I'm babbling. "I'm definitely interested."

His stern, elegant face lights up as if the sun's just come out. He looks happy, genuinely happy, in a way that seems quite astonishing in a man so obviously worldly and experienced.

"Splendid!" He sets down his glass, and leans forward. "I'm so glad."

Without any warning, he leans down and dusts my lips with a tiny, fleeting kiss.

"For luck. To seal our agreement." A wry, strange smile flits across his face. It's almost as if he's surprised somehow, but not by me. "Come then."

He takes my hand and leads me back toward the fireside.

When he reaches his armchair, he sits down in it, all elegant, languid grace, and draws me between his outstretched thighs. I suddenly feel very small. Like a naughty little girl, and as that registers, I realize it's exactly what he wants me to feel. Suddenly I'm staring at my toes, too embarrassed to look at him, even though he's the most beautiful thing I've ever seen.

"Ah, now then, my Rose…" He reaches out, lifts my chin with the tip of his finger and makes me look at him. His brown eyes are electric, gleaming and wickedly dark. Just for a second his tongue tip flashes out and licks the center of his lower lip, and it's as if in that instant someone's thrown a switch and changed everything in the room.

We're playing.

"So, do you normally go around prying into people's private belongings? Or is it just me that you spy on?"

I don't know how to answer. I don't even know if I should answer. But he prompts me.

"Well, Rose?"

"Um…no, not normally, but I was interested. I wanted something to watch."

"And you didn't think to ask first?"

"No, my lord…sorry, my lord…."

His title slips perfectly off my tongue, so sweet and so dangerous in this context.

"I think I should be punished," I add rashly, suddenly wanting to move on and get to the heart of the game.

"Really?" His voice is arch, slightly mocking, but I can still hear the joy in it. "In that case, my dear, bold

Rose, I think we should oblige you, shouldn't we?"
He's still holding my hand, and unexpectedly he brings
it momentarily to his lips before releasing it.

For several long moments, he just watches me,
peruses me, looks me up and down as if he's planning
something demonic, and then he says simply,
"Undress."

Oh God, I wasn't expecting this. I thought it might
come afterward—after, I suppose, my first spanking.
I'd been picturing myself across his knee, maybe with
my skirt up and my knickers down...but not totally
naked and exposed.

When he says, "Did you hear me, Rose?" in a soft
tone of remonstration, I realize I'm just standing here
dithering.

I peel off my cardigan, and to my surprise he takes it
from me and places it over the arm of the chair. Nothing
too frightening there. But next, it's my little buttoned
top, and I fumble with the fastenings as if I have five
thumbs.

The marquis sighs softly, gently puts my hands down
at my sides and then undoes the top himself, divest-
ing me of it with precise efficiency as if he undresses
clumsy women all the time. Maybe he does. Well, not
necessarily clumsy ones...but who knows whom he
sees when he's not here at the manor overseeing the
renovation.

Now, on top, I'm left just in my bra, and the marquis

studies it, doing that little head tilt thing of his again, as if he's grading me on the quality of my underwear. I swallow hard, wondering how my choice stands up. It's a delicate white lace number, my best…I hope it passes muster. I hope my breasts do as well, beneath. They're not big, but they're perky, and right now my nipples are as pink and hard as cherry stones. Something the marquis takes note of by reaching out to squeeze one. I moan like a whore as he twists it delicately through the lace.

Lust and blood and hormones career wildly through my body. It's as if I've got too much energy to fit inside my skin. I close my eyes tightly, ashamed of my own wantonness as my hips begin to weave in time with the delicate tweaking. But the marquis says, "No," and with his free hand he cups my chin. "Look at me, Rose. Give me your feelings. Don't deny me them."

I open my eyes, aware that they're swimming, but it's not from the pain. It's that overflow again, that wild abundance of emotion and sensation; it's welling over in the form of sudden tears.

The marquis's eyes are amazing—deep as the ocean, unfathomable and yet on fire. He reaches for my other nipple and as he plays with that, I wriggle anew as if my pelvis had a wicked life of its own.

"You're willful, sweet Rose," he purrs, tugging, tugging, first one nipple then the other. This simple punishment is far more testing than any amount of smacking or spanking, I sense, and suddenly I'm proud to be put to such a test.

The marquis's eyes glitter as if he's read my sudden thought, and he permits me the beneficence of a slight smile. Then he draws a deep breath and leans back in the chair, abandoning my breasts.

I feel bereft until he tells me, "Continue."

Slipping off my bra, he gives my breasts and my rosy, swollen nipples a swift once-over, as if without covering they don't interest him quite as much. I hesitate and he nods to indicate I should take off my skirt.

First I slip my feet out of my shoes and kick them away, then I unfasten the button and zipper of my skirt. For a moment, I clutch at it, suddenly nervous despite everything. Then I let it drop, and kick it away, standing as proudly as I can in just a very tiny G-string.

I keep my own smile inside, but elation geysers up inside me as the marquis can't disguise his grin.

"Oh, how splendid…how splendid…." he murmurs, and that naughty pink tongue of his slips out again, touching the center of his lush lower lip. Reaching out, he runs the backs of his fingers over the little triangle of lace, and over the fluffy pubic hair that peeks out on either side. Fleetingly, I wish I'd had a chance to visit a salon and get a Brazilian, then I change my mind as his fingertips coil in my floss and gently tug it. He seems to like me *au naturel*, and whatever the marquis likes, I like too.

He tweaks a little harder and the tension transfers directly to my clitoris. I'm so excited I almost come; I'm so close to the edge. As it is, I let out a groan, I just can't help myself.

The marquis pulls again, making a tiny pain, a little hurt, prick and niggle at the roots of the little curl he's playing with. But at the same time, he reaches up with his free hand and places his fingers across my lips.

"Now, now, Rose, you must learn to control yourself," he reprimands quietly but without rancor. "A good submissive is quiet and still, bearing discomfort— he twists a little more tightly "—with perfect grace and fortitude. You have a long way to go yet, my dear, but I hope that you'll learn."

The tears trickle down my face. This isn't quite what I expected, and somehow I feel reduced to some kind of wayward little girl for a moment. But this excites me, and inside, deeper than my confusion, is a brighter glow. It's a game, and my body loves it even though my mind is still learning.

It isn't only my tears that are trickling.

As if he too has detected my welling arousal, the marquis's nostrils flare eloquently. His deep chest lifts as if he's breathing in my foxy, fruity smell. A slow smile curves his lips and I half expect him to lick them again, savoring my aroma.

A moment later, I'm gasping, fighting for breath,

desperate to obey his wishes, and at the same time on the point of shouting out and jerking my hips.

In a sly, deft, sleight-of-hand motion, the marquis has abandoned my pubic curls and slid his fingertips into my cleft beneath the lacy triangle of my underwear. One finger zeroes in like a guided missile and pushes right inside me. He presses in deep and lifts his hand, and I rise on my toes, speared and fluttering.

When he rocks the digit inside me, I grab his shoulders, almost fainting as I come. My resolution crumbles when he squashes his thumb down flat onto my clit and I groan like an animal, lost in pleasure.

Pulsing, sweating, burbling nonsense, I lose all strength as my knees turn to jelly. The marquis's free arm snakes around my waist to hold me up, while between my legs, he both supports and manipulates me, his finger lodged inside me while his thumb presses and releases, presses and releases, presses and releases…tormenting me by lifting me to orgasm again and again.

I hold on. My body clamps down on him again and again. Time passes.

Eventually, the tumult ebbs and I flush with shame and a strange, tangled happiness as I regain the ability to stand up straight.

The marquis's strong, straight digit is still inside me.

And it stays there, his hand cupping my mound, as he speaks to me.

"You have so much to learn, sweet Rose, so much to learn." He looks into my face, his beautiful brown eyes gleaming with sex, yet somehow almost regretful. "And we have so little time, you and I, don't we? Just a week or two."

What the hell is he talking about? I could stand here forever, possessed by him, my sex his plaything.

And then I remember that all this is temporary. There's my dream job of a lifetime waiting for me in the Caribbean in a few weeks and I'll be thousands of miles away from the marquis and his hand, his eyes, his body.

The shock must show on my face because he smiles kindly. "Don't worry, my dear. All the more reason to make the most of things while we can." His finger crooks inside me and finds a sweet spot, forcing me to grunt aloud, flex my knees and bear down. "Usually, I start with a little pain before the pleasure. But in your case, I couldn't resist handling your delightful pussy and making you come."

He flexes his finger a little more.

I cry out, "Oh God!" and come again.

It's quick. It's hard. It satisfies, yet primes me for more. But instead of either working me to more orgasms, or just pushing me down on the rug, unzipping and thrusting into me, the marquis withdraws his finger, suddenly and shockingly, and offers it to me.

My head whirling, I wonder what he means, but then it dawns on me that he wants me to clean it off.

My face flaming, I suck my own musk from his warm skin as more flows between my legs to quickly replace it.

I feel bereft when he withdraws the digit and then dries it methodically with his perfectly laundered handkerchief.

"And now to business," he says briskly, as if implying that I've deliberately kept him from it with my orgasms. "I think I'd like to bind you. Are you okay with that?"

Speechless, I nod like an idiot as he reaches down the side of his chair and pulls out a length of soft, silky cord. I feel it slide over my hip and flank as he turns me to face away from him, and then, bringing my hands behind me, he fastens them at the wrist.

I think that this is it, but suddenly he produces another length of cord and, pulling my arms back tighter, he winds it around my elbows, drawing them together.

Twice bound like this, I start to sweat even harder. While not really painful, the position is uncomfortable, and what's more, it forces my breasts to rise and become more prominent, vulnerable and presented.

When he spins me around again, I feel almost faint as he leans forward and slowly licks and sucks each of my nipples. His silky hair swings and slides against the skin of my midriff and the scent of an expensive man's shampoo fills my nostrils.

As he torments me with his tongue, I feel his fingers at my thong. He plucks at the lace and elastic and tugs the thing up tight into the division of my sex lips. When the sodden cloth is pressing hard on my clit, he reaches around behind me, working beneath my shackled wrists, and makes a little knot somehow at the small of my back, to keep it taut.

He licks at me a moment or two more, then leans back, almost indolent in his great chair as he cocks his head to one side and regards his handiwork.

I feel like a firecracker in a bottle, an explosion of sexual energy and need contained by my bonds. I'm desperate to come again, but I'm reaching and yearning for more than just simple gratification. The marquis smiles as if he understands me completely.

"And now we really begin," he says softly, taking me by the waist and pushing me from between his knees. Then, settling himself more comfortably in the chair, and setting his booted feet more squarely on the floor, he nods to me, his eyes dancing with lights and a subtle smile on his handsome face.

I know what he's indicating. That I should assume the position.

It's difficult to settle elegantly across his lap with my hands tied, but I do the best I can, not wanting to disgrace myself. Even so, he has to more or less grapple me into place, setting me at precisely the right angle and elevation and disposing my limbs and torso in the optimum position to present my bottom to his hand.

I wait for the first spank. The first real one…the tap the other day was nothing, I suspect.

But it doesn't come yet.

"Mmmm…"

It's a low, contemplative sound, and as he utters it, the marquis gently cups my bottom cheek, testing its resilience. The feeling is entirely different this time; his fingers on my bare skin feel like traveling points of electricity, sparking me and goading me as they rove. He grips me harder and I have this sense of some kind of computer in his brain calculating, calculating. How hard to hit. How high to lift his hand for the downstroke. How many slaps is optimum.

"Ready?" he asks, to my surprise. I'd expected him to just take what he wanted. He's in charge, after all.

And yet, is he? I bet if I said "no," even now, he'd immediately desist and help me restore my clothing to decency and propriety. But no way would I do that. I want what I want and it's what he wants too.

"Yes," I whisper, barely able to hear my own breathy voice over the bashing and thudding of my heart.

"Good girl."

And then he spanks me.

Oh, dear God! It hurts! It hurts so much!

What a shock! I'd expected a tingle, a little burn…something that's as much pleasure as pain.

Bloody hell, how wrong can you be?

It's like he's slapped me with a solid hunk of wood rather than his strong, but only human, hand. For a moment, both mind and bottom are numbed by it, but then sensation whirls in like a hurricane, I shout out loud—something indistinguishable—and my left buttock feels like it's on fire.

And that's just one blow.

As more and more land, I realize in astonishment that in that first shot, he was actually holding back….

Slap! Slap! Slap!

Spank! Spank! Spank!

The whole of my rear is very quickly an inferno, and the heat sinks like lava into the channel of my sex, reigniting the desire, the grinding longing I felt before my orgasms, and rendering it slight and inconsequential.

I know I should be quiet and still and obedient. I know I should just accept my punishment like a good little girl. Instinct tells me that a master appreciates that in a supplicant. Perfect poise. The perfect ability to absorb the punishment with grace and decorum.

But me, I'm rocking and wriggling about, struggling against my bonds, plaguing my own clit with my wild pony bucking and jerking that makes my pulled-tight thong press and rub against it.

I feel as if I'm going out of my mind, and yet I know, in some still-sane part of it, that I've never been happier in my life. Despite the pain and the strangeness and the sheer, unadulterated kink of what's happening to me, I know that this is where I should be and who I should be with.

The marquis lands a particularly sharp blow, and I let out a gulping, anguished cry. But it's not from the impact, or the raging fire in my bottom cheeks.

No, what pains me the most is that in two weeks I'll be thousands of miles away from the hand that's spanking me.

Still squirming about, my backside still in torment, still almost about to orgasm, I begin to cry piteously, completely out of control and racked by raw, illogical heartache.

As if he were plugged right into my psyche on the deepest level, the marquis stops spanking me immediately.

Strong and sure, he turns me over as if I were as light as a feather across his lap. I gasp as my sore bottom rubs against his denim jeans, but he takes the exhalation into his own mouth as he swoops down to kiss my very breath.

With his tongue still in my mouth, he unfastens my hands and elbows, then, with a swift, sharp jerk that snaps the lace like a cobweb, he wrenches the thong from between my legs and replaces it with his fingertips. His gentle fingertips that love me to a swift, sweet, pain-stealing orgasm.

I moan into his kiss, pleasure sluicing through my loins, rising through my body and my soul and soothing my aching heart. He touches me so tenderly, coaxing me to the peak again and again. As I twist beneath his touch, I realize, distantly, that I'm clinging on to him for the dearest life, yanking at his dark shirt and digging my nails into his back, perhaps inflicting a tiny percentage of the pain I've just experienced.

Finally, we both lapse into silence and stillness. He holds me. I hold him. We're two breathless survivors of a whirlwind.

How long we sit like this, I have no real idea. My entire world is his strength, his scent, his sure, steady breathing and the beat of his heart in his chest where I huddle against it. After a while, though, another physical factor begins to impress itself on me.

I'm on the marquis's lap, and in the cradle of that lap there's the hard knot of an erection.

I start to feel hot again. My cheeks flush with shame at my own selfishness. This spanking was something he wanted to do, but it was really as much my idea as his…and I've had the pleasure of it—several times—and he's had nothing in the way of sexual release.

He's been stiff all through this strange interlude and I've made not the slightest offer to do anything about that. Even though he's seen to *my* satisfaction…repeatedly!

I wonder how to broach the subject. He seems to be quite content for the moment just to hold me, despite the fact that he must be in a fair degree of discomfort. Something that's dramatically illustrated when I shift my position slightly and he draws a swift, sharp breath.

"Um…your lordship…er…shouldn't we do something about that?"

Not exactly eloquent, but I drive my point home by moving again, cautiously rubbing my sore bottom against the solid bulge that's stretching his jeans.

If I've been expecting a positive response and an enthusiastic segue into the next delicious stage of the proceedings, I'm completely wrong. He remains silent, perfectly silent, for several long moments, and when he does utter a sound it's a soft, regretful sigh.

"That's a sweet offer, my lovely Rose, and I'm very tempted." I gaze into his face and suddenly discover that he looks quite sad. "But perhaps it's not the best idea…not really."

"Why not?" I demand, my submissive role suddenly a thing of the past. His eyes widen, and for a moment I wonder whether I should apologize and grovel a bit, but then he smiles and shrugs, the movement of his shoulders transmitting itself to me more through his erection than anything else.

"I…" He looks away, distant for a few seconds, and then returns his gaze to me. He looks rather sad, almost wistful, and then he smiles again. "I prefer to just touch and play and give pleasure, rather than receive it."

What?

"But…um…don't you need to come?"

He laughs. "Of course I do. But I'll deal with myself later, Rose." He tips his head back, as if looking heavenward for inspiration, his night-black hair sliding away from his face with the movement. "It's hard to explain, but basically, if I get too intimate, I want too much…and I'm not really a good prospect for relation-ships." A heavy sigh lifts his chest. "I'm a widower, but I wasn't much good as a husband. Or even a boyfriend. Too wild…too selfish…. I've settled down a lot now, of course—" he makes a vague gesture as if to encom-pass his responsibilities at the Manor "—but now I'm saddled with debts and commitments, and anyone who takes me on takes all that on as well."

I can see what he means, but suddenly, in the midst of that thought, a bright revelation shatters the gloom.

Oh God, even though he's expressing his short-comings and his wariness of relationships, the fact that he's actually mentioned a relationship—marriage even—must mean that he feels more for me, and sees me as more than a temporary employee and a casual spanking playmate.

Mustn't it?

"Look, please, let me…let me touch you…or maybe we can even fuck? I won't expect more than just that.

All it'll be is a bit of pleasure with no commitments. Um…just friendship with a little bit of extra, really, nothing more."

It's out before I've really thought about it. But thinking about it, I know I do want more, despite what I say.

Even though it's possibly the stupidest thing I've done in my life, even crazier than agreeing to be spanked by my temporary boss, I've only gone and fallen head over heels in love with the marquis, haven't I?

And he's right, there's no future in it, is there? None at all…. Soon I'll be leaving for the Caribbean, to take up my chance-of-a-lifetime job!

He looks at me and his dark eyes are still sad, but strangely yearning. It's as if he's just read my thoughts, and feels the same bittersweet emotions that I do.

"You're a wonderful girl, Rose." He touches my face, the same fingers that punished me now a tender, caressing curve. "You're far too wonderful for me. If I take more from you, I'll just want more than that. And more…and more…and that's not fair of me."

I could weep and scream. He *does* bloody well care!

Acting on impulse, I turn my face into his gentle hand and kiss his palm. He groans and mutters, "No!"

But I know I've got him. His whole body shakes finely, and beneath me, his cock jerks and seems to harden even more, if that were possible.

"I shouldn't…I shouldn't…"

"It's all right. It'll be 'no strings,'" I whisper against his palm, then inscribe a little pattern, a promise, with my tongue.

"Oh hell," he almost snarls, and then he's kissing me, tilting me back on his lap and going deep with tongue and lips…and heart?

I embrace him, writhing on his knee again, the discomfort of my spanked bottom forgotten. Wrapping my arms around him, I try to silently say all the things that are too difficult and irrational to say.

Like…

To be with him just a little while, I'll pay any price, do things his way and never ask for more.

Like…

I'm prepared to take my chances on his lack of prospects and commitments.

Like…

Who needs a fucking job in the Caribbean, after all?

This last one shocks me, but just as I think it, the marquis deepens the kiss even further. His arms slide around me, holding me tight, and yet with delicacy, as if I'm precious to him.

And then, somehow, we're on the rug, and he's lying over me, great and dark, like a shadow that's so paradoxical it's also light. The light of revelation….

His hands rove over my body, exploring with reverence this time, and great emotion. And the touch is a thousand times more sexy than when we played. With a gasp, he straightens up momentarily and rips open his shirt, sending buttons flying in his impatience. Then he embraces me again, skin to skin.

His body is hot, feverish and moist, with a fine sheen of sweat that seems to conduct electricity between us. I moan, loving the communion, almost feeling that this might even be as good as sex in some mysterious way. But then my cunt flutters, reminding me I want more.

Still kissing me, the marquis deftly unbuckles his belt and then unfastens his jeans. But just as he's about to reveal himself, and allow me to feast my eyes on that which I've been fantasizing about since the moment he cordially and quite impersonally welcomed me to the manor and the work team, he lets out a lurid, agonized curse.

Then says, "I don't have a condom. I wasn't expecting to need one."

A part of me thinks, whoa, he really did mean all that stuff about not fucking! But another part of me gives thanks for the fact that hope always springs eternal.

"Er...I've got one. It's in the pocket of my skirt."

He gives me a look that says he thinks I'm a saucy, forward minx, but he's more than glad of the fact, and then he scoots gracefully across to where my skirt landed, and locates the contraceptive in my pocket.

Back close again, he hesitates, and gives me a beautiful, complex look, full of hunger, compassion, yearning again...and a strange fear. I nod. I feel just the same.

And then he reaches into his jeans and reveals himself.

Involuntarily, I make a little "ooh" sound.

He's big. Stunning. Delicious. His cock is as handsome and patrician as his face, magnificently hard and finely sculpted. He's circumcised and his glans is moist and stretched and shiny. I've never seen a prettier one, and it's almost a shame when he swiftly robes it in latex.

I reach for him, expecting him to move between my splayed thighs. But with all the authority of his centuries-old title, he takes hold of me and moves me into his preferred position. With his arm around my waist, he scoops me up and places me on my hands and knees and moves in behind me.

It's not what I would have chosen but I'll take what I can get. And I understand his reasons. This way is more impersonal, not too intimate and less dangerous to his emotions and to mine.

At least I think so, until he moves in closer, pressing his condom-clad penis against my still-tingling buttocks while he leans over me and molds his bare chest against my back so he can reach to give the side of my neck a soft kiss.

I sway against him, loving the kiss, loving his skin, loving his scent…and loving him. His weight is on one hand, and with the other he strokes me gently and soothingly, hot fingertips traveling over my breasts and my rib cage, then skimming my waist before finally settling over my sex. He cups me there, not in a sexual sense, but in a vaguely possessive way that's almost more intimate than a blatant attempt to stimulate me.

Then his long finger divides my labia and settles on my clit.

I moan, long and low, already fluttering as he rubs in a delicate, measured rhythm. He's trying to make me come first, I realize, and perversely I resist for a few seconds, holding out for our union. But he's far too clever and too skilled, and I crumble, coming heavily and with an uncouth, broken cry.

As I'm still pulsating, he pushes in, the head of his cock finding my entrance with perfect ease.

Oh God! He's big! He feels even bigger than he looks, so hot and imposing. I pitch forward onto my folded arms as he ploughs into me, making a firm foundation from which to push back at him.

The impact of his penetration shocks my senses for a moment, and pleasure ebbs while I assimilate what's happened to me.

I've got the marquis's cock inside me. I'm possessed by this strange, elegant, deeply personal and mysterious man that I work for. We are one, for the moment; joined by flesh.

But when he starts to move, I'm back in my body and the pleasure reasserts itself.

We rock against each other and he thrusts in long, easy, assured strokes. At first he grips my still-tingly bottom cheeks, but as things get more intense, he inclines right over me, taking his weight on one hand again while with the other, he returns his loving attention to my clit.

Somehow he manages to stroke me in exactly the way that suits me, a firm rhythm, devilishly circling, but not too rough. God alone knows how he manages it. Maybe it's pure instinct or something? Because, judging by the way he's gasping and growling, he's just as out of it as I am.

Sublime and miraculous as all this is, I can't hold out for long. And I don't. Within moments, I'm growling too, like some kind of she-wolf, and climaxing furiously. Dimly, I sense the marquis trying to contain himself, conserve himself as long as he can, to increase my pleasure. But I'm not having any of that—I want *his* pleasure too!

I milk him hard with my inner muscles, and he lets out such a string of profanities—in his immaculate upper-crust accent—that I find myself laughing just as wildly as I'm coming.

Then he laughs too, pumps hard and fast and shoots inside me. I feel the little bursts of his spurting semen even through the condom, and despite it being very stupid, I suddenly wish the rubber protection wasn't there. As we both tumble forward in a gasping, sweating, laughing, climaxing heap, I have fleeting but dangerous thoughts about one or two or three little marquises or honorables or whatever, all running around the place looking as dark and aristocratic and beautiful as their daddy.

Lying on the rug, wrapped in his arms as he cradles me spoon-style—his still partly clothed body warm and protective against mine—I fight with a huge case of genuine post-coital *tristesse* this time.

This is all there is, Rose, I tell myself. A couple of weeks of this. A bit of naughty spanking and sex play by mutual consent. Maybe a friendly, but not too personal, fuck or two.

And then you're off to your lovely new job and a new life of opportunity.

While he stays here, in the heart of England, tending to his great house.

Outside, I hear it start to rain again.

* * *

Two weeks later, it's still raining. In fact, there's a raging thunderstorm outside and it's really scaring me.

But in a way, this is a good thing. It's taking my mind off the fact that tomorrow, I'm supposed to be leaving. And though I won't miss this cold, English rain one bit, there are a lot of things I am finding very hard to leave.

This funny old house has really grown on me, and I wish I was going to be here to see it finished.

I'm going to really miss being spanked and tied up and given mock orders in a mock-stern, beautifully cut-glass English voice. Oh, I'm sure there'll be a man somewhere in the Caribbean who'll oblige me, but it won't be the same, it won't be the same.

And pleasure, oh how I'll miss the pleasure. Not just any pleasure, but the bliss gifted to me by a man who seems to know my every thought, my every response, inside out.

I'll miss the sex, too, even if I never do get to see his glorious face as he comes inside me. But even if he won't face me, I still don't think I'll ever find anyone with his finesse, his strength, his sweetness, his consideration…and his mastery.

Yes, it's the marquis. I fear he's irreplaceable.

And it's our last night.

Lights flicker along the passage as I make my way to the little sitting room, and just as I knock on the door, as I always do now, the lights dim and then go out. There's still some rewiring to do and this happens now and again, but this is the first time the power's gone out in a storm.

There's a loud crack of thunder, and lightning flashes almost simultaneously.

I shriek with fear and the door to the study flies open.

If I wasn't so terrified of the storm outside, I would laugh out loud. It's just like a Dracula movie, with a venerable old house, a wild storm and a beautiful, dramatic aristocrat dressed from head to foot in black.

I squeak again as he gathers me to him and hustles me into the softly lit room.

"I didn't think you'd come tonight, Rose. I thought you'd be down with the others in the kitchen, all seeing out the storm together."

I would be annoyed that he'd think that of me, except that the joy in his eyes at the fact that I did come is patent. He looks as if I've just given him a supremely magnificent gift, and that expression binds me to him far tighter than any length of rope ever could.

Mad, mad thoughts gather in my mind. They're thoughts that have been circling for the past two weeks, nipping at my resolutions and my every idea of what I've always wanted for my future.

But they're so crazy that I find it hard to acknowledge them, and when thunder cracks again they disappear, along with almost all my normal ones.

The marquis wraps me in his arms, softly cooing to me in low, comforting tones, and it's only as I settle that it dawns on me that I just shouted out incoherently again.

The embrace isn't sexual, it's protective. And yet I can still feel him hard against my belly. I hope he'll make love to me tonight, seeing as it's our last time. He doesn't always. Sometimes he's still hard when he escorts me to my little room, high in the old servants' quarters, and I can only assume he deals with his own needs after, alone.

His hold on me is too nice, too sweet and tempting. I struggle out of his grip and try to sink to the floor and kneel…to begin the game.

But he holds on to me, his big, strong hands gripping my shoulders.

"Not tonight, dear. You're too frightened, aren't you?"

He gazes at me, his dark eyes full of complicated emotion. He *does* want to play. I can tell by his erection and the tension in his body that these games of ours seem to release just as much as actual sex does. But there's more, so much more on his mind.

Turbulent joy rushes through my veins. He's going to miss me! My marquis is going to miss me!

And it's for more reasons than just the obvious one— because he likes to spank my bottom….

Amazingly, for one so confident and masterful—both by birth and by inclination—he snags his lip like a nervous, unsure boy. And in this sudden, weighted moment, I sense another, far more real, chance of a lifetime.

"Where's your bedroom, Christian?"

His given name, on my lips for the first time, comes out so naturally. He looks perplexed for a moment. Not angry or confused, just amazed really. I can almost see him rapidly processing an array of new factors in our brief relationship. Then his sculpted, intelligent face lights with joy.

"Not far," he says, suddenly gruff as he grabs my hand and leads me swiftly out of the room. His long stride eats up the yards and I have to trot to keep up with him.

As we round a corner onto another corridor, a particularly violent crack of thunder seems to shake the entire manor, and I yelp again and falter, despite my eagerness to follow wherever he leads. He spins around, his long, night-black hair whipping up as he turns, and in one smooth, effortless move, he sweeps me up in his arms, and then we continue on our way, me being carried and with my arms wound tight around his neck.

The storm, his knight-errant act and his intoxicating and spicy male fragrance all make me dizzy. Everything feels unreal, yet more real than anything that has ever happened or will happen.

As he kicks open a door, there is no job, no Caribbean, no life plan…just the marquis…no…just Christian and his bedroom and his bed.

His room is big and dark and lit by just one rather anemic bedside lamp—rather gloomy. It's nothing like what one would expect in a stately home, but then it's not a public area, just actual living space. The bed isn't even made, so I guess he does his own housework up here. My gaze skitters around and I notice there's a black shirt flung across a rather saggy armchair in the corner, a bottle of gin and a glass on the sideboard and a heap of books beside the bed, all with old, well-worn bindings.

It's like the cell of some rather libertine type of monk.

But he won't be particularly monkish for much longer, if I get my way.

Christian carries me to the bed, sets me down on it and sits down beside me.

His face is still a picture of enigmatic emotions, as if there's a war going on inside him. But at least one part of the battle is quickly resolved, because drawing in a deep breath, he sweeps his hair back to one side and then leans down to kiss me.

It starts gently, but quickly takes fire, his tongue possessing me face-to-face in a way his cock never has. Adjusting his position without breaking lip contact, he stretches out alongside me, then half over me, reaching for my hand and a lacing his fingers tightly with mine.

For a long time he just kisses me as if he were fucking me, his tongue diving in, exploring and imprinting its heat on the soft interior of my mouth. I can't believe how exciting it is, as stirring in its own way as any of the naughty sex games we've played. And yet, for all its power, it's a simple kiss.

When my jaw is aching and my lips feel full and red and thoroughly marauded, he sits up again, and mutters, "Oh God, I shouldn't do this…."

"Yes, you should!" I insist, not sure what it is he shouldn't be doing, but every instinct screaming that if I don't get it now, I'll just go mad.

For a moment, he tips back his head and looks to the somewhat discolored ceiling moldings for inspiration. His sublime hair slides back, accentuating his profile, and giving him the look of a fallen archangel contemplating his sins. And then he swoops back down again and starts undressing me, his hands working deftly at first, and then more frantically. I swear if I didn't help him, he'd probably have torn my flimsy knickers to get them off.

Thunder peals again, and though I don't cry out, I still can't help but flinch. Instantly, he's holding me to him, stroking and cherishing and protecting, his still fully clothed body creating a piquant sensation against my bareness.

But when the noise from the heavens ebbs, I spring into action. I don't want to be just held. I want to be fucked! I want him inside me, face-to-face, possessing every bit of me.

And now it's my turn to tear at clothes, wrenching open his shirt as he first heels off his boots and kicks them away, then fumbling with his belt and his jeans button and struggling to free him from his jeans. Between us we achieve our objective and he sinuously wriggles clear of the restriction of the denim.

He's glorious naked. Utter perfection. Long and lean,

yet powerful, his enticingly defined chest dusted with a scattering of dark hair. And there's more of that dark hair clustered below, adorning the base of his belly and the root of his eager, jutting cock.

He's everything I've ever wanted in a man, and I want to be worthy of him, a graceful, dexterous, intelligent lover.

But instead, I squeal like a scared kid and hurl myself at him for protection when thunder roars again, right overhead. The crack is so loud I'm convinced the manor has been struck, but it seems not to have been when all Christian does is gather me into his arms and hold me tight against his warm, hard body, stroking my back and murmuring sweet, reassuring bits of nothing.

The heavens rage and bellow, lightning illuminating the room, even though the obviously ancient and rather shabby curtains are quite thick. One powerful arm still wrapped around me, Christian tugs at the bedclothes—old-fashioned linen sheets, woolen blankets and a quilt on top—and pulls them right up and over our heads, sealing out the light show and some, if not all, of the noise.

"Better?" he whispers, his voice echoing strangely in our frowsty little nest. He tightens his arms around me again, and snuggles me close. The heat under all this bedding is really quite oppressive, but the sensation of safety, and of being cared for, more than makes up for that.

And the fact that he's still erect, and his delicious penis is pushing against my belly and weeping warm, silky fluid, makes matters infinitely more interesting and sensual.

"Yes…." I whisper, adjusting myself to rub against him and let him know that my fear of the storm hasn't killed my desire for him. In fact, the more I feel that long, hard, fabulous tower of flesh against my skin, the less I seem to be noticing the muffled booming of the thunder.

"Well, we'll have to pop out sooner or later, or we'll suffocate." He pauses, then chuckles. "And I'm going to need some air if I'm going to make love to you properly. A guy needs plenty of wind in his lungs for a good performance."

As if by magic, the next roll of thunder sounds much more muted, more distant. And the one after that even more so, far less fierce.

"I think I'll be all right now." I place my hand flat against his belly, then slide on down. When I fold my fingers around his prick, he gasps and tugs at the quilt, so we emerge.

"Are you sure? It could still come back again. We could wait a little while, if you'd like."

He's still concerned, thoughtful, caring. Even though his penis is like a bar of fire in my hand, and the satin flow of pre-come is yet more copious.

"I don't think I can wait."

It's true. My own body is flowing for him too. I'm wetter than a river down below. The thunder chunters again in the background, and though I flinch, my need for Christian is far greater than my remaining fears.

I part my legs and he gets the message and starts to touch me, his fingertip settling lightly, yet with authority, on my clit.

The pleasure comes quickly, as wild and elemental as the storm, and just as electric. Within seconds, I'm climaxing hard, rocked by the intense, hungry spasms in my sex, and fighting a battle with myself not to grip Christian's cock too roughly.

But he just laughs kindly, and pushes toward me while I pulse and pulse.

When I get my breath back, I stare at him as he looms over me in the low light from the bedside lamp. I'm still holding his erect penis, but there's more than sex in his eyes. They're dark yet brilliant, a chiaroscuro of turbulent emotions. They seem to say so much, yet the message is still scrambled, unclear. I sense some of it, and it takes my breath away again.

"I want to make love to you." His voice is husky, low, intent. "No spanking, no mind games, no ropes or bondage. Not tonight."

I don't know what to say, but he seems to read my thoughts. He gives me a little smile, then rolls away from me for a moment and pulls open a drawer in the bedside cabinet, and fishes around in it without looking.

It takes next to no searching to produce a foil-wrapped condom. He puts it into my free hand.

My fingers shake as I dress him in it, rolling the superthin latex over his silky skin and encasing the iron-hard strength of his erection. When he's covered, I hesitate.

What will he want? His usual position? Taking me from behind?

I start to roll into position, but he stops me, a firm but gentle hand on my flank.

He smiles, pushes me flat against the mattress and then parts my legs and moves swiftly and elegantly between them.

For a moment, he just rests there, the head of his cock nestling tantalizingly at my opening, almost quiescent.

"I've so been wanting to do this," he says, his eyes grave. "Wanting it, but knowing I shouldn't."

I want to say *why not?* But I think I know why.

Games of spanking and bondage are just that. Games. Beautiful and life-enhancing. Sexual fun.

But this, this is serious. This is more.

I sense a different kind of bond breaking as he enters me. It's a restriction. An artificial barrier we've set between ourselves, and it's shattered now.

All is open. All is honest, dangerous but wonderful.

"I love you," he says quietly, then starts to thrust.

I can't speak, but I show him with my body that I feel the same. By holding him in my arms as tightly as

I can while still allowing him to move. By hooking my legs around his body, and undulating my hips to press against him.

If only I could mold our two forms so closely together that we could become one, be inside each other's skin.

We rock and surge against each other, our heated perspiration almost fusing us in the way I crave. Christian's thrusts are short, shallow, urgent, almost desperate. He braces himself on one arm for leverage, and clasps me tightly to him with the other, his fingers digging into my flesh, not in cruelty but in possession and fierce need.

The joining is manic, almost animal, and yet at the same time soaring and transcendent. Holding him, being held and owned and fucked by him, I'm aware of my life changing as my flesh throbs with pleasure and clutches at his.

I gasp those three words too as my future changes shape.

In the morning, the park outside is fresh and clean and bright with sunshine. It's like a brand-new world after the storms of last night, a tangled paradise as I stare out from the window.

On the mantelpiece, Christian's clock reads a little after 6 a.m., but I'm wide-awake, anticipating a busy day ahead. I've so much to do and I don't know how to start.

So instead, I return to bed...and my man.

We said very little last night. Our bodies spoke for us. But this morning, I have to confirm not just my hopes and fears but my beloved's.

I know he probably wants what I want, but will his ancestral notions of duty and honor stop him from taking it? He might feel he has to set aside his needs for what he thinks is best for me.

Time to persuade him that he can't live without me.

Lifting the sheet that covers him, I feast my eyes on his magnificent body for a few moments, loving his tousled hair and the faintly sweaty early-morning aroma of his skin. His patrician face looks younger in repose, and his long, lush eyelashes are two dark fans against his cheekbones.

I wonder whether to bend down and take his cock in my mouth. It's already thickening, as if it's awake even if Christian himself isn't quite yet.

But instead, I try something different. Lying down against him I press my bottom against his thighs, and then draw his sleeping hand against its rounded shape, hoping he'll respond.

Yours, I think as his fingers automatically curve and cup me. *Yours until the end of time, to spank and play with at your leisure.*

"You do know what you're asking for, doing that, don't you?"

His voice is sleepy, yet still full of masculine power.

He squeezes my cheeks briskly, already waking and ready for his treat.

"Um…yes, I think so."

"You know, there isn't really time, my love." There's regret there, but it's tempered with typical British stoicism. As if he's bracing himself already for what he dreads. "Isn't your taxi coming at eight? Shouldn't you be packing?"

I can't speak. Now that I have to tell him about my decision, I'm scared. I know I've read him right, and I know he cares, but still…

"I'm not going."

There's a long silence. His hands are still upon me, but they're quiescent.

And then he laughs. And squeezes again.

"You're a very silly girl. You know that, don't you?"

"Yeah, I do know it…but it doesn't change things." I press myself back into his hold. "I've decided that I like rain, and I want to hang around here, stay on the team and see what this old heap looks like when the renovation is finished."

"Is that all?" I hear the smile in his voice as he rolls me onto my front, still palpating my bottom in a way that's utterly sensual and full of delicate, delicious menace. "I do hate it when someone I care about keeps things from me." He lifts his hand, and that's more menacing than ever. "Now, tell me the whole truth…or I shall be forced to punish you."

"You might think I'm a bit forward."

"I'll be the judge of that, Rose. Now tell me."

I hesitate again. Deliberately.

He makes a soft tutting sound, and though I can't see him, I imagine him shaking his head, and his gorgeous black hair rippling.

A little tap lands on my right buttock. It's light, barely a smack at all, but my sex ripples in luscious excitement. He barely has to touch me and I'm soaring toward pleasure already.

Another tap lands and I swirl my hips, rubbing my mound against the mattress, trying to stimulate my clit.

"Keep still. Don't be naughty."

He's fighting not to laugh, and his voice is so warm, so affectionate that I begin to melt in an entirely different way. My spirits sing as I work my crotch, happily defying him.

He smacks again and again, a little harder, warming up my hind parts to match the glow in my sex and in my heart.

"Tell me…tell me everything." He smoothes his free hand down my back and my flank, the other still softly slapping at my bottom.

It's hard to answer now because I'm so turned on I can't think straight to form words, and it's also getting difficult to keep my hips still against the sheets.

I grab at the pillows, clutching the linen of the pillowcase hard in an effort to concentrate.

"I…I've decided that I'd quite like to find out what it's like to be a marchioness!"

There's a pause, during which I hold my breath, then I feel a kiss settle on the small of my back like a butterfly.

"Well, I can tell you what that will be like." His breath is hot against my skin, wafting over my bottom, which is already even hotter. "You'll never have any money. You'll spend your life enslaved to a great monster of a house that'll never ever stop needing attention." He kisses me just one more time, and then straightens up again. "And you'll probably get your bottom smacked at least once a day, if not considerably more often!"

Spanks begin to rain down. Hard, loving, rhythmical and stirring. I surge against the mattress, my clit pulsating and my heart thudding and leaping with the purest love.

* * *

A while later, I've been spanked and I've been fondled and I've been comprehensively fucked…and I've been brought to climax again and again and again. And with each smack, each stroke, each thrust and each orgasm, I've been told that I'm cherished and adored.

Christian's gone back to sleep now, and I'm lying here savoring the peace and the closeness of his beloved body. Pretty soon I'll have to start making phone calls and explaining a lot of things to a lot of very astonished people. But for now, I'm just listening to my darling's breathing and the sound of a new, teeming downpour outside.

British weather? It's not so bad…in fact, I love it! Almost as much as I love the man who's at my side.

12 Shades left you wanting more?

Read on for an exclusive extract of Tiffany Reisz's
Shockingly powerful full-length story
The Siren – available *now*!

The Siren

By Tiffany Reisz

Numbing.

As an editor Zach often forced his writers to dig deep, cast aside the obvious and find the perfect word for every sentence. And the perfect word to describe this book release party he'd been forced to attend? *Numbing*. Zach stalked through the party saying little more than the occasional hello to various colleagues. He'd only come because once again J.P. had twisted his arm, and Rose Evely— the guest of honor—had been a Royal House writer for thirty years now. What a ludicrous party anyway—someone dimmed the lights to create a nightclub sort of atmosphere but no amount of ambience could turn the banal hotel banquet hall into anything other than a beige box. He wandered toward a spiral staircase in the corner of the room to surreptitiously check his watch. If he could survive two hours at this party, maybe it would be long enough to placate his social butterfly of a boss.

Scanning the crowd, he saw his twenty-eight-year-old assistant, Mary, trying to talk her new husband into dancing with her. J.P. stood with Rose Evely. Both J.P. and Evely had been happily married to their respective spouses for decades but nothing stopped J.P. from chivalrously flirting with any woman who had the patience to listen to his literary rambles. Everyone seemed to be enjoying themselves at this miserable party. Why wasn't he?

Once more he glanced down at his watch.

"I can save you, if you want," came a voice from above him. Zach spun around and looked up. Smiling down at him from over the top of the staircase was Nora Sutherlin.

"Save me?" He narrowed his eyes at her.

"From this party." She crooked her index finger at him. Zach's better judgment warned him that climbing that staircase could be a very bad idea indeed. Yet his feet overruled his reason, and he mounted the steps and joined her on the platform at the top. He raised his eyebrow as he cast a disapproving gaze over her clothes. That morning at her house, she'd worn shapeless pajamas that concealed every part of her but her abundant personality. Now he saw on full display what his mind had before only imagined.

She wore red, of course. Scarlet red and not much of it. The dress stopped at the top of her thighs and started at the edge of her breasts. She had miraculous curves that the dramatic floor-length red jacket she wore over her dress did nothing to hide. Even worse, she wore black leather boots that laced all the way above her knees. Pirate boots and a roguish grin on a beautiful black-haired woman…for the first time in a long time Zach felt something other than numb.

"How do you know I want to be saved from this party, Miss Sutherlin?" Zach leaned back against the railing and crossed his arms.

"I've been watching you from my little crow's nest here since the second you walked in. You've said maybe five words to four people, you've checked your watch three times in as many minutes, and you whispered something to J.P., which, guessing from the look on his face, was a death threat. You're here against your will. I can get you out."

Zach cocked a self-deprecating smile at her. "Unfortunately, you're right. I am here against my will. I have to wonder, however, why you're here at all. Didn't I give you homework?" he asked, remembering his rash decision this morning to give her one chance to impress him.

"You did. And I was a good girl and finished it. See?" He tried and failed to look away as she reached into the bodice of her dress and pulled out a folded piece of paper and handed it to him. The paper was still warm from her skin. "This is it?" he asked, seeing only three paragraphs on the page.

"Don't judge a book by its mother. Just read." Zach glanced at her once more and wished he hadn't. Every time he looked at her, he found something else to attract him. Her jacket had slipped down her arm and her pale sculpted shoulder peeked out. Sculpted? His petite little writer had some muscle to go along with her impressive curves. Tougher than she looked.

Remembering himself, Zach turned from her, tilted the page into a patch of light and read.

First she noticed his hips. The eyes might be the windows to the soul, but a man's hips were his seat of power. She doubted he'd chosen those perfectly fitted jeans and that black T-shirt that belied the tautness of his stomach for the purpose of flattering his lower body, but he had and now she lost herself in the thought of caressing with her lips that exquisite hollow that lay between smooth skin and elegantly jutting hip bone.

She had to meet his eyes eventually. With reluctance she dragged her gaze to his face, as dignified and angular as the rest of him. Pale skin and dark Brutus-cut hair contrasted with eyes the color of ice. Glacial, she decided his eyes were—they spoke of hidden depths. A stark beauty, he was a man made to be admired by intelligent women. Lean and tall but with the substantial mass of an athlete, he was utterly masculine. The world had fallen away in his presence and now that he was gone, she was left in the equally potent presence of his absence.

Zach read the words one more time trying all the

while to ignore the annoyingly pleasant image of Nora Sutherlin caressing his naked hips with her mouth.

"I've noticed you usually shy away from long descriptive passages in your books?" he said.

"I know people think erotica is just a romance novel with rougher sex. It's not. If it's a subgenre of anything, it's horror."

"Horror? Really?"

"Romance is sex plus love. Erotica is sex plus fear. You're terrified of me, aren't you?"

"Slightly," he admitted, rubbing the back of his neck.

"A smart horror writer will never put too much detail in about the monster. The readers' imaginations can conjure their own demons. In erotica you never want your main characters to be too physically specific. That way your readers can insert their own fantasies, their own fears. Erotica is a joint effort between writer and reader."

"How so?" Zach asked, intrigued that Nora Sutherlin would have her own literary theories.

"Writing erotica is like fucking someone for the first time. You aren't sure exactly what he wants yet so you try to give him everything he could possibly want. Everything and anything…" She enunciated the words like a cat stretching in sunlight. "You hit every nerve and eventually you'll hit the nerve. Have I hit any nerves yet?"

Zach clenched his jaw. "Not any of them you were aiming for."

"You don't know what I was aiming for. So what do you think of the writing?"

"Could be better." He refolded the page. "You use 'was' too much."

"Rough draft," she said unapologetically. She stared at him with dark, waiting eyes.

"The last line's the strongest—'*the equally potent presence of his absence.*'" Zach knew he should give the page back to her but for some reason he stuck it in his pocket. "It's good." She gave him a slow, dangerous smile.

"It's you."

Zach only stared at her a moment before pulling the folded page back out.

"This is me?" he asked, his skin flushing.

"It is. Every last long, lean inch of you. I wrote it right after you left this morning. I was, needless to say, inspired by your visit."

Swallowing hard, Zach unfolded the sheet again. *Brutus-cut black hair...ice-colored eyes...jeans, black shirt...* It *was* him. "Excuse me," Zach began, trying to regain control of this conversation, "but didn't I repeatedly insult you this morning?"

"Your kvetching was very fetching. I like men who are mean to me. I trust them more."

She tilted her head to the side and her unruly black hair fell over her forehead, veiling her green-black eyes.

"Forgive me. I might be speechless right now."

"Your orders," she said. "You told me to stop writing what I knew and start writing what I wanted to know. I want to know…you."

She took a step closer and Zach's heart dropped a few feet and landed somewhere in the vicinity of his groin. "Who are you, Ms. Sutherlin?" he asked, not quite knowing what he meant by that question.

"I'm just a writer. A writer named Nora. And you can call me that, Zach."

"Nora then. I'm sorry. I'm not used to being hit on by my writers. Especially after verbally abusing them." Nora's eyes flashed with amusement.

"Verbal abuse? Zach, where I come from 'slut' is a term of endearment. Want to see where I come from?"

"No."

"Pity," she said, sounding not at all surprised or disappointed. "Where should we go then? I promised to save you from this party, didn't I?"

"I really shouldn't leave," Zach said, terrified what would happen the second he found himself alone with Nora.

"Come on, Zach. This party sucks and not in the good way. I've had pap smears more fun than this." Zach covered a laugh with a cough.

"I must admit you do have a way with words."

"So you'll edit me then? Please?" She batted her eyelashes at him in mock innocence. "You won't regret it." Zach glanced up at the ceiling as if it could give him some hint of what the hell he was getting himself into. Nora Sutherlin… He had only six weeks left in New York until he left for L.A. Why was he even considering getting involved with Nora Sutherlin and her book? He knew why. He had nothing else in his life right now. He liked Mary and enjoyed working for J.P. But he'd made no friends in New York, no connections of any kind. He hadn't allowed himself to even consider dating. One day he'd taken off his wedding ring in a fit of anger and couldn't find a reason to put it back on. He wouldn't consider inflicting himself on any woman right now. At least working with Nora Sutherlin might give him a much-needed distraction from his misery. She seemed like the type of woman who'd help you forget about your headache by setting your bed on fire.

Won't regret it? He already did. "You do realize that working with you could be bad for my career," Zach said. "I do literary fiction, not—"

"Literary friction?"

"I can't believe I'm doing this." Zach shook his head. Nora leaned in close to him. He was suddenly and uncomfortably aware of the long, bare curve of her neck. She smelled of hothouse f lowers in bloom.

"I can." She breathed the words into his ear.

Zach exhaled slowly and pulled, reluctantly, away from her.

"I'm a brutal editor."

"I like brutal."

"I'll make you rewrite the whole book."

"Now you're trying to turn me on, aren't you? Shall we?"

"Fine," he finally said. "Save me then."

"Let's do it," she said. "If J.P. gives you shit about leaving the party with me, tell him it was my idea for us to go work on my book. J.P. won't spank me."

"I'm not certain of that," Zach said.

"I knew I liked that man for a reason."

"I need to say a few goodbyes if we're leaving." J.P. for one. Then Mary. And he hadn't met her husband yet. And Rose Evely, too.

"Nope. Can't do that," Nora said. "Never say good-bye when you leave a party. That way you leave a mystery in your place. They'll have so much more fun talking about us than they ever would talking to us. Can't you already hear them? *Zach Easton just left with Nora Sutherlin. Are they…surely not…of course they are—*"

"We aren't," Zach said with finality.

"I know that. You know that. They don't know that." Zach looked around the room. Everywhere he looked he saw eyes glancing furtively in their direction. The most intense gazing came from Thomas Finley, his least favorite coworker. Zach noted that Finley didn't so much stare at him as he did at Nora. And the look in his eyes wasn't particularly friendly.

"I prefer not being a topic of gossip," Zach said.

"Too late. At least with me, it'll be really good gossip." She strode down the staircase with an audacious kick of her heels on each step.

Zach followed in her wake. The crowd parted for her as she cut a bloodred swath through the center of the room. Finally free of the suffocating party, Zach threw on his coat and breathed in the bracing winter evening air. A cab stopped within seconds for Nora and she slipped gracefully inside. He took a sharp breath as her black-booted legs disappeared into the cab. One more time he asked himself what the hell he was doing before sliding in next to her. Nora said nothing as he joined her, only turned her head and gazed out at the night. She seemed to be trying to stare down the city. He had a feeling the city would blink first. Nervously, he rubbed the empty spot where he'd once worn his wedding band. Nora reached out and wrapped her hand around his ring finger. Facing him now, she raised her eyebrow in a question.

"Grace," he answered.

Nora nodded. "You married a princess."

Princess Grace—her mother called her that.

"She hates being called 'Princess.'" Zach heard the anguish in his voice.

Nora lifted his hand and brought it to her neck. She pressed his fingers into her throat. Her pulse throbbed through her warm, soft skin.

"Søren," she said and met his eyes. In those dark, dangerous depths he saw a glimmer of something human—not merely sympathy but empathy. And he felt something inhuman in response—not passion but pure animal need. For a brief moment he imagined his hands digging into her thighs and the bite of her leather boots on his back. He tore his gaze away before her uncanny ability to read him saw that image in his hungry gaze.

She released his hand just as the cab pulled up in front of Zach's apartment building. He opened the door and got out. He wanted to ask her up, wanted to spend a few hours forgetting his pain and all the reasons for it. But he couldn't, could he? Because of Grace, not that she would care anymore. Zach opened his mouth but before he could ask Nora up, she reached out to shut the door.

"See, Zach? I told you I'd save you."